1st March 2003

For Clare with best wishes,

D Eric Sturdy

Operation Gan

D Eric Sturdy

First Impression—2003

ISBN 0-9544449-0-6

Published by D Eric Sturdy, 22 Stow Park Circle,
Newport, South Wales NP20 4HF.

Printed in Wales by Gomer Press, Llandysul, Ceredigion SA44 4QL
Distributed in Great Britain by Welsh Books Distribution Centre, Aberystwyth, Ceredigion SA23 3AQ

*This book is dedicated to my grandchildren –
Claire and Sarah Whitefield, James Sturdy,
William and Brodie Coghlan – in recognition of the
pleasure they have given myself and my wife, Meriel,
over the years and in the hope the book will serve to
remind them of their adoring grandparents.*

Acknowledgements

The Royal Air Force flew out of Gan twenty six years ago, on 29th March 1976, when the Maldivian Government achieved full independence from Britain and to acquire a flavour of 'things as they were' during Gan's thirty year British occupation, I am indebted to several ex-servicemen. In particular I wish to express my thanks to the following, recorded in alphabetical order and not seniority – Wing Commander C S Burns, Air Chief Marshal Sir Michael Knight KCB AFC, Air Commodore K H Minton BSc and Squadron Leader Tony Tucker all of whom provided me with information on the Royal Air Force College Cranwell and with technological details for Russian transport planes and British strike forces in combat in March 1976. The RAF Museum, Hendon, kindly provided aerial photographs of Gan as it was in the sixties. For my research on the Maldives in general I am greatly indebted for information on local history and traditions to Mm. Toni de Laroque, otherwise known as 'Toni the Maldive Lady' and herself an authoress of considerable repute. My granddaughter, Claire Whitefield, in collaboration with Miss Ester Ranes, both BA graduates from Chilterns University College, Buckinghamshire, designed the cover for my book. Finally, and by no means least, I wish to record my grateful thanks to Mrs Rosanna Carnevale who painstakingly and expertly compiled and typed my manuscript and to the staff of Gomer Press for their expertise and professionalism in printing my book.

Chronology

The Ides is the 15th day of March, May, July or October, or the 13th day of the remaining months, in the ancient Roman calendar. The date was immortalized in a prophetic prediction, 'Beware the Ides of March', by Emperor Julius Caesar who was assassinated on this day in 44BC by Cassius and Brutus and whose life terminated in his equally famous dying words 'Et tu Brute'.

1292 'The flower of the Indies', Marco Polo, an Italian traveller and the Pope's emissary to the Far East and the Indies.

1334 'The most agreeable place I have ever seen and truly one of the wonders of the world', Ibn Battuta, a wealthy Arab cowrie-shell trader.

1922 'A delightful spirit of ease and contentment seems to prevail universally', H C P Bell, a British vice consul and antiquarian.

29th March, Maldivies' Independence Day, declared on final evacuation of the Royal Air Force from Gan airbase on this day in 1976.

By the same author under pseudonym David E Scott

BLOOD BROTHERS

Minerva Press, London

ISBN 1 86106 096 3

During Crete's turbulent history no period was more vicious than the island's occupation by German and Italian forces between June 1941 and April 1945. Into this atmosphere of hostility, passion and intrigue destiny leads earstwhile blood brothers David Green and Manfred Schmidt. Fate has entwined their lives and ultimately insists on a final confrontation between the British and the SS officer on the partisan-infested killing fields in Crete. Blood brothers in their youth, it took a bloody vendetta truly worthy of the Cretan past, for the men to be finally reunited.

The BULLDOG, the WHIPPET, the BAT and the FALCON

Minerva Press London

ISBN 0-75410-924-0

The Bulldog – Winston Churchill, Britain's saviour in 1940 in her darkest hour.
The Whippet – Neville Chamberlain, arch appeaser with Italy and Nazi Germany and Churchill's bitter political rival in the pre-war thirties.
The Bat – Admiral Canaris' Wehrmacht agent who cultivates Chamberlain's affection and ultimately gains access to the Cabinet War Rooms in Whitehall.
The Falcon – A fanatical Nazi hit-man nominated to carry out the Fuhrer's instructions to assassinate Winston Churchill and his wartime cabinet council.
The Plot – Kept secret at the time and still classified until 2042, a failed attempt to assassinate Britain's wartime leaders in the Cabinet War Rooms during the early hours of July 4th 1942.

Contents

Chapter One

Ministry of Defence (Air)
4th January 1975

"THERE ARE NO CROWS ON GAN" was Mike Townsend's standard reply to all inquiries about his remote command in the Indian Ocean. The pretty, elegantly turned-out, prim-nosed flight lieutenant, sporting an insincere smile, asked about Gan out of courtesy. Wing Commander Townsend was in no mood for idle chatter and the flight lieutenant looked perplexed. "I beg your pardon wing commander?"

"There are no crows on Gan and that tells you everything about the place," Townsend repeated and sat down heavily in a commodious leather chair, scowling at the self-important female. She withdrew into her shell and busied herself shuffling some papers on her desk and sorting out a stack of unopened mail. Mike took stock of his surroundings. The air commodore's outer office was capacious and air-conditioned and the fittings leather and polished mahogany. There was no comparison between these palatial surroundings and his pokey little command post in a Nissen hut on Gan. He sighed. Mike's day, so far, had been trying to say the least. An early train from Grantham had been an hour late arriving at Kings Cross and a taxi ride from the rail terminal to a military outfitters in Cambridge Circus was a traffic-induced nightmare. His brand new service dress, tailored to measure, did not sit comfortably on his lean frame and needed readjustment while he waited around for an hour in a vestibule at Moss Bros. His new, light blue, British warm overcoat was a size too large but would have to do and, at least, there would be no use for it in Gan's tropical climate. The tailors worked wonders and a handsomely overpaid cabbie dropped him off at precisely ten minutes to twelve outside the Ministry of Defence building in Whitehall. As far as Mike was concerned he was dead on time and now, at twenty minutes past twelve, he was still waiting to see Air Commodore Sir Charles Lampton and the smiling virago behind the desk was none too helpful. Despite air-conditioning he was beginning to feel hot and uncomfortable and beads of sweat percolated gently down the nape of his neck and inside his starch-stiff shirt collar and under the armpits of his brand new service dress.

As he sat and waited he reflected that he, himself, should be occupying the inner office on the other side of the oak-panelled door instead of sweating it out as base commander of a remote RAF staging station in the Maldives. He had all the necessary qualifications but, during his thirty-two year service career, he had crossed swords with too many senior officers and they had never forgiven him for his gaffe during the Dresden raids in 1945 when, as 'tail end Charlie', he had unnecessarily exposed his crew to danger by flying his Lancaster over the burning city on a second strafe so that they all had a better view of the holocaust below. Still, he got home to base safely and intact and, in common with many bomber pilots involved in the Dresden raids, he received a Bar to his Distinguished Flying Cross from King George VI. Already known familiarly amongst his peers as 'Mad Mike', the accolade was strengthened by the Dresden escapade and was to stick with him for the rest of his service career. And what had the pompous twit, Charles Lampton, done to deserve promotion and a knighthood? Though he enlisted in 1940 Lampton had seen little active service. He had not strayed far from Cranwell and the Air Ministry and his real claim to fame was masterminding the Berlin airlift during the fall of 1948 and the spring of 1949. He had also married the daughter of a French air force general and, perhaps, the reasons for his rapid promotion were none too difficult to fathom. It hurt to think that a desk-bound wallah, with roughly the same length of service as himself, could rise two ranks above a fighting airman with over thirty sorties to his credit and a DFC and Bar to boot. He had met Sir Charles Lampton socially on a few occasions and had not taken to the man. They were totally incompatible and Mike found him a dull, pompous bore and on his dignity at all times. Mad Mike was about to meet him again.

The buzzer on the flight-lieutenant's desk purred and flashed green at 1225hrs. She looked up from her task and the plastic, sickly smile returned to her face. "Follow me, please, wing commander."

She held the door open for Mike to enter the sanctum sanctorum. There were two senior officers seated behind a mahogany desk with portraits of Queen Elizabeth II and Lord Trenchard hanging on the oak-panelled wall behind their backs. Mike stood to attention and formally saluted the officer in the centre. He immediately recognised the second seated figure. Wing Commander Tony Widgeon, best man at his wedding, sat with a grin on his face and greeted Mike with a mischievous wink. The stern-faced air commodore waved his hand to indicate Mike to sit in an upright wooden chair opposite the desk and wasted no time in coming to the point. "For the past twelve months the Maldivian government has had its eye on Gan for use as a civilian airport. We have no immediate plans to grant their request but I have to inform you that our staging airbase at Gan will be handed back in the foreseeable future. This is classified information and a defence white paper, announcing closure of the base, is in the pipeline and will be published by the Government in the spring. When the handover date is confirmed you will be the first to know and you will return to Gan on the tenth and resume your command."

The air commodore paused and tugged at the bristly end of his grey, military moustache, an irritating habit accentuated during periods of stress and deep thought. He cleared his throat and continued, "Your task will be to carry out an inventory of all moveable equipment and fixtures on the base and to evacuate such equipment, item by item, over the next twelve months. When we hand over to the Maldivians the base must be clear of MoD property. You will also take personal charge of the handover. It will be a low key affair but your rank is sufficiently senior to represent Her Majesty's armed forces. I have no doubt a high-ranking consular official will be there to support you. After handover you will return to Cranwell where you will be demobilized. Are there any questions?"

Mike was so stunned he could not think of anything to ask. The air commodore, tugging vigorously at the brush of his moustache, continued, "I wish to broach a delicate subject. Have you overcome the drink problem you had at NATO?"

Mike was devastated by the unexpected question and spoke up in self-defence. "There never was a serious problem and I'm surprised, Sir Charles, you brought the subject up but, now that you have, I can assure you I'm not drinking to excess."

Tony Widgeon was embarrassed and diverted his gaze away and Mike's brain was racing like a well-tuned motor engine. So much for General Geoffrey Baxter's promise of confidentiality! Air Commodore Lampton would have, by now, spread the news at MoD and at last Mike became aware of the possible reason for his 'punishment' posting to Gan. So, what the hell!? His long-standing antipathy to the establishment and his support of the Russkies now made more sense. He glared aggressively at the air commodore and there was a deathly silence in the office for a full minute. The impasse was finally broken, dismissively, by Sir Charles Lampton. "Very well, Wing Commander Townsend, if you have nothing to add that will be all" and, casting an envious glance at Mike's pristine new service dress and impressive medal ribbons which outclassed his own decorations, he added, "By the way, you should not wander around London in uniform. The IRA have issued a warning that all British subjects in uniform in Ireland, and on mainland Britain, are fair targets and subject to attack. Show Wing Commander Townsend out group captain."

Tony Widgeon ushered Mike out of the office past the preening, smiling Madonna, down a spiral, marble staircase, past two 'MoD Plod' guards and out into Whitehall. Nine inches taller, Tony stood on the road and Mike stood on the kerb where, eyeball to eyeball, they confronted each other and Mike broke into a torrent of abuse directed at Commodore Lampton, "That was below the belt and completely unnecessary, Tony. Lampton abused my confidentiality and the bastard has spread the muck at MoD. All my chances of promotion have now been blown away and I see clearly the reason for my posting to Gan."

Tony Widgeon chose his words carefully. "Steady on, old boy. Commodore Lampton is not all bad. He's still feeling his way around in his recent appointment and we'll have to make allowances for him. Look, old chap, I can't hang around for a chinwag at the moment. Can you stay on in town tonight? If you can I'll meet you in Rodriguez's wine bar in Frith Street at six o'clock."

Mike, still in a daze that at the age of forty-nine he was being thrown out on the slag heap, answered mechanically, "Yes, Tony old boy, I'll be there at six o'clock."

With a mischievous twinkle in his eye Tony turned to leave and spoke hastily over his shoulder. "I don't suppose you wish me to invite old Lampey to join us for a drink?"

"Not bloody likely! I don't wish to see that chap ever again if I can avoid it."

"Cheerio old chap. Must dash. See you at six o'clock."

Standing alone on the busy thoroughfare Mike was suddenly engulfed with rage. Who the hell did they think they were kicking about and what had he done to deserve early retirement? He'd show them and to hell with the IRA! Mad Mike was in town and he feared no one. Let the buggers try it on and he'd soon put their noses out of joint! With a determined stride he surged up Whitehall to Trafalgar Square and crossed over to St Martins Lane and into Leicester Square. He ate a solitary lunch at Manzi's fish restaurant and then walked to Moss Bros where he changed into civilian clothing. Carrying his new service dress and his British warm in separate parcels he arrived at Rodriguez's wine bar in Frith Street at ten minutes to six and took a seat in a dingy cubicle near the bar. Tony Widgeon arrived just after six o'clock and he was not alone. The man with him was called Bobby Davidson and, though Tony hinted that his companion was a naval officer, it soon became evident that 'Bobby' had no connection with the sea and his thick, guttural accent suggested he would be more at home in the Polish army rather than Her Majesty's Royal Navy. The presence of a stranger put paid to any private discussion of the day's events at MoD. Rodriguez's Cuban bar, frequented by Hooray Henrys and city-slickers, was a sleazy clip-joint partitioned into small cubicles and serviced by mini-skirted waitresses of dubious character and morals. The unsophisticated wine list offered a choice between red, white, or rosè house plonk or an inferior, but expensive, Spanish bubbly which was reluctant to fizz until air was blown into it through a straw. The three men sat huddled around a small table and drank the lukewarm, flat champagne. Tony Widgeon sympathised with Mike's predicament but pointed out that a successful handover of Gan would almost certainly lead to recommendation for a big gong. Somewhat mollified, Mike set about drinking the unpalatable Spanish hooch with gusto. At one point Tony excused himself to go to the toilet and was away for fifteen minutes and, in that time, Bobby lowered his voice and assumed a conspirational attitude. "In 1949 you volunteered to serve my party. My comrades in Moscow now order you to honour your contract."

"I only did it for a bit of fun," Mike retorted defensively omitting to mention he had already been 'used' by Moscow during his time at Commandement du Nord in Versailles and at NATO Headquarters in Brussels.

"You have no choice in this matter. Your services will be required soon. When you hear from my comrades you must carry out their instructions to the letter."

"And what if I refuse?" Mike asked half-jokingly.

"You are married Comrade Townsend? You have a beautiful wife and her father was a high ranking officer in the British army. You will not wish to do anything to harm them?"

Mike thought long and hard. He wished no harm to Vanessa, or her irascible father, and saw his collaboration with the Russkies as a means of getting his own back on the Establishment. Dangling a medal in front of his nose was all well and good but he knew how things worked in the services and the chances of a wing commander, serving on a remote outpost, getting an OBE or a CBE were very slim. He decided to play along with the Russian conspirator. He lowered his head and nodded. "Okay. I'll do it."

By the time Tony reappeared Mike and Bobby were in earnest conversation and had ordered a third bottle of bubbly. They drank solidly for the next two hours and Mike laced the Spanish pop with shots of brandy poured from a complimentary Moss Bros silver hip flask. After a mad dash across London in a taxi he caught the last train from Kings Cross to Grantham by the skin of his teeth. On the journey north he debated whether he should tell Vanessa about the new development but decided against it for the time being. Vanessa's father was, supposedly, suffering from cancer though there were no outward signs of his immediate demise. He ate heartily over the festive season and was not averse to a brandy, or two, and a cigar after dinner. Vanessa's visit to Gan in December had been a disaster and she evidently would not wish to return to the Maldives with him. She had been hinting for days she was needed at home to nurse her precious, ailing Daddy. Bobby's veiled threats were still ringing in his ears and, without Vanessa, he would have a free hand back at Gan. No, definitely not, Vanessa must not be told about his future prospects in the RAF. He would return to Gan, bide his time, and play along with the Russian agents.

As the express hurtled northwards through the night, comfortably seated and alone in a first class compartment, Mike had time to reflect and plan his future. He refused to contemplate a life of leisure as a country gentleman at Belvoir Hall. That would be utter purgatory. Perhaps he could find an appointment as military adviser to one of the Arab states or with the Colonial Office in Africa? The obvious answer was to remain in the RAF but future promotion prospects were spelt out to him that morning at the MoD briefing and the man preferred by High Command was obviously Tony Widgeon. Rumours, on the service grapevine, were rife that Tony and Sir Charles Lampton were an item. Earlier in the year Lady Lampton, a French pseudo-countess, had returned to her family villa in Biarritz and Sir Charles had moved into a suite at the Ritz Hotel. Across Piccadilly, at the exclusive Athenaeum Club, Tony had his bachelor quarters. Socially, and at work, the two officers were inseparable. At station inspections, mess dining-in nights, cocktail parties and official banquets, Lampey and Widgey, as they were irreverently known, were seldom apart. Tony had always been a loner. In his younger days, handsome and attractive to the ladies, his affairs seldom lasted more than a couple of weeks and it was strange he had never married, or proposed marriage. Of late he seldom entertained lady friends and spent his time at the Athenaeum Club, a bastion of male dominance. Tony Widgeon had certainly played his cards right. Ensconced at MoD, and with an air commodore as his personal mentor and partner, he made no secret he was angling for a top job and was heir-presumptive to the next senior appointment. Mike smiled ruefully as the train pulled into Grantham station. His conscience was clear and he had never sucked up to, or curried favour from, the Establishment. He should have changed tactics years ago but now it was too late. He was for the chop at the end of his time in Gan and there was nothing he could do about it.

Chapter Two

A Cranwell Society Wedding
July 10th 1960

MICHAEL LIONEL TOWNSEND, the only son of a retired diplomat, was born in Torquay on 10th May 1924. Educated at Wellington School he emerged, in June 1942, with creditable examination results. At Wellington he was a bit of a loner and his impulsive nature frequently led to trouble with the school authorities. His school reports described him as 'above average' in intellect, lazy and haphazard in his approach to essay writing and arithmetic and prone to bouts of instant aggression which led to confrontation and a severe caning from the headmaster on more than one occasion. His one redeeming feature was his complete dedication to the school's Air Training Corps and his single-mindedness and determination to become an RAF pilot. In October 1942 he volunteered for the RAF and was sent for basic training to an officer cadet unit near Blackpool. Much to his disappointment he was turned down for fighter pilot training on the grounds that he was too aggressive and cocksure and on his luke-warm Wellington School reports. At that time the RAF were desperately short of bomber pilots and, as second best, Mike was drafted to Bomber Command for flying training.

In December 1942 he sailed for Halifax, Nova Scotia, where he was taught to fly. His six months in Canada was not without incident. He managed to prang a Handley Page Halifax whilst executing a half-loop at low altitude, a manoeuvre only suitable for high speed fighters a quarter the weight of his cumbersome crate. He was reprimanded but not taken off the course. A few weeks later, for his own convenience, he tried to 'park' another Halifax too near the officers' mess and clipped a wing which brought a final reprimand. Mike Townsend got his wings in the summer of 1943 and flew home to the UK where he was posted to an operational heavy bomber squadron based at Waddington in Lincolnshire. Flying Lancasters on night raids over Germany, Mike's war started in earnest in November 1943. He brought with him to Waddington a reputation of being a bit 'mad' and very soon he was living up to expectations. At pre-raid briefings he was always the first to volunteer his crew to fly in the lead plane, having worked out that the first attackers over the target came as a surprise to the German defenders on the ground. And so it proved on most of his early sorties when he, and his crew, returned home unscathed while the 'poor beggars' at the tail end of the sortie got shot up. In early 1944 RAF night bombing tactics changed and Mosquito pathfinders were sent ahead to light up the target for the bombers. The surprise element was now lost and the first bombers 'in' caught the full brunt of German anti-aircraft defences. Mike now volunteered his plane, and crew, for tail end duties on the premise that the bombers arriving ahead of his plane would have 'bombed the shit' out of the German ground defences. The main danger of flying 'tail end Charlie' was from German night fighters who were constantly improving their effectiveness in combat. All in all Mad Mike's wartime strategy paid dividends. He flew thirty-two sorties over enemy territory and returned with his crew and plane intact from each and every one of them including his final strafe over Dresden on 16th February 1945. Ordered by Winston Churchill and masterminded by Air Chief Marshal 'Bomber' Harris, Mad Mike and his Lancaster crew were involved in the second successive night raid on the German city on the banks of the Elbe. Realising the war would soon be over he treated his crew to an extra 'run' over the target and, at a thousand feet, dipped the plane's wings in salute, 'a la' Spitfires and Hurricanes in the Battle of Britain. The Dresden raids produced violent repercussions from Herr Goebbel's propaganda ministry and Lord Haw Haw, in his nightly broadcast to the British people, claimed that low-flying aircraft had machine-gunned helpless, fleeing German civilians on the ground. Mad Mike had carried out his final strafe as a lark, insensitive to the fact he was unnecessarily exposing his crew to danger. Smithy, his sergeant rear gunner, might have let off a few rounds to celebrate their successful raid but, such was the intensity of smoke from the fires below, it was absurd to suggest that civilians had been targeted and visibility over the burning city at 800 feet was virtually zero. Mad Mike's lark generated a stern rebuke from his station commander but for his part in the Dresden raids he was awarded a Bar to his DFC. The war in Europe ended on 8th May 1945 and by this time Mike Townsend had made up his mind to pursue a career in the Royal Air Force.

In September 1948 Flight Lieutenant Mike Townsend was seconded to the London School of Economics on a three year Bomber Harris scholarship to read politics and Russian. London was slowly recovering from the ravages of war and the dashing flight lieutenant, with his impressive war record and a row of medals on his chest, had little difficulty in pulling the birds. Within a fortnight of his arrival at LSE Mad Mike was living up to his reputation. Organizer and leader of student rags, convener of legendary pub crawls, instigator of pyjama parties and the inevitable orgy to follow at his Sloane Street flat and a prankster and practical joker in lectures and the common room, he soon became a legend at LSE. To be in Mad Mike's set was a much sought after honour especially for impressionable female students. Mike always had a long-haired, frequently shabbily-dressed, blonde clinging to his arm and hanging on to his every word. For the impecunious students, often eeking out a miserable existence on the breadline, Mike was a wealthy man. His regular income as a flight lieutenant and payment of his course fees and lodgings from an RAF bursary, ensured he lived the life of luxury and, at the same time, entertained lavishly. He grew his hair long and cultivated a pony tail, an original hippie in the pre-hippie era. He also found great enjoyment and stimulation from smoking pot.

Within a few days of starting his course Mike came to realise that most of his fellow students were rabid socialists and many were overtly communist. He stimulated interest and fun amongst the student body by conducting witch-hunts and holding mock trials and gradually developed an empathy with the 'commies' who were hell-bent on propagating their ideology among the politically-motivated students. Mike egged them on just for the fun of it. He took part in debates on the policies and economy of the USSR more often than not, and with tongue in cheek, upholding the party line. As a result of his liaison with the rough and ready pseudo-Marxists he found himself, one evening, smoking pot at a party with his current girlfriend in a seedy basement flat in Earls Court. Easily distinguished by their open-toed sandals, unwashed smelly bodies and unkempt straggly beards, political activists at the party openly plied their trade and spread the communist gospel amongst a receptive audience. Mike had learnt early on how to deal with these dedicated evangelists but the man who seduced him into joining the Russian secret service was a different kettle of fish. He was elegantly-groomed and well-dressed in a blue suit, white shirt and polka-dot tie. Clean-shaven, and smelling of an exotic deodorant, he was clearly well-off and had expensive tastes. Though his English was faultless, a faint middle-European accent intruded insensibly into his speech. His approach to Mike was subtle and friendly without banging tables and high-pitched shouting. He kept the conversation to mundane matters and laughed about Arsenal losing to Liverpool at Highbury and discussed at length the latest opera at Covent Garden. He told Mike he worked in the City, announcing his name was Edward but everyone called him Teddy and would Mike please call him Teddy? By this time Mike was floating on a pot-induced cloud nine. When he woke up the following morning with a thumping hangover, lying next to a blonde girlfriend, he only vaguely recollected the charming young man and the events of the night before.

A fortnight later Flight Lieutenant Tony Widgeon, a flying pal from Waddington, turned up unannounced. He was in London for a couple of days and had little difficulty in coercing Mike into a series of pub crawls and wild parties. Tony was a typical, prototype RAF officer and a gentleman to his fingertips. Tall, good-looking, and sporting a black, neatly-trimmed moustache, his brylcreemed black hair and deep set dark-brown eyes made him a dead ringer for George Raft. Though he attracted females like bees to a honeypot, his 'flings' with the opposite sex, curiously, were short-lived and a weeks' romance was a long time in Tony Widgeon's social calendar. On his last night in town Tony arranged to start off drinking at the Prospect of Whitby in Wapping and, when he arrived, he was not alone. His companion turned out to be Teddy who did not let on that he and Mike had met each other at the rave-up in a basement flat in Earls Court. Teddy showed great interest in Mike's Russian studies. So far Mike's main contribution towards Russian culture at the LSE had been to promote vodka as a staple drink in the students union bar. Teddy was an experienced drinker and vodka was his tipple. After a pub crawl of the East End they ended up at Lyons Corner House in Charing Cross Road for a late brunch and made their separate ways home, and to bed, in the early hours of the morning.

Out of the blue, four nights later, Teddy appeared in Ye Old White Horse, LSE's 'local' public house in St Clements Lane. He took Mike into a quiet corner of the pub and very quickly revealed his intentions. He wanted to recruit Mike into the Russian secret service. Mike took it as a joke, a laugh, a bit of fun and goaded the Russian agent to see how far he would go. Teddy was deadly serious and went all the way. He demanded a definite 'yes' or 'no' and Mike agreed to think matters over. In a sober moment, on the following day, he ruminated over his position viz-à-viz the secret agent and his daily contact with left wingers and commies at the LSE and made up his mind to string along with Teddy. Two nights later the elegantly dressed agent was back at Ye Old White Horse.

"What is your decision comrade?"

"I agree," Mike replied solemnly, "what's in it for me?"

"You'll be paid handsomely when you perform a service for us. You won't regret your decision. My comrades will be pleased with their new recruit."

Two quick vodkas later Teddy left and Mike never saw him again. For a fortnight after his meeting with the Russian agent Mike had a guilty conscience but he soon forgot all about the affair and returned to his life of pleasure and debauchery.

Flight Lieutenant Michael Townsend graduated from the LSE in May 1951 with passable results in his two subjects. In October, now sporting a standard RAF haircut, he became a political and language instructor at Cranwell College and a year later came promotion to squadron leader and an operational posting to Bückeburg in Germany. A second three year term of operational duty followed at Akrotiri in Cyprus and then it was back to Cranwell as a deputy staff officer. Mad Mike left his mark in both overseas stations. As president of the mess committee in Bückeburg he supervised party games after mess dinners. Most of the games ended in a demonstration of physical prowess or inventiveness and, in one unfortunate incident, two young officers suffered serious injuries when ordered by the PMC to parachute-roll off a windowsill. Mike Townsend was severely reprimanded. And then, at Akrotiri, he was again up before his commanding officer when, in a drunken state, he rode a motorcycle through the mess causing considerable damage to fixtures and fittings. Both messes had reason to remember Mad Mike's term of service with a mixture of regret and pleasure. By May 1959 he was back again in Cranwell with high hopes of promotion and a command of his own. But, by this time in his life, the powers that be had made up their minds that Michael Lionel Townsend was a liability and not destined for elevation into the higher command echelons of the Royal Air Force. He was deemed to be an efficient workhorse but temperamentally unsuited for higher command. During his second term of service at Cranwell, on the 20th December 1959, Mike met his wife-to-be at a hunt ball at the George Hotel in Grantham and this meeting changed the direction of his life and his future career in the Royal Air Force.

Vanessa Henrietta Willoughby, the only daughter of Brigadier Sir Charles and Lady Willoughby, was born at Belvoir Hall, the family ancestral home in Leicestershire, on 12th April 1929. A pupil at Rodean during the war she furthered her education at a secretarial and language finishing college in Geneva. Having completed her education she returned to Daddy's mansion in Leicestershire in 1952 where, protected and venerated by the old brigadier, she lived the genteel life of a county gentlewoman. At college she attained a halting command of French but had very little aptitude, or inclination, for secretarial work. Never an atheletic sportswoman Vanessa had an all-abiding love of horses and everything horsey. Conveniently Sir Charles, snubbed by the Belvoir Hunt, had made himself master of the Lincolnshire Border Hunt and Vanessa rode to hounds at every possible opportunity. The brigadier subscribed to a private box in the Royal Enclosure at Ascot and was a steward at Windsor Great Park Polo Club. He graced these venues with a timid, and overwhelmed, Lady Willoughby on one arm and his daughter Vanessa on the other. And it was as a direct result of the brigadier's mastership of the Lincolnshire Border Hunt that thirty year old Vanessa met her husband-to-be.

Vanessa was a curious combination of classic facial beauty and corporeal ungainliness. She had a perfectly-shaped, oval, peaches-and-cream face, fully-rounded lips and regular, pearly-white teeth. Widely set, innocent pale blue eyes and a mop of natural blonde hair completed the picture of a ravishing English rose. The finely-chiselled head was supported by a long swan-like neck. When God, with the Willoughby's connivance, made Vanessa his creative talents stopped short at her collarbones. Vanessa's long, angular torso was S-shaped and a kyphotic thoracic spine pulled the front of her chest inwards. To say she was flat-chested was an understatement and her pubescent breasts could hardly be classified as 'fried eggs', a popular yardstick of breast size in common usage at the time. To compensate for bowing of her upper spine, the lower half of her body pushed forwards producing a permanent abdominal protrusion, reminiscent of a six month pregnancy. Her pot belly sat atop splayed-out iliac crests which gave a shelf-like appearance to her pelvic girdle. Vanessa's thin body was supported by long, spindly legs set so far apart that uncharitable escorts often commented 'You can drive a bus between her legs'. Fully aware of his prospective wife's inadequacies Mike's comments were hardly flattering, 'I'm not a bum or tit man. Give me a pretty face any day of the week. After all it's nice to look at a beautifully arranged mantelpiece when you're poking the fire. Don't you agree?'

And everyone agreed with Mad Mike.

Vanessa was an out-and-out snob and had been groomed by her parents to become lady of the manor. Waited on hand and foot, her upbringing led her to expect attention and acclamation and menial tasks, such as washing, ironing and cooking, were completely without her capabilities. Her physical disproportions were cleverly concealed by the expertise of London's Bond Street haute couture houses. At the hunt ball, in her long, pink evening gown suitably padded in strategic places, she looked stunning. Mike fell for her that night and it was her face that carried the day. He thought she would make an acceptable model for a Degas or Picasso oil but, in truth, these venerable artists would probably be more interested in her thin, S-shaped body than in her facial beauty. When Vanessa stood upright people feared she was about to topple backwards and frequently proffered a supporting hand.

The Lincolnshire Border Hunt Ball was held annually at the George Hotel in Grantham during the week leading up to Christmas. As befitted the Master, Sir Charles Willoughby entertained the Lord Lieutenant and two senior retired army cronies and their ladies on the top table. Lady Willoughby sat subserviently next to the Lord Lieutenant and Vanessa was parked at the end of the table next to a doddery old cavalry colonel who had overindulged before he arrived at the ball. In fact he had reached a stage of no recovery when the band struck up a waltz and as is customary on these occasions the whole top table, with the exception of Vanessa and the drunken colonel, took to the dance floor. A boisterous party from YHOM, Cranwell's York House officers mess, arrived late. They had missed the meal and a couple of boring speeches and dancing was well on the way when they burst on the scene. Mike Townsend had been coerced into joining a mess party by the younger blades who promised six 'smashing' WRAF officers but only three materialized. Pairing off started in earnest at the champagne session in YHOM and it soon became evident that the squadron leader was an odd-man out. "Bad luck old chap," one of the young flight lieutenants commiserated, "we didn't know the birds were going to be Waafs, which excludes senior officers!" Mike smiled at the impetuous young flyer as he envisaged himself in the young man's shoes ten years previously. There were two wallflowers at the hunt ball: the one, the female on the Master's table, and Mike Townsend on the YHOM table. Surreptitious glances winged to and fro across the dance floor and, after ten minutes, Mike got up and asked Vanessa for a dance. The brigadier gave his permission and noted with satisfaction Mike's senior rank and impressive campaign ribbons. Conversation on the dance floor was almost exclusively about horses.

Vanessa: "Do you ride to hounds?"

Mike: "No."

Vanessa: "Do you go racing?"

Mike: "No ma'am."

15

Vanessa: "Do you watch polo? I often meet the Duke of Edinburgh playing a chukka or two at Windsor Great Park."

Mike: "No ma'am, I've never seen a polo match."

Vanessa: "What do you do for recreation squadron leader?"

Mike: "I fly aeroplanes, ma'am."

Vanessa: "How interesting. And have you been doing this for a long time?"

Mike: "Since 1943, ma'am."

Vanessa: "You flew in the war?"

Mike: "Yes ma'am. I was in Bomber Command."

The dance ended but, as soon as the band struck up another waltz, Mike was on his feet and across to the top table to lead Vanessa on to the dance floor. They danced together all night and, in between dances, Vanessa reported to Daddy that the officer paying court was a wartime pilot.

"Bomber Command and all that. Must be a good chap, Vanessa. I see he's got a Bar to his DFC. I'd like to get to know him better. Why not invite him over for Christmas lunch? Christmas Day is a beastly time in any mess. If he's not made other arrangements ask him to join us at the Hall."

The brigadier had obviously given his seal of approval to Mike's advances. With no definite plans for celebrating Christmas Day Mike was surprised to hear himself saying "Thank you, Vanessa. I will be delighted to have Christmas lunch with your family."

That was the beginning of an affair which led to a formal proposal of marriage in March 1960. The engagement lasted three months and a wedding date was fixed for July. One minute Squadron Leader Michael Townsend was a free agent and the next everything went pear-shaped and wedding bells were about to chime. All arrangements for the wedding were supervised by the brigadier who sorely wanted to see his daughter wed. Lady Willoughby, totally overwhelmed by the bustling brigadier, had little say in the matter and to a large extent Vanessa was in the same boat. She had learnt at an early age to obey her father and as she often repeated, 'Daddy always knows best'.

Ever since the announcement of their engagement in The Times at Easter 1960 the Townsend-Willoughby wedding promised to be one of the premier society events of the year. Brigadier Sir Charles Willoughby

16

mobilized all his old army cronies and influential relatives. There was a tenuous family connection on Lady Willoughby's side with the Kents and Sir Charles was flattered when the Duke and Duchess accepted his invitation. The old chap assumed control of all arrangements and was determined that his one and only little filly should have a good send-off. Vanessa and her mother were only allowed one chore – selection and fitting of the bridal gown and even this task was largely delegated to Hardy Amies, the London haute couturier. Mike's personal guest list consisted of his ailing and widowed father and two maiden aunts from Clacton-on-Sea. He bolstered his numbers with a few pals from his flying days and the entire officer complement of York House officers mess together with their spouses or partners. All in all two hundred guests were expected to attend the wedding. The ceremony was destined to be conducted by the senior chaplain of St Michael and All Angels Church in Cranwell, followed by a reception at College Hall officers mess, abbreviated to CHOM by the airmen. Weather permitting, seating for guests had been arranged under red, white and blue awnings on the cadet parade ground in front of the mess. The band of RAF College, Cranwell was booked to play during the wedding breakfast and a dozen officer cadets had been mobilized to form an arcade of honour when the married couple emerged from the church to run the gauntlet of well-wishing confetti throwers. The brigadier ordered two white Rolls Royces for the bridal party and a four-tier wedding cake surmounted by a marzipan replica of a Lancaster bomber and the figurine of a mounted horsewoman. With military precision, Sir Charles made meticulous preparations for the biggest day in the life of his one and only daughter. In one respect, over which he had no control, his planning failed dismally. The unseasonable weather on 10th July 1960 was atrocious. It rained heavily all day.

Mike Townsend insisted on having Tony Widgeon as his best man and he flew in from Malta to RAF Brize Norton three days before the big event. Together with four officers from YHOM they went on a stag-night pub crawl of local hostelries on the eve of the wedding and, very much the worse for wear, the party ended up at a seventeenth century coaching inn five miles from Cranwell. By around 2.00 am the last two left standing at the bar in the Greyhound at Folkingham were Mike and his best man.

"Tell me, Tony, how do you rate our chances for promotion? I've been in the RAF for seventeen years, and so have you, and here we are still squadron leaders."

Tony Widgeon fiddled with his whisky glass and slurred, "The way I see it, Mike, is this. Too many chaps stayed on after the war and our promotion has been blocked by senior colleagues. And now they're cutting back on bombers and the accent is on fast fighters with masses of electronics. You need a degree in maths and physics to fly these new kites. I can just about manage a Meteor but the new-fangled machines are out of my league. My job in Malta is almost purely admin and I'm virtually grounded. I can't see me going much further up the ladder."

Mike digested his friend's comments for a few seconds. "I get your point old chap but you stand a better chance than I do. You've kept operational and I haven't flown a kite for over four years. I can't see a hope in hell of promotion."

Tony's brow furrowed as he concentrated on Mike's words. "You did three years at the LSE?"

"Yes," Mike replied, "but I read Russian and politics."

"Ah! Politics is a growing commodity in the service. Command needs political wallahs to deal with the Khrushchev's of this world. Mark my words! You'll be at the top of the ladder long before I get there." And then, as an afterthought, he added, "and what you're about to do tomorrow will do your promotion chances no harm. Vanessa has county pedigree and is well connected and her Daddy's big in the army."

He winked at Mike and continued, "And what about top table at the reception? You'll get noticed and remembered and, bingo, you'll have extra rings on your sleeves in no time."

They lapsed into silence broken by a question from Mike. "You mentioned the LSE? Whatever happened to that chap you brought along to the Prospect of Whtiby?"

"Oh, that fellow Teddy? I haven't seen or heard of him since. That night I bumped into him in a pub in Chelsea and only brought him along to the Prospect for a lark. Do you know, Mike, I think he was a Pole, or a Russian? He tried to get me to enlist in some sort of organization. I told him to bugger off! He didn't bother you did he?"

Mike gulped down the last of his whisky, "No. He didn't sound me out," he lied, "If he had I would have given him the same reply."

Mike felt uneasy, and inexplicably uncomfortable, at the thought he was unable to reveal the truth to his best friend. He changed the subject abruptly. "How about your love life, Squadron Leader Widgeon? Any unattached females on the horizon?"

Tony Widgeon's face suffused with colour as he replied without conviction, "There's plenty of crumpet about but I have no special woman. I'm enjoying myself playing the field."

Mike made a joke of it. "You'd better hurry before your cannon gets clogged-up and rusty through under-usage!"

They burst out laughing. With an effort Mike squared his shoulders.

"Okay, Squadron Leader Widgeon, we'll have one for the road and that's it."

Clutching a refilled glass of whisky, Tony proposed a toast. "To our lasting friendship and rapid promotion, old pal."

Mike mumbled 'promotion'. They clinked glasses and downed their tumblers of whisky in one.

When Sir Charles Willoughby and Vanessa left Belvoir Hall in a chauffeur driven white Rolls Royce the skies overhead were grey and overcast and by the time they were half way down Lighter Than Air Road and approaching the church at Cranwell, it was raining cats and dogs. Sir Charles was uncharacteristically nervous. He cast one eye skywards and the other at his gold half-hunter pocket watch and, leaning forwards, eased his well padded frame inside his tight-fitting number one dress. "We're going to be very late Vanessa. Let's hope the rain eases off."

He gently touched the back of his daughter's hand. She was near to tears. "Daddy! I don't want to go through with the wedding. I look a mess and this dress is digging into my ribs."

"Don't be silly Vanessa! All arrangements are made. The Duke and Duchess are there and you can't let them down. Pull yourself together darling! You're marrying a good man with excellent prospects. Besides, you look beautiful in that Hardy what's-his-name dress. So buck up my little filly."

The insensitive, gruff old brigadier did not realise that his daughters' reluctance to go through with the ceremony was as much based on her fear of the sexual demands of marriage and the honeymoon as the imagined discomfort she was suffering from her exquisitely ribbed and padded wedding trousseau. By the time they pulled up outside the Church of St Michael and All Angels, Vanessa had cheered up a little but her tears were never far away from the surface.

As the wedding day wore on matters went from bad to worse. On arrival they had to be escorted into church sheltering under two multi-coloured umbrellas. Even so, the driving rain soaked Vanessa's billowing white skirts which rapidly became speckled with daubs of muddy-brown soil. The church was full to overflowing and smelt musty from the soaked uniforms and clothing of the rain-sodden congregation. After the ceremony Mike proudly escorted Vanessa down the aisle but, because of the rain, the guard of honour outside the church had been cancelled. In a grave error of misjudgment, Sir Charles insisted the wedded couple should walk the four hundred yards, alongside the cricket pitch on the Orange, from the church to the reception at College Hall. In his prenuptial plan the brigadier envisaged a sunny day and a game of cricket on the Orange but the scheduled match between Cranwell and the Adastrians had been called off mid-morning. Outside the church a few enthusiasts threw cascades of confetti which clung to Vanessa's white bridal gown and, from the waist down, she looked like a speckled harlequin. The tables and chairs on the parade ground had all been removed and the Cranwell College band abandoned their platform under a canopy in the open and were relegated to a crowded minstrels gallery surrounding the spacious dining room in Cadet House officers mess.

The top table guests consisted of an impressive array of senior ranking officers from both services. Apart from the bride and groom and Brigadier and Lady Willoughby, the Duke and Duchess of Kent, one air vice marshal and a major general, two air commodores and a group captain and their ladies were seated in a row with Tony Widgeon, squatting like an unwanted appendage at one end of the top table, sloshing down champagne as if there was no tomorrow. He conducted the ritual duties of best man with exaggerated aplomb. Sir Charles made a pompous and starchy speech and Mike Townsend replied in traditional style pointing out the Willoughby's were not losing a daughter but gaining a son. And then it was Tony Widgeon's turn to propose a toast and, at this point, the wedding breakfast disintegrated into a farce. Tony was well over the top and unable to speak coherently. He digressed at length on Mike's years at Wellington School and recounted in detail his frequent visits to the headmaster's study for corrective punishment. Then came Mike's war service. Laudatory at first, Tony soon settled on the theme of 'Mad Mike'. The audience laughed, sniggered and clapped until, finally, Tony got lost in a morass of incomprehensible gibberish. There were shouts from the floor of "Get on with it Widgey old boy" and "Get to the point Widgey" and, less reverently, "Cut the crap Widgey". Squadron Leader Tony Widgeon eventually got to the point, "And here we have a man with a DFC and Bar. In my book two DFC's are equivalent to a VC."

There were loud cheers from the floor as Tony slurred onwards, "Mad Mike's first DFC was well deserved. He flew thirty two sorties over Germany but his Bar is more dubious. All he did was to fly twice over the target and the second run was superfluous to requirements."

A deathly, embarrassed silence descended upon the audience. Mike looked at his fingernails while Vanessa, at his side, sat ramrod stiff. The brigadier was on the point of exploding and the Duke of Kent smiled politely to hide his discomfiture. But Tony was not finished and tried to dig himself out of the hole he had created for himself, "What I mean to say is there was no need for the second run over Dresden. But here we have a 'mad' personality and it is in his nature to take risks. After the war he spent three years at the LSE learning Russian. Russian my foot! I should know. He spent his time womanizing and drinking and Vanessa should be made aware of his wild days at the LSE."

There were boos from the audience. Tony then gave details of Mike's clashes with authority and each incident was minutely described until the boos became shouts of "Pack it in Widgey". At long last Tony Widgeon came to the end of his speech, "So there you have it, Vanessa. That's the madman you married today. As an expert horsewoman I know you will keep Mike on a tight rein and the 'Mad Mike' we have all known, and come to love over the years, will be no more."

There was a long pregnant pause and Tony gulped down a mouthful of champagne. "Traditionally the best man proposes a toast to the bridesmaids. In the absence of such ladies I have the honour to propose long life and happiness to Mad Mike and Vanessa."

The guests mumbled "To the bride and groom" and Tony Widgeon slumped heavily into his seat and passed out. The best man's speech rekindled doubts in the minds of the senior brass present about Mike Townsend's suitability to command. One by one they made their excuses and left hurriedly in their staff cars, leaving Mike to wonder why his best pal had painted such a discrediting picture of his service life. And then he realised that at the root of Tony's vilification was the dirty word 'promotion'.

The wedding had been solemnized at 2.00 pm and by 5.30 pm CHOM was empty of senior guests. Vanessa went away wearing a beige, two piece, 'new look' outfit which would have been entirely appropriate ten years previously but was out of place in the mini-skirted sixties. She was acutely aware that her thin legs and lower body were not designed for the popular pussy pelmet. Awkward to the end, she tossed her bouquet into the air as they ran through the driving rain to the waiting Humber staff car and the decorative nosegay landed fairly and squarely on the brigadier's balding head. The trials and tribulations of the day were not yet ended. The Humber developed two punctures about three miles south of Stilton and the driver abandoned the car and hired an old Ford Consul from a local garage. Bedraggled, wet and tired, the newly-married couple arrived at the Savoy in the Strand at 10.00 pm to spend the first three nights of their honeymoon in the bridal suite.

As soon as they were alone Vanessa's resolve cracked and she burst into tears. "What a disastrous day!" she sobbed, "I never want to see that horrible man Widgeon ever again. How could he say those awful things about you in front of the Kents and all those high-ranking officers? Daddy was furious." And she again broke down and started another sobbing fit.

Mike tried to console her. "Tony was drunk and made up most of the stories. I thought he was quite funny."

"Be that as it may, he had no right to run you down in public" and, with a woman's intuition, she added, "It won't do your promotion chances any good at all."

She then lay fully-clothed on the bed and announced she had a headache and was going to sleep which became a feature on the subsequent two nights of their honeymoon.

After two days at the Savoy Hotel in London they crossed the Channel by boat train to spend a week at George V Hotel in Paris. Vanessa's demeanour changed radically. The opulence of the hotel, the dress sense of the Parisienne ladies and the variety of food and fine wines suited her aristocratic taste down to the ground. She became gay and light-hearted, almost flirtatious, and the chance to practice her rusty French gave rise to endless amusement. Encouraged by Mike, she used her newly-rediscovered talent on their frequent shopping forays and for ordering meals at posh restaurants. All in all the Paris sojourn was a great success and their shared enjoyment was reflected in Vanessa's attitude to Mike. She flirted openly with him and their nightly lovemaking had the intensity and passion of two young lovers discovering each other for the first time. But all good things come to an end and, on the eighth day, they bid farewell to the magical city where they had consummated their love and spent happy, sun-kissed days amidst its boulevards, museums, shops and restaurants. The September issue of the Tatler carried a full report of the Townsend/ Willoughby wedding of the month. The heavily-padded article displayed photographs of the Duke and Duchess of Kent and notable dignitaries and their spouses but only included one photograph of the happy couple as they stood, arms linked in traditional fashion, in the driving rain outside the Church of St Michael and All Angels.

Cranwell College's married quarters, at the northern end of Lighter Than Air Road, were controlled by a station families officer and strictly allocated to married personnel ranging from type 1 houses for senior officers to type 5 flats for airmen on the permanent staff. When he married, Mike was half way through his tour of duty at Cranwell and, though he applied for a quarter when he became engaged to Vanessa, he was still on the waiting list in August 1960. He resigned himself to continue messing at York House in Cranwell, while Vanessa went to live at home and, when off duty, Mike had to be content with weekend visits to Belvoir Hall. In the course of the following weeks his marital troubles began escalating and involved Brigadier Willoughby who sprang to Vanessa's defence at the drop of a hat. She was obviously the apple of the brigadier's eye and, as such, could do no wrong.

To say that the Willoughbys were fanatical blood sports enthusiasts would be a gross understatment. The brigadier rode to hounds two or three times a week, forcing his wife to comply, and Vanessa needed no coaxing whatever to join in. She was as fanatical about foxhunting, if not more so, than her father. In the close season the Willoughbys went salmon fishing to Scotland in May and September and rarely missed a day grouse shooting every year on the Yorkshire moors on 'the glorious twelfth'. To complete their lust for blood they were syndicate members of two local pheasant shoots and had fishing rights on the Test in the summer months. Privately, Mike loathed blood sports of any description but, to keep the peace at Belvoir Hall, he pretended to be mildly interested. If invited to participate he usually found an excuse claiming pressure of work and the brigadier, a military man to his fingertips, understood that sadly, but honourably, duty came first. Following their trip to the Spey during the first week in September 1960, conversation at the Hall was almost entirely confined to recollections of the salmon 'grassed' and, with increasing fervour, arrangements for the foxhunting season due to start in October. Much to Mike's displeasure anticipation was mounting daily and, due to his lack of interest, he felt a complete outsider. What galled him most was Vanessa's dedication to the cause and her rejection out of hand in discussing matters relating to their marital arrangements and fulfillment of their sacred vows.

Matters came to a head at Belvoir Hall on the third Saturday in October when the Willoughby's had guests for the weekend. A pheasant shoot, which Mike deliberately avoided, had been arranged in the daytime and he turned up at the Hall for Saturday night dinner. On this occasion the invited guests were a Mr Claude Bernard and his wife. As befitting his position as a multi-millionaire Mr Bernard lived in a secluded mansion on the outskirts of Hampstead Heath. How he accumulated his wealth was unclear but rumour had it he dabbled in arms dealing and made a fortune after two lucrative deals with the Lybian government. He was one of the noveau riche and was attempting to buy his way into aristocratic society. Rumour also had it he was in line for a knighthood, recommended by the government of the day for services to industry, but what that entailed remained a complete mystery to the populace at large. Sir Charles' interest in the

Bernards was purely pecuniary and, for a mere twenty thousand pounds, the wealthy entrepreneur would be made Deputy Master of Foxhounds to the Lincolnshire Border Hunt. With this in mind the wily brigadier had been working on him all day and Claude Bernard, with his thirst for social elevation, was an avid candidate. The dinner that night was something of a celebration of a pact they had concluded during the shoot but, eventually, the whole arrangement went horribly astray. After the ladies retired for coffee the men sat at the dining table passing around a vintage port in the traditional clockwise direction and puffing on Havana cigars. Conversation continued to be about foxhunting and the Lincolnshire Border Hunt and Mike, rather the worse for wear, was getting short tempered and irritable. Out of the blue he interrupted Sir Charles in mid-sentence, "Tell me, Mr Bernard, what is the name of your company?"

"I have no company, as such, squadron leader. You could say I'm a one-man company."

There was a frosty silence. The brigadier coughed and tried to rekindle conversation with a hunting story but Mike persisted, "I must say I've never heard of your company's title."

The thin, dark-eyed, weasely-faced guest cast a withering, disdainful look at Mike, "No! You will not have heard of my organization as I'm on secret contract to the government. I'm a bit like you, squadron leader, as we're both employed by the government."

Mike, feeling his hackles rise and disliking the stranger even more, interrupted the brigadier's attempt to intervene. "With all due respect, Mr Bernard, I cannot see how your business in any way resembles mine unless, of course, you are involved in flying aeroplanes" – the latter words spoken with sarcasm and hostility.

The brigadier exploded. "That's enough, Michael. It's no concern of ours what business Claude is conducting."

A sudden pregnant silence descended on the trio when, quite suddenly, Claude Bernard's face broke into a wolfish grin reminding Mike of Nazi wartime cartoons of Herr Goebbels and Himmler. Inebriated and aroused, Claude Bernard spat out his story. "You wish to know about me squadron leader? I was born in Amsterdam of Jewish parents. My name then was Klaus Bernstein and I was arrested by the Gestapo and sent to Buchenwald in 1943. We were liberated by the English and, after the war, I emigrated to England. I was penniless and found work in a shoe factory in Stepney. Then it's a long story of hardship until I got a job with Ferranti and this led to my present government contract. You see I sell tanks, guns and planes to foreign countries and I get a commission from the government. That's how I made my money and I've worked hard for it and run risks. It's a bit like the risk you take in the Air Force, squadron leader. I stand a chance of getting shot at every day."

Mike's brain was sharp and incisive and his words came out in a vitriolic torrent. "Your job, sir, doesn't compare in any way with my career in the Royal Air Force. All my activities are just and above board. Yours are clandestine and under the counter and it sounds as if they're on the boderline of legality most of the time."

"Yes, Mr Townsend. I work from the shadows and in strict secrecy. I've supplied arms to all the Arab countries, Israel and Eastern Europe."

With a plastic smile on his face and wishing to further impress his listeners Bernard continued, "Let me tell you about last month's deal. At great risk to myself I went to Dresden to speak to the East German government. They bought two obsolete Meteor jets and four Crusader tanks from me. From the deal I made a cool half a million in commission. Much more lucrative than flying for the Air Force wouldn't you say Mr Townsend?"

Sir Charles was on his feet in a rage. He glared in turn at the antagonists, "Gentlemen, gentlemen, that's enough! Please calm down."

Mike leapt to his feet, trembling with anger. "I bid you both goodnight. I'm returning to the College where I know I'll be serving the Queen and not only looking after number one."

He stomped out of the dining room and curtly bid goodnight to the ladies. Driving a drunken pathway towards Cranwell he reflected on his reactions and attitude towards the Jewish immigrant who had made vast sums of money arms dealing with the Arab world and, in particular, with the Communist Bloc in Eastern Europe. And yet, who was he to pass judgement? He had made a vow to serve Moscow but, thank God, he had not heard from them for over ten years. Hopefully they had forgotten all about him and, in the meantime, he had to smooth over the cracks in his relationship with the Willoughbys and with Vanessa.

First thing Monday morning Mike was on the telephone to Brigadier Willoughby. "I wish to apologise for my behaviour on Saturday night, Sir Charles. I was extremely rude to your guest and that's unforgivable."

There was a lengthy pause, as if the brigadier was struggling to formulate an answer, and when his gruff voice spoke up it was sharp and incisive but not entirely unsympathetic. "I'm disappointed in you, Michael. For what its worth I couldn't stomach that business about selling arms to East Germany. The Israelis I don't mind but not the blasted Krauts! Herr Bernard packed his bags early yesterday morning and announced he would place his sponsorship elsewhere. Our Hunt lost twenty thousand pounds as a result but there's a principle involved. Still, you had no reason to be rude to a guest."

"Thank you, sir. I shan't do it again. I drank too much at dinner and downed too many port wines afterwards. May I speak to Vanessa please?"

Vanessa came on the phone, "Daddy's told me all about the argument. How could you Michael? The fellow was Daddy's guest. I didn't take to him, or his wife, but that's no reason to be rude. Anyway they went home early on Sunday morning."

"I've apologised to your father. He's taken it very well."

"The Hunt is poorer by a few thousand pounds but we'll manage. We're starting out to hunt on Wednesday but the first major meet of the season will be on Saturday. Will you be able to join us?"

"No, Vanessa. I'll give Saturday a skip. I'll turn up for lunch after church on Sunday. Have a good day out and happy hunting."

Mike was glad to get out of a commitment and had no intention of riding to hounds. The time would come when he would have to explain his objections to Vanessa and the Willoughbys. The present, just after healing a rift with his in-laws, was not the right time and this turned out to be only a temporary respite.

At the end of November Mike was informed by the families officer that a type 4 apartment would become available in mid-January. Neither Vanessa, nor her parents, seemed thrilled with the news and the brigadier quickly voiced his objections, "It could not come at a more inconvenient time for the Hunt. The January meets have already been scheduled and Vanessa is a tower of strength in my organization.

She's done it for so many years, I would be unable to run the show without her. May we defer a decision until the hunting season is over in March?"

Due to his recent faux pas Mike was in no position to argue. He asked lamely, "What are Vanessa's wishes?"

"Ask her yourself dear boy! You'll find Vanessa agrees with me."

And Vanessa, true to form, agreed with her father as, in her opinion, 'Daddy always knew best'.

Mike was forced to continue a bachelor's existence at YHOM where his fellow officers often teased him about a separate existence from his new wife. He countered by claiming his temporary separation was inevitable due to lack of a suitable married quarter, a position which would soon be rectified. But in his heart of hearts, he was depressed and wondering where he went wrong. He was certainly not strong enough to stand up to the combined willpower of Vanessa and her bullying father. He was prepared to let matters rest for the time being if an event of the utmost importance had not occurred in the second week of December. Vanessa announced she had been to see a doctor and was eighteen weeks pregnant. On hearing the news Mike rushed off to Belvoir Hall.

"I'm thrilled with the news Vanessa. I'm very proud and happy for you" and, turning towards the Willoughbys, "Are you excited, sir?"

Sir Charles Willoughby spoke on behalf of his timid wife in a loud, blustery voice, "Congratulations old boy. We're extremely pleased with the news. It does mean, of course, that my little filly won't be able to complete the hunting season. She'll have to give up riding in a couple of months."

Vanessa chirped in, "Nonsense, Daddy! I'll complete the course without any trouble. I'm fit as a fiddle."

Mike was flabbergasted and blurted out, "There's no question of Vanessa riding again until the baby is born."

The brigadier spoke for the whole family. "Rot and balderdash! Doc McDonald says she could ride for a further six to eight weeks and he's my authority on the subject."

Mike tensed and held back his anger with difficulty. "The life of our unborn child is at risk. As Vanessa's husband, my wishes are for her not to ride again before our child is born. I wish to make my position clear."

The brigadier was taken down a peg or two but he was still adamant, "To coin a phrase, 'Vanessa is as strong as an ox'. The Doc gave her M and D and until he says 'stop', the show will go on."

Mike gave way reluctantly. Later, alone with Vanessa, he voiced his objections again but found she was completely in accord with her father, "I trust my father and Dr McDonald implicitly. They would not advise it unless everything is perfectly safe."

Neither the brigadier, nor Vanessa, felt it necessary to mention that Dr McDonald was a prominent member of the Lincolnshire Border Hunt and had a vested interest in keeping Vanessa actively involved in hunting for as long as possible. For once Vanessa should have listened to Mike and saved herself a basketful of trouble.

Five days before Christmas Day 1960, the Lincolnshire Border Hunt was holding a meet in preparation for their traditional Boxing Day event at which Mike would have to participate. He had no stomach for this day of carnage and, much less, for the hunt ball which would be held, as usual, at the George Hotel in Grantham on Friday night. He was sitting at his office desk, musing over some new Queen's Regulations and recollecting how he met Vanessa at the ball exactly a year ago, when the telephone rang and interrupted his reverie.

"Squadron Leader Townsend speaking."

"This is Sister Francis from BUPA Hospital, Grantham. Your wife has been admitted to the emergency ward. She's not seriously hurt and has asked for you. Can you come across urgently?"

"Of course, sister. I'll be there in twenty minutes. Are you able to tell me what's wrong?"

"I'm afraid not, sir. All I can tell you is she was brought in by ambulance from the hunt."

"Thank you, sister. I'll be with you as quickly as I can."

Mike drove at breakneck speed to Vanessa's bedside. When he arrived two white-coated orderlies and a staff nurse were about to wheel her on a trolley down to the operating theatre. Vanessa was pale and white as a sheet and woozy from her premedication. Mike grasped her hand and her eyes flickered open for about ten seconds. She whispered in a dry-mouthed croak, "I'm sorry Michael. I fell off my horse and I'm bleeding a bit down below. Daddy knows I'm here but I insisted he should carry on with the hunt."

Before Mike could reply her eyes wandered and closed. Mike bent over and kissed her cool, lifeless lips. The staff nurse whispered urgently, "You'll have to excuse us, sir. They're waiting for Mrs Townsend in theatre."

In a trice Vanessa was whisked away leaving Mike standing in the empty cubicle. With that Sister Francis appeared and took him into her private office. "Quite a shock for you Squadron Leader Townsend. I couldn't tell you much on the telephone but I can now put you in the picture. Your wife came off her horse while jumping a fence at the hunt. No bones are broken but she's losing blood heavily and there's a good chance the surgeons will be unable to save your baby."

Mike shook his head incredulously and felt nauseated. His worst fears had materialized. Why had the stubborn brigadier not seen sense? He was near to tears of frustration and impotence. "Thank you Sister Francis. I'm sure the surgeons will do all they can. How long will my wife be under the anaesthetic?"

"The operation will take about an hour but Mrs Townsend will be flat out for three hours. I've tried to get in touch with Sir Charles, or Lady Willoughby, but they're still out hunting. I'll keep trying. If you will sit in the waiting room I'll bring you a pot of tea."

Mike sat in numbed silence in the empty waiting room staring vacantly at the tiled walls and ceiling. Sister Francis looked in twice and, about half past two, ushered in a dapper, white-coated doctor whom she introduced as the gynaecologist. He shook hands with Mike and took a seat next to him. "Squadron Leader Townsend, I'm pleased to say Mrs Townsend is fine and all she now needs is a few units of blood and rest. She will be home in three days, in good time for the Christmas festivities. I regret to tell you that we failed to save her baby. He was a perfectly-formed seventeen-week male foetus. I'm sorry to bring you bad news but there was no alternative available to us. Your wife will be back in the ward in another hour and don't be alarmed when you see her. She's very pale and drowsy and on a blood drip into her arm. But, as I've said, Mrs Townsend will be home in good time for Christmas Day."

The gynaecologist stood up and shook hands before departing to finish off his operating list. Mike, left alone again, began to brood silently. One minute he was thanking God, and the doctors, for

Vanessa's safe recovery from her operation and the next minute he castigated himself for not having been firmer in insisting she must not go riding during her pregnancy. If only Vanessa had a normal, sensible parent instead of the bluff old nannygoat who ruled her life.

Just before four o'clock Sister Francis appeared and took Mike to Vanessa's bedside. She was lying flat on her back, sleeping peacefully, with a blood transfusion in her left arm and pale as the white sheets draped around her body. She surfaced momentarily from her coma and smiled wanly but her efforts to speak were practically futile. She occasionally slurred some incomprehensible jargon of which Mike could only decipher one word clearly: 'Daddy'. Within the hour Sir Charles Willoughby, resplendent in his hunting pink, was ushered into the private room. He looked at Vanessa's pale, comatose figure lying on the bed and then at Mike and bellowed in his booming voice, "And how's my little filly, dear boy? Sister told me what's happened. Damn bad luck, what? Doc McDonald assures me the chances of this happening are one in a million. Still, better luck next time! My Vanessa will get through this without any bother but I'm afraid she'll miss the hunt ball on Friday."

Mike stared at the pompous, insensitive fool in amazement. Had he no feelings of compassion or remorse? He sprang to his feet and ushered the brigadier out to the corridor realizing that, though Vanessa was still under influence of an anaesthetic and virtually flat out, her sense of hearing could be quite acute. "Keep your voice down, sir. Vanessa has had a rough time and all because she was allowed to go riding against my will. And, worse still, she has lost, and I have lost, our first baby, a perfectly healthy, well-developed boy incidentally."

The brigadier slapped Mike on the back in a forlorn effort to cheer him up. "Perk up old chap! Its not the end of the world. Dr McDonald assures me Vanessa can have another brace of healthy boys."

Something snapped inside Mike's head and a surge of anger rose like a tidal wave within his chest. He took a deep breath and looked Sir Charles straight in the eye, "To hell with Dr McDonald! He's made a bloody mess of things so far and so have you, sir. I intend sitting with Vanessa for the rest of the day and overnight but, if you're going to be around, I'm taking my leave now."

It was the brigadiers' turn to get flustered, "Take it easy old boy. I know you're upset and not thinking straight. I'll get out of your way after I've said goodbye to Vanessa. If you need me I'll be at the Hall."

At first Vanessa's recovery and convalescence went according to plan. She was home at Belvoir Hall for Christmas Day and saw off the hunt from a wheelchair on Boxing Day. Then things started going wrong. Her blood loss intensified and she was re-admitted for two days in the second week of January 1961 for blood replacement and another 'minor' operation for evacuation of retained products of conception. Home again she suffered a sequence of bleeds throughout January culminating in a massive hemorrhage on the third of February. Severely shocked, and almost exsanguinated, she was rushed into the BUPA Hospital and had an emergency hysterectomy. Vanessa remained in hospital for six weeks and during that time it became abundantly clear that Belvoir Hall, with its bevy of servants, was the only suitable place for her continued convalescence.

By July 1961 Mike was again making overtures to persuade Vanessa to move into their married quarter at Cranwell and, in early August, she consented on a trial basis. Her stay in the apartment lasted only a fortnight and her objections were voiced in no uncertain terms: "This is a quaint little flat! I'm not at all happy with our neighbours. They have noisy children and I cannot stand mixing with some of the other ranks. They're a bit too common for my liking! Still I'll put up with it if I have to and why are we quartered with the other ranks? Considering your seniority we should have a house in the senior officers' compound."

"We are only here for a short time, Vanessa, and I don't qualify for a house. This is quite a nice apartment really."

Vanessa screwed up her nose. "I don't like it. I'll see if Daddy can use his influence."

"You will do nothing of the sort, Vanessa. I forbid you to use your father. It might do my career a lot of harm. So forget it."

But much to Mike's displeasure and on Vanessa's prompting, Sir Charles inquired on the 'old boy net' and Mike had to placate the camp commandant and assure him that Brigadier Sir Charles Willoughby was an interfering old busybody. Vanessa steadfastly refused to mix with the other wives, most of whom had young families and their days were committed to carting their offspring to school, music lessons and a host of sporting activities. Accustomed to servants waiting on her hand and foot she had no intention, or inclination, of doing domestic chores and insisted in having her meals brought to the apartment. And, inevitably, she took every opportunity to run off home to Belvoir Hall and her beloved Daddy. Mike's marriage became a fiasco especially when Vanessa refused sexual intercourse on someone's dubious advice at BUPA hospital. Rows and altercations became more frequent and, after a fortnights' trial, it became obvious that living together in the apartment was not going to work out and Mike reluctantly agreed Vanessa would be better off with her parents at Belvoir Hall. The Willoughby's returned from grouse shooting on the 22nd of August and Vanessa was home in good time to join them salmon fishing on the Spey in September and in plenty of time to prepare for the 1961-62 hunting season. Mike's marriage was nearly on the rocks, blamed mainly on the overbearing brigadier and he seriously considered separation and eventual divorce. His visits to Belvoir Hall became less frequent and his reception by Sir Charles and his Lady was frosty. Vanessa was cool and disinterested and fully occupied in planning pheasant shoots and foxhunting engagements for the Lincolnshire Border Hunt.

Still based in Malta, Tony Widgeon was in the UK for a flying visit over the 1961 Christmas holiday. He popped up to Cranwell for one night and teamed up with Mike, lending a sympathetic ear to his marital problems. He hinted that, after his Maltese tour of duty, he might well be landing up in Cranwell. They drank to a happy reunion sometime in 1962 and toasted each other's hopes and aspirations for rapid promotion. Following an unhappy and frustrating night at the 1961 hunt ball Mike had concluded that it was time for separation from Vanessa but Tony Widgeon's sage advice prompted him to think otherwise. He mulled over the problem throughout January and then, out of the blue, the answer came from MoD. In May he was being posted as liaison officer to the French Air Forces' Commandement du Nord based outside Versailles. On the anniversary of Vanessa's major operation, Mike arranged to dine with her at the Greyhound Inn at Folkingham. Over coffee he outlined his proposal. "I heard this week that my next attachment will be to the French Air Force. I would dearly love you to come to Paris with me. If you feel you don't wish to do so I have no alternative but to file a separation order and, at the end of my Paris assignment, I will be asking for a divorce. I'm driven to this as we can't go on living as we are for much longer."

Mike's proposal hit Vanessa like a bombshell. Her face hardened and a steely glint reduced her clear blue eyes to mere slits, "There's no question of divorce. Daddy wouldn't allow it under any circumstances."

Mike expected Vanessa to flare up and greet his request with a torrent of abuse, even to go as far as storming out of the pub in high dudgeon. But wonders never cease! As quickly as it appeared the hard glint in her eyes softened to be replaced by a coquetish 'come hither' look and her beautifully-chiselled face broke into a faint smile. "I've always wanted to revisit Paris. I'll have to discuss it with Daddy. Give me a week to work on it, Michael, and I'll give you my final answer."

Vanessa rose to go and, for the first time in ages, she kissed Mike on the cheek.

Back in Cranwell Mike had little hope that his plan would succeed. But, for once, Vanessa got the better of a heated argument with Sir Charles. She was desperately keen to live in Paris for a few years and he was swayed by the ignominy of a threatened messy divorce so soon after what he had come to regard as the society wedding of the year. After hours of debate and soul-searching the brigadier eventually gave his blessing to the proposed move. Five days after their private dinner at the old coaching inn Vanessa rang Mike Townsend's office. "Hello Michael. I have some good news for you. The answer is 'yes'. Daddy has agreed to the move and I will accompany you to Paris."

Mike was over the moon.

"Thank God for that! God bless you darling. We'll meet soon to work out all arrangements."

And so the Townsends planned their move to Paris for May 1962.

Chapter Three

The French Connection

ON THE EVENING OF 14th MAY 1962 at the end of a gloriously sunny day, Mike and Vanessa arrived at their new home in St Cloud, on the outskirts of Paris. Their third floor, two bedroomed flat overlooking the Seine had been sublet to the RAF by the British embassy and the remaining apartments were occupied by senior embassy officials and two army colonels and their families. The Townsends' palatial apartment was elegantly furnished and decorated with contemporary French masterpieces. As soon as she put her foot inside the door Vanessa was enthralled. "I love this apartment, Michael. I'll be happy here!" And when she stood on the balcony overlooking the river, her eyes sparkled. "Just look at the view. It's a typical French scene, the sort one only dreams about, or sees, in a Cezanne painting."

She moved rapidly to the bedroom balcony overlooking a busy street. The sun was setting behind the buildings opposite and, on the pavement, people were scurrying to and fro with a constant stream of noisy traffic hooting its way along the illuminated thoroughfare. Vanessa took a deep breath and turned her face towards the setting sun.

"Can't you feel the ambience, Michael? There's a faint aroma of freshly-brewed coffee and the unique smell of freshly-baked bread and *croissants* from the *boulangerie*. And just look at that quaint old café and the bistro next door! We won't starve in this place. It brings back memories of our lovely honeymoon. It's magical and I'm in love with Paris already."

Mike had not seen Vanessa so enthusiastic about anything since their honeymoon. He glanced at her smiling, radiant face and snatched a quick peck on her cheek. "The RAF have come up trumps for a change. There's no comparison between this apartment and the one we had at Cranwell. I'm glad you like it, Vanessa."

Thus began the happiest three years of their married life.

Commandement du Nord Headquarters shared the same building with a fighter squadron operating from an airfield halfway between Versailles and St Cyr and was responsible for eight fighter and four heavy bomber squadrons, stretching from Abbeville in the west to Verdun in the east. Twelve flight commodores and their staff were responsible for sections of northern France's air defence and the HQ was commanded by a General Maurice Niemes, a veteran Free French pilot of the second world war. Across a courtyard in the same building Colonel Pierre Daladier, commander of the St Cyr/Versailles fighter squadron, had his own staff of six senior officers and eighteen fighter pilots. Though completely separate for operational purposes, all the officers messed in a communal dining hall and mingled freely with each other, which enhanced fellowship and *camaraderie* in the HQ mess. The appointment of British liaison officers to French commands began in 1962 and was a direct result of President Charles De Gaulles' defence policy. In 1960 De Gaulle, who was in reality Frances' dictator of military strategy, came to the conclusion that, on development of its own nuclear deterrent, France would act independently of NATO. Behind his decision was an inherent mistrust of the Belgians and his egoistic jealousy of the selection of Brussels, ahead of Paris, as NATO's Headquarters. He foresaw that when the time came to split with NATO, France would need access to decisions of NATO's integrated command structure. Among the liaison officers appointed in the sixties, Squadron Leader Michael Townsend became the first to be seconded to Commandement du Nord.

The Townsends settled into a French lifestyle very quickly. They were allocated a maid-cum-cook by the embassy and Vanessa never lifted a finger to help with household chores, which suited her down to the ground. She was able to concentrate on socialising and soon developed a circle of embassy and Parisienne friends whose sole preoccupation was browsing around fashionable dress shops, daily visits to the hairdresser, lunching at expensive restaurants and partaking in coffee mornings and cocktail parties. Vanessa's forte was providing a typical English tea party at their flat at no physical effort to herself. A *patisserie* across the road provided cakes and succulent cucumber sandwiches and her maid dispensed tea and waited on the elegant ladies of leisure. After a few weeks her circle of friends enlarged to include French officers' wives from Commandement du Nord and her halting French improved by leaps and bounds. Very soon she came to be regarded as one of the most fashionable English hostesses in St Cloud *arrondissement.* Her enjoyment of life was reflected in her demeanour and attitude towards Mike. Gone was her bitchy, snapping repartee and, instead, she glorified in gossipy conversation centred around details of shopping excursions and coffee mornings with her socialite girlfriends. Encouraged by Mike her social calendar was fully occupied and, if Vanessa was ever really happy during their marriage, the years spent in their apartment at St Cloud would be classified as her halcyon days.

With his friendly outgoing personality Squadron Leader Townsend rapidly fitted into the daily routine at Commandement du Nord and in the course of his duties he developed firm friendships with the French officers. His sparse knowledge of French was, at first, a considerable handicap but he soon learnt the French trick of gesticulation and shrugging of the shoulders with a downcast look on his face. Much to his amusement he found most of the French officers spoke perfect English but declined to do so until they were sure about the pedigree of their British counterpart. A stickler for protocol and a confirmed bachelor, General Maurice Niemes was a quiet, reserved commandant and his senior staff were courteous, helpful and polite. They were under strict instruction to make the British squadron leader's transition into his new post as trouble-free as possible. After a few weeks in office it became clear to Mike that two nights of the working week were devoted to Headquarters business and, every Wednesday, officers of the St Cyr/Versailles squadron went for a night out on the town. On Mondays at 1800 hours, with perverse Gallic logic, General Niemes held a senior staff conference. At that meeting the commodores of each northern sector presented their reports and proposals for operations and exercises for the forthcoming week. Mike was ordered to attend and advise on sorties which might infringe on British and NATO airspace, especially in the English Channel and over the North

Sea. Though General Niemes and two of his senior commodores had flown with the RAF during the war, they were still extremely sensitive about France's capitulation to the German Luftwaffe and Mike had to bear this in mind at all times in his dealings with HQ staff. Monday night's briefing, a 'must' for Mike, usually went on until 9.00 or 10.00 pm and ended with a round of cognac and coffee. The second 'must' was the combined headquarters dining-in night, always held on a Friday and presided over by the French general. It was a grand banquet and according to General Niemes cemented relationships and was invaluable for *'espirit de corps'*. Mike looked forward to the interesting all-male dinner with superb food and excellent wines. During his first week at Nord HQ he was made an honorary member of the St Cyr/Versailles Mess and in deference to their commanding officer, Colonel Pierre Daladier, he invariably found himself joining in their Wednesday boys' night out. Strictly, he was not required to attend this jamboree but, as he explained to Vanessa, these three mess functions were written in tablets of stone. Anticipating a tirade of abuse and disapproval she was, unexpectedly, in a benevolent mood and completely immersed in her own social circle.

"I fully understand, Michael. I appreciate your job requires you to integrate with the French officers. I will be safe and sound with my new found girl friends."

Mike swallowed hard.

"The functions are very late affairs. I should be home by eleven o'clock on Mondays but it will be early hours of the morning on Wednesdays and Fridays. At least, once every three months, you can accompany me to a ladies night at the mess. Will you feel safe on your own, Vanessa?"

"Don't worry about me, Michael. I'll be fine. I'll curl up in bed with a good book."

Mike was given the go-ahead when he was expecting vehement objections and a tantrum. Life in Paris was certainly suiting his headstrong wife! He might easily have got out of Wednesday night's binge with the boys but, in truth, it promised to be more entertaining than the formal mess dinners. And so it turned out to be over the succeeding months.

By September 1962 Squadron Leader Townsend was well-established at Commandement du Nord Headquarters and enjoying both the operational and social side of his appointment and home life at his apartment in St Cloud. Whilst sat at his desk one wet September morning, out of the blue, a telephone call came from London from Tony Widgeon. "Hello, Mike, you old reprobate, how are you?"

"I'm fine, Tony. Where are you calling from?"

"I'm at MoD for the day. I'm home on compassionate leave to visit my mother. She's had a stroke but she's recovering quite well."

"I'm sorry to hear about your mother," Mike replied solemnly, aware Tony had a close relative in the Bournemouth area.

"How's Vanessa?"

"She's very well and has got over her operation. She's very happy with life here in Paris."

"Tell you why I rang Michael. I've got three days to make a dash across to Paris. I want to pop over and see you before I fly back to Malta."

For a few seconds Mike's brain went numb. He had no wish to shatter Vanessa's dream world and he knew that Tony Widgeon would be *'persona non grata'* at their St Cloud apartment. As it happened, Tony soothed his worries. "I'm booked into George Cinq hotel for two nights and I'm arriving tomorrow. Can you be free on Wednesday night?"

"Yes, of course, Tony. We'll paint the town red. Headquarters mess have a night out every Wednesday and we dine at Auberge du Sanglier Bleu in Boulevard de Clichy. I'll pick you up at George Cinq at 1900 hours."

"That'll be fine, Mike. Will Vanessa be with you?"

"No. It's strictly a boys night out."

"Okay, old boy, it sounds fun. See you on Wednesday" and he hung up. It was a surprise to hear from Tony again and, on reflection, Mike thought it wiser not to upset Vanessa by telling her about his best man's forthcoming visit.

Tony Widgeon and Mikes' night out with the French airmen was a huge success. Tony's lively personality, *bonhomie,* and fund of amusing wartime escapades went down well with the French flyers. Added to this, and to Mikes' surprise, Tony was more than competent in his command of the French language and this embellished his wartime stories. The dinner at Auberge du Sanglier Bleu was more prolonged than usual and the party broke up at around 11 o'clock when the airmen departed for their base and Mike, Tony and Colonel Pierre Daladier were left at the dining table. With a mischievous twinkle in his eye Tony broached the subject, "How would you both like to accompany me around the corner to a late show at the Moulin Rouge?"

"*Magnificent!*" the Colonel responded "but at this hour the *places* will be *complet* and we shall not get in."

"Leave it to me old chap. I've never failed yet."

Mike was impressed by Tony's versatility and contacts in Paris. He seemed to be a close friend of the manager and *concierge* at George V Hotel and the doorman at the Moulin Rouge reacted rapidly to the surreptitious passage of a hundred franc bill into his tunic pocket. The theatre manager, similarly, showered the trio with respect as he ushered them by torchlight into a private cubicle in the auditorium. It appeared to Mike at the time that their visit had been pre-arranged and pre-booked. The show had already started and their personal waiter, upon receipt of another large bill, uncorked a bottle of the house's best champagne and opened a bottle of Scotch whisky. They then settled back to enjoy the show, punctuated at regular intervals by bevies of near-naked dancing girls. When the lights went on during the first interval Tony scanned the crowded auditorium and suddenly burst out, "Well I'll be damned! There's Arnaud. I haven't seen him in years" and he waved his hand, vigorously, at a stocky man with jet black, brylcreemed hair plastered to his scalp and wearing dark glasses. The man detached himself from the clutching arm of a blonde woman and lumbered across the floor to their table. Tony hugged and kissed him on both cheeks and introduced the newcomer, "This is Arnaud Baillier, a friend of many years' standing. He owns a famous night club just off the Champs Elysees."

The dark, heavy-jowled heavyweight bowed and exposed a row of irregular, blackened teeth, attempting a smile but more of a grimace than a smile. Mike and Pierre shook hands with him formally and Pierre inquired, "And where is your night club Monsieur Baillier?"

The Belgian, still standing, growled in a gravelly voice, "The Katzen Keller in Rue Marceau just off Elysees. You and your friends must come as guests to see my floorshow. It's the best in Paris, much better than this one. Bring as many persons as you wish. I will be pleased to entertain friends of Monsieur Widgeon."

Pierre, with traditional French courtesy, thanked the stranger. At that moment the theatre lights were dimmed and, with an *'Excusez moi s'il vouz plait'*, Monsieur Baillier waddled off to rejoin his own party. Tony was full of enthusiasm for the suggested invitation and Colonel Daladier saw it as a good excuse for a Wednesday night out. Mike was not so sure and had reservations. Arnaud Baillier, with his lop-sided grimace which substituted for a smile, his limp handshake and his menacing demeanour, spelt danger and, though he was unable to put his finger on it, the man could probably not be trusted. Tony Widgeon flew out from Orly the next day. His last telephone call before departing for Malta urged Mike and the French officers to take advantage of Arnaud Bailliers' generous offer adding, "After all it's not a tinpot setup. I've been there on a few occasions. Arnaud will look after you royally and the French boys will have a great time. It's a unique Club, quite different to anything you'll have seen before, and I wish I could be with you. Give my best regards to Colonel Pierre and his lads."

A week later Mike came in late to his apartment to find Vanessa curled up on the sofa, wide awake and in a gossipy mood. After a peck on the cheek and an exchange of pleasantries, her face lit up with a 'spreading the muck' smile and she waded straight in. "I had coffee this morning with the gals from the mess. They told me you intend going to a naughty night club with the boys. Is that true, Michael?"

Mike felt his face colouring and swallowed hard, "Yes, Vanessa. We plan to go to the Katzen Keller to celebrate one of the flyers' birthday. I'm told the Club is a bit *risque* but I have to stay in Colonel Pierre's good books."

Vanessa persisted with a twinkle in her eye, "And is it on recommendation of a mysterious English officer?"

Mike took the bull by the horns and decided to come clean. "I didn't wish to upset you but Tony Widgeon dropped in last week for twenty four hours and insisted on joining our mess party on Wednesday. Afterwards he took Colonel Pierre and myself to the Moulin Rouge."

Vanessa's reply was utterly unexpected. "That's alright, Michael. I don't mind a bit. Thank you for not involving me with that vile person. I still haven't forgiven him for ruining what should have been the happiest day of our lives."

Mike breathed a sigh of relief. "Tony's not all bad, Vanessa. He's quietened down quite a lot. He asked me to pass on his best regards."

Vanessa screwed up her face in disgust.

"Don't bother, Michael. I can do without that cad's regards."

Colonel Daladier wasted no time in organizing a Mess party at the Katzen Kelller on a Wednesday in October and Tony's prediction that the Club was unique was fully justified. A party of fourteen from St Cyr/Versailles Mess were personally met by Monsieur Baillier who immediately announced that all drinks and refreshments were on the Club. The food was served by two males of dubious sexuality only wearing G-strings and red plastic aprons. Customers were encouraged to remove their clothing and sit around in their underpants. Pierre Daladier and half a dozen of his young officers thought it a huge joke, and obliged, but Mike's only concession to stripping was to remove his jacket. During the show there were numerous all-male cabaret acts which culminated, on two occasions, in an erotic homosexual orgy. The French contingent entered into the spirit of the occasion but Mike, despite his outward appearance of jollity, was thoroughly disgusted by the performance. Monsieur Baillier looked in from time to time and, during one visit invited Mike along to his private office. Mike declined politely but later, when he paid a visit to the washroom, he was waylaid by Baillier who virtually pushed him into a private room. Once inside the overweight bully came belligerently to the point, "Monsieur Townsend, I have a message. You are to go to the Etoile Vert, a restaurant in Rue Brey, off Wagram, at 8.00 pm tomorrow. There you will meet a man called Henri and you will dine with him. Henri will be wearing a red polka-dot tie and a red pocket handkerchief. You must not fail to turn up. That is all. You may now go back to your party."

Mike was dumbfounded and decided to stall. "I don't understand Monsieur Baillier. Who is this Monsieur Henri?"

"I've given you the message and now it's up to you. If you don't turn up I will have great pleasure in making your life a misery. Now get out" and, with a dismissive wave of his hand, he half-pushed Mike out into a darkened corridor where he stood collecting his thoughts for fully five minutes. He guessed the source of the message but could not think of a way out of his dilemma. For a fleeting moment he considered whether Tony Widgeon's sudden appearance had any significance but put it down to a chance coincidence. It was strange that at his first contact with the Russians fourteen years ago, Tony Widgeon had been present and now, for a second time, he was on hand when Arnaud Baillier came on the scene. Apart from having to convince Vanessa he had to be absent for a second night running, there was the hideous fact that Baillier meant business. The man was undoubtedly a thug and a hit man and Mike had to go along with his instructions. Vanessa was easily placated with a lie that he had to meet a high-ranking friend of Colonel Daladier and this kept the coast clear for him to keep his assignment with the mysterious Monsieur Henri.

Mike arrived at the restaurant at precisely four minutes to eight. The Etoile Vert, fifty yards down Rue Brey from Avenue Wagram, was a typical French bistro with an L-shaped dining area and run by the Benodet family of whom Madame Benodet was the principal owner and head cook. Popular with local French families, the place was full to capacity by the time Mike arrived. He found Monsieur Henri sitting at a table in the L-shaped extension tucking into a mountainous plate of *moules mariniere*. He was easily identified by the polka-dot bowtie and a billowing, bright red pocket handkerchief. On Mike's approach Henri signalled him to sit on the only empty chair in the establishment and thrust a plastic-covered menu into his hand, "Have a look and order. First we eat. Then we talk."

While glancing at the menu Mike took a peek at Henri himself. He was a short-statured, sinewy man of about forty years of age, with a bald patch on the crown of his head and unkempt, wispy brown strands of hair across his forehead. His pale-blue eyes were shielded by a pair of thick-lensed glasses and his protruding buck teeth and receding chin were covered by a straggly, grey moustache and goatee beard. Henri never smiled. With an authoritative wave of his hand he summoned a plump, homely waitress and spoke to her in immaculate French. "I will order for my friend. He will have a *douzaine escargot* to start followed by your delicious *bifstek*. And bring us a carafe of *vin ordinaire*."

43

The waitress scurried away and Henri again concentrated on his plateful of molluscs. At the conclusion of the meal he ordered two espressos and cognacs and made a great show of stirring his sugar into the coffee. He looked across the table at Mike with myopic eyes and spoke in broken English, "Now we talk. These are your instructions. You will report to me here, at times I shall specify on the telephone, the schedule of flights and any special exercises, or sorties, that are conducted from St Cyr/Versailles airfield and ordered by Commandement du Nord Headquarters. In particular, you will report on tactical and nuclear heavy bomber flights and any secret information that passes through Nord Headquarters. Is that all clear?"

Mike spoke for the first time. "But, Monsieur Henri, St Cyr/Versailles is a fighter base and I have few links with the heavy bomber squadrons."

"Even so, you must keep me informed of anything happening out of the ordinary. We'll dine here at least once a fortnight. It's quite safe and I have yet to hear the locals speaking English. Before you go I will need a direct telephone number to your office and I will only telephone your home in an emergency. When I ring I shall call you *Michel* and I will tell you the date and time for our next meeting. We shall always meet at this table. Now finish your coffee and you may go."

Mike took his leave and slowly walked out into the cool, slightly misty night, along Rue Brey and up Wagram towards the Arc de Triomphe. He did not think for a moment that this fellow, Henri, was an important Soviet agent as the information he demanded was unimportant and could be obtained by slipping a mess waiter a few francs. After all the flight schedules were posted up in the orderly room every Tuesday morning for all to see. He surmised Moscow was testing his loyalty, presumably in preparation for something important ahead. To make certain and to keep his nose clean, Mike determined to pass on accurate information as he was suspicious that Moscow might be cross-checking on his every report. And so the sporadic meetings with Monsieur Henri at the Etoile Vert continued for the next two years. On a few occasions Mike attempted to humour the man and learn about his past but the Russian agent kept a poker face at all their meetings. How they got away with passing on military secrets in a crowded bistro Mike would never know. Henri seemed to lead a charmed life and gambled on the fact that French families, frequently seated not more than four feet away, were more interested in their food and wine than in the conversation of an eccentric odd-ball and his well-dressed English friend. In a way Mike began feeling sorry for Monsieur Henri with his stereotyped, clandestine existence but his warmth was never reciprocated. Even to the very end, when Mike was due to leave for the UK and they were dining together at the Etoile Vert for the very last time, Henri's final words were still strictly formal. After finishing his coffee and cognac he stood on his feet and, for the first time during all their meetings, shook Mike limply by the hand and whispered, "*Adieu* Monsieur Michel."

And that was the end of Mike's clandestine meetings with Monsieur Henri.

Mike and Vanessa moved from their St Cloud apartment in July 1965. They were sorry to leave, more so Vanessa who was devastated at having to give up her luxurious lifestyle. Mike left his post with mixed feelings. In three years he had become somewhat disillusioned with an increasingly stuffy atmosphere at Commandement du Nord Headquarters but he would sorely miss his liaison with the commandant and airmen of St Cyr/Versailles officers mess. On the other hand he was genuinely relieved to be away from the clutches of the Russian agents in Paris and, in particular, the psychopathic hit-man Arnaud Baillier from the Katzen Keller. He wondered if Moscow would chase him across the Channel to Cranwell and why had they waited fourteen years to contact him? Time would tell. In any case he was now involved in their dirty business and had no alternative but to sink or swim.

Chapter Four

Cranwell College and NATO

DURING THREE HAPPY YEARS IN PARIS Vanessa had only returned to Belvoir Hall on a dozen occasions but kept in touch with her parents by telephone at least twice a week. Latterly the news from home was disturbing. On the 25th of June Sir Charles was rushed into Grantham Hospital with retention of urine and underwent an emergency prostatectomy. Post-operatively things did not go well and he suffered a pulmonary embolus, followed a week later by a heart attack. He was still in hospital when the Townsends crossed the Channel on the 2nd of July 1965 and made their way directly to Belvoir Hall, where Vanessa decided there and then to take control and supervise her father's recovery. Mike gave in gracefully. His appointment as college adjutant at Cranwell normally carried the rank of wing commander but, as it was hastily explained, his position was temporary and would be reviewed in a year's time. His ego was further dented when he heard Tony Widgeon had recently been promoted wing commander and was now in charge of tactical operations at RAF Akrotiri in Cyprus.

On arrival at Cranwell the Townsends were allocated a type 3 married quarter but Vanessa had a ready excuse for staying at Belvoir Hall. By mid-October the brigadier was well on the road to recovery and increasingly concerned about the imminence of the hunting season and arrangements for running the Border Hunt during his enforced convalescence. The obvious choice was Vanessa and, encouraged and directed by her father, she took on his mantle and ran the show. Sir Charles was unable to attend the 1965 Christmas hunt ball, organised with exemplary efficiency by Vanessa, and Mike went along as a bystander. The pink-coated huntsmen and their elegantly-gowned wives ignored Mike but showered Vanessa with plaudits confirming her destiny and duty to carry out Sir Charles' instructions and supervise his affairs. As the brigadier's influence grew so she became more estranged from Mike and, despite repeated efforts to coerce her to Cranwell, he eventually threw in the towel and admitted defeat. His visits to the Hall became less frequent and he again took up residence in YHOM. He could not converse sensibly with his wife and Vanessa's obsession with her father prevented her appreciating the selfish old duffer was using her for his own vicarious purposes.

Despite a setback at missing promotion Mike was enthusiastic about his appointment at the college. As adjutant he was responsible for the smooth running of the cadet school and was also influential in allocating married quarters and, if Vanessa had been co-coperative and not dismissive of the offer out of hand, a type 2 house would have become available to the Townsends. As Vanessa explained, "Daddy's illness is paramount. He needs me around him all the time and I have to run the Hall and the hunt on his behalf. There's a pack of hounds and eight horses to look after and I have to pay the gamekeepers and huntsmen. It's a full-time occupation. You do understand don't you Michael?"

At first he was prepared to give Vanessa the benefit of the doubt but, after a year, he was less and less convinced she needed to be continually at her father's beck and call. When the 1967 hunting season came around Mike was again reaching a conclusion that his only course of action would be to seek a divorce. His chief constraint was the memory of happy times they spent in Paris and his final decision was influenced by a visit from Wing Commander Tony Widgeon, home on leave from Akrotiri over the Christmas holiday and eager to flaunt his recent promotion.

In January Tony came to stay at York House officers mess for two nights. The first night out was a preliminary celebratory drink in the mess followed by a pub crawl of local hostelries as in days of yore. The second night was a more sombre occasion at which they drank heavily, without getting drunk, and Mike had a heart-to-heart conversation with Tony. "You see Tony, I'm disappointed I missed promotion in my present post which is normally filled by a wing commander."

"Now, look here old boy, I'll tell you something confidentially. I've just come from MoD where I spent some time with Group Captain Lampton. You'll remember Lampey from the old days? He's in charge of posting at MoD and I'm told on good authority they're lining you up for a job with NATO and you'll be promoted before you go. So put that in your pipe and smoke it!"

"I'll believe that when it happens. In any case Vanessa will refuse to go abroad again!"

"It's essential she goes with you Mike."

"I'm on the point of breaking up with her."

"Don't do that at any price. NATO wants stable characters and marriage is an important criterion. So take my advice and stick with Vanessa at all costs. I thought she enjoyed Paris?"

"So she did. We were very happy but, since she's at the Hall again, she's more and more under the influence of Sir Charles and it's getting me down. Still, I'll try and convince her to come to Brussels with me."

Tony downed his scotch and changed the subject abruptly. "Do you recall our night out at the Moulin Rouge?"

"Yes, Tony, it was a superb party."

"How's Pierre Daladier? What a character and raconteur!"

"The last I heard he's been promoted air commodore at Commandement du Nord."

"I heard you visited Arnaud's night club. Did you go there often?"

A fleeting thought flashed through Mike's brain. How on earth did Tony know about their visit to the Katzen Keller?

"The French lads went fairly regularly. I only went once and found it disgusting. The place was full of homosexuals."

"I know, Mike. That's why I told you it was different. I've had some very good nights out at that place."

"I bet you have you old ram. The Keller would be right up your street."

Tony Widgeon blushed, as he always did when anyone referred to his sexuality and in a flash again changed the subject. "A good pal of Group Captain Lamapton, a chap called Claude Bernard, spent a weekend with the Willoughbys about eight years ago. Did you happen to bump into him?"

Mike was stunned to hear Tony mentioning the unwelcome visitor to the Hall and answered defensively, "I thought he was a bit of a charlatan. He packed his bags and left in a huff on the Sunday morning."

Tony pulled a wry face, "It's a great pity. Lampey thinks the world of him," and, with that, conversation returned to mundane matters. Mike took Tony's advice and deferred his decision on separation until he heard officially from MoD his promotion was through and his secondment to NATO Headquarters in Brussels was fixed for May.

Throughout March and April Mike had his work cut out convincing the Willoughbys Vanessa should accompany him to Brussels. At first Vanessa was lukewarm but she was swayed by the argument that Brussels was a replica of Paris and social life would be equivalent to, if not better than, the living in Paris. Sir Charles was against her going until he learnt the British commander at NATO was a Major General Geoffrey Baxter who had served under him as a subaltern during the war.

"General Geoff is a good fellow and a superb soldier. I'm proud one of my boys has done so well. I'm not one hundred per cent recovered but, at a pinch, we can survive without Vanessa for a couple of years. After all Brussels is no distance away and Vanessa can come home as often as she wishes. If there's any trouble about getting away you only have to mention my name to General Geoff."

Having made the decision Sir Charles entered enthusiastically into arrangements for the move in May and, so it was agreed, Vanessa would accompany Mike to his new post in Brussels.

In April 1949 a North Atlantic Treaty Organization, NATO in short, was formed as an alliance between free and sovereign Western European and North American countries with the objective of mutual defence in the event of an armed attack on one, or other, of the constituent nations. NATO Headquarters' permanent home was established on the north-eastern side of Brussels, six miles from the city centre and two miles from the International Airport. It was protected by a high fence enclosure with Belgian police guard posts at its three main entrances. Constructed in the austerity years after the war from reinforced concrete, steel girders and glass panels, the two-storey building had an ornate front façade draped with the flags of the Allied Nations. Inside the building each nation had its own office accommodation and a central council chamber, library, restaurant and cafeteria served the needs of employees. Recreational facilities were provided in a gymnasium, an indoor swimming pool and a tennis and squash court. Entrance to NATO's main building was strictly limited to political, military and secretarial staff of the participating nations who had to display official passes for admission. Accommodation for employed personnel was provided in town houses and apartments within striking distance of NATO Headquarters. The British Government requisitioned a block of luxury apartments in the village of Evere where the Townsends were quartered when they arrived in Brussels. From the beginning Vanessa was not enthusiastic about their accommodation and, compared with the chic ladies of Paris, their neighbours seemed boring and frumpy. She longed for the intimate coffee mornings, lunches and shopping sprees she had so much enjoyed with the Parisiennes. Contrary to what she had been led to expect Brussels itself was a poor imitation of Paris, lacking in a number of elegant stores and high-class restaurants. The local population lacked the gaiety and *joie de vivre* of their French counterparts and many refused to speak English, or French, preferring the harsh Flemish dialect. Very soon Vanessa had doubts about their move and on discovering there were three British Airways flights each day from the nearby International Airport, she popped over to see her family at every opportunity, especially during the foxhunting season when she spent more time at Belvoir Hall than she did with Mike in Evere. The excuse was always Daddy's health which was only partially true as, by now, the brigadier missed very few social and sporting occasions. By the end of the year Mike was again at his wits end and remonstrated with Vanessa but to no avail. She was adamant her presence at home was vital for her father's well-being and if Mike didn't like it, he could lump it. To preserve their marriage Mike fell in line with her unreasonable demands which continued for two years but, eventually, he threw in the towel and accepted she could come and go as she pleased. Daddy had won the day again and there was very little he could do about it. He stuck out his chin and made the most of a tricky situation, regularly concocting cover-up stories for the absences of his wayward wife.

Major General Geoffrey Baxter, Britain's Commander at NATO, was a confirmed bachelor and, as such, had the mentality, punctiliousness and foibles of a single man living on his own. Nicknamed 'Monty' from his resemblance to the famous wartime general he was a short, dapper ex-gunner with a sharp, pointed nose, a grey, clipped moustache and two crystal-clear, piercing blue eyes. A vegetarian all his life, he was a stickler for physical fitness which he demanded from all ranks under his command. For some inexplicable reason, possibly due to his connection to Brigadier Willoughby, the General took a liking for Mike in preference to a naval commander and an army lieutenant colonel on the campus. Mike became his confidant and go-between with other sections of the organization and with the main kitchen where he collaborated with the head chef, a Monsieur Jean Duprè. Mike had to be precise with the general's vegetarian diet and any slip-up brought a sharp reprimand, always delivered in a charming manner but with the cutting edge of a well-honed butcher's knife. General Monty's daily routine was strictly stereotyped beginning at 6.00 am with a glass of yoghurt and followed by a twenty minute workout in his private gym. He then showered and breakfasted in his quarters on museli, fresh fruit and all-bran and was always at his desk in the NATO building from 7.30 am until noon, when he donned a track suit and went jogging in a nearby park for an hour before a light lunch in the mess. After a further hour and a half at his desk he completed fifty lengths in the compound's indoor swimming pool before retiring to his quarters to relax and listen to music in preparation for his main vegetarian meal of the day at 7.00 pm, preceded by one glass of dry sherry beforehand. He was invariably in bed by 9.00 pm. General Monty's routine only varied when he was away on inspection or at a conference and even then he usually managed to get to a swimming pool during the day and stuck rigidly to his diet. Mike thwarted the general's attempt to get him involved in his daily routine but to humour his commanding officer and keep in his good books, he joined in a swim most days of the week.

Wing Commander Michael Townsend had not been in Brussels long before he realised that a large element of jealousy and mistrust existed between officials of the fifteen constituent nations and even his own naval and army counterparts were reserved and kept themselves to themselves. Social intercourse between families was a rare occurrence and the Townsends, or when Vanessa was absent Mike on his own, attended an occasional starchy cocktail party and the monthly dinner in the mess which was remarkable for its elegance and grandeur but completely lacking in warmth and *espirit de corps*. As intelligence officer with a knowledge of Russian, Mike's brief at NATO was to collate and process reports from spy-planes and secret agents on Russian nuclear and satellite activity behind the Iron Curtain. He found this aspect of his work fascinating but, otherwise, life at NATO Headquarters was one string of routine meetings and sterile planning conferences which rarely got anyone anywhere. Without Vanessa's support, and with no real friends in the married quarters, life became dull, boring and monotonous which, after a few months in post, made him depressed and eventually drove him to bouts of heavy drinking. In the solace of his apartment Mike often consumed a bottle of scotch at night. When Vanessa was present he was ultra-abstemious but, no sooner was she away, he returned to the bottle for the comfort and the euphoria which alcohol temporarily provided.

Mike's depression was further heightened by an event which occurred during the week leading up to Christmas 1968. Vanessa was away at Belvoir Hall joining in the foxhunting fraternity's pre-Christmas functions and Mike had volunteered to be on duty at NATO over the festive season. One morning he received an urgent summons to General Baxter's office. Fingering a sheet of paper, the general wore a perplexed look. "What do you make of this memo from MoD instructing us to host a government official for a day? They've cleared him with NATO but omit to tell us the purpose of his visit. That's the worrying bit. Still, we have to comply with the order."

Mike looked askance at the general. "Am I allowed to know the name of the VIP, sir?"

"Yes, of course, Michael. I'm leaving him in you hands while he's here. Sir Claude Bernard, that's his name. I gather he's an industrialist of middle-European extraction."

Mike winced visibly. "I know the man, sir. He was a guest at a shoot on Brigadier Willoughby's estate about eight years ago. I've heard he's friendly with Group Captain Lampton at MoD. I wonder what his mission is all about?"

"We'll soon know, Michael. Today is Friday. He'll be with us on Monday morning. I'm meeting him here in my office at 1100 hours and I expect you to be present. That'll be all, Michael."

Throughout the weekend Mike hit the bottle hard and pondered on the possible reasons for a visit from the obnoxious entrepreneur who had been knighted since he last saw him. He was also concerned as to why Tony Widgeon had made a point of mentioning Claude Bernard's friendship with Group Captain Lampton. It was all very strange and the answers to his queries came on Monday when he learnt a little more about the mysterious Claude Bernard.

At 1044 hours on a Monday morning Mike reported to the general's office and, at precisely 1100 hours, Sir Claude Bernard was ushered into the room. He flashed a glance of recognition in Mike's direction before General Baxter made formal introductions. The weasely-faced visitor displayed a beaming smile but his deep-set, dark eyes were cold and threatening. "Wing Commander Townsend and I are acquainted. We met at dinner at Belvoir Hall a few years ago. May I congratulate you, sir, on your promotion to wing commander and your appointment here at NATO?"

Mike was taken aback by the affability of the man and replied courteously, "Congratulations to you too, sir, on your knighthood."

General Baxter interrupted the exchange of pleasantries. "I have read your introduction from MoD but we are not clear at this end, Sir Claude, as to the precise purpose of your visit?"

"I am acting in an unofficial capacity on behalf of the Department of Trade. My brief is to negotiate with military establishments to purchase obsolete armaments and to recycle them to underprivileged and third world countries. My superiors recognise there must be a vast wastage in NATO and I am prepared to pay top book for second-hand armaments. You will realise the government itself cannot act officially in this matter and my contacts with you must remain secret. I may add, if NATO cooperate, it will be a source of considerable revenue for your organization."

General Baxter tugged at his moustache and asked, pensively, "How will we be able to assist you in this, umm-er, enterprise?"

"I wish to have a private meeting with your NATO commanders to outline my proposals and, if possible, to get their agreement to go ahead."

General Baxter responded promptly, "There's a council meeting of commanders this afternoon. I'll find a slot for you at 1500 hours and, in the meantime, Wing Commander Townsend will show you around our headquarters and take you to lunch in the mess. I'll meet up with you later Sir Claude."

For the next two hours Mike showed Sir Claude Bernard around the main departments at NATO. The visitor took a particular interest in the satellite monitoring and telecommunication's rooms and the eastern European chart room and, all the while, he was affable and chatty and had a permanent smile on his cadaveric face. But when they retired to Mike's private office prior to lunch in the mess his mood changed dramatically. He sat down and stared scornfully at Mike. "Well, Mister Townsend, since we last met the boot's on the other foot. I'm running the show now and you'll do as I say. Is that clear?"

Mike's face reddened in anger. He offered a feeble protest but was violently stopped dead in his tracks, "Listen, Mister, and don't interrupt me again. My intention to sell arms to third world countries is all bullshit. I'll sell NATOs armaments to our comrades in the Communist Bloc and out of it I'll make a handsome profit. Moscow has instructions for you. You are to collect information on NATO secret schedules and proposed actions and pass it on to our agent. We used you at Versailles and, in the same way, you will obey this order to the letter. Otherwise you will be exposed and face a fate worse than death. Agents who don't comply with our orders usually take their own lives in preference to the disgrace of a court martial and imprisonment."

Mike was completely deflated and dismissed any thoughts of argument with the double agent. He lowered his head in subjugation and mumbled, "I will do as ordered. Where will I meet my contact?"

"Be in no hurry! Just wait and see. Now it's time to go to the mess for lunch."

By the time Mike and Sir Claude reached the main restaurant it was approaching 1.30 pm and the place was rapidly emptying of diners. Sir Claude was again smiling and full of bonhomie and ordered a bottle of expensive claret with his lunch. By the end of the meal they were the only two left in the mess and Sir Claude, apparently impressed with his lunch, asked to see the chef. Monsieur Jean Duprè, Mike's adviser on the general's vegetarian diets, hurried to their table and bowed deferentially. Claude Bernard smiled wryly. "Wing Commander Townsend. This is your contact. Monsieur Duprè will pass on any messages to the appropriate authorities."

The blond-haired chef grinned slyly, "You can pass on information to me anytime, Wing Commander. I'm on duty in the mess most days of the week."

After lunch Sir Claude Bernard returned to General Baxter's office in time for the 1500 hours conference and flew back to London in the evening. Mike never saw him again. The double agent was unsuccessful in his bid for an arms deal with NATO, for which Mike was eternally grateful. Apparently American arms dealers were already involved in this capacity. In contrast to Claude Bernard who made money out of both sides of the coin, Mike's motives were much more altruistic and, in his own mind, honourable and he had not received any payment for services rendered. And now he was up to his neck in it again and had to obey Moscow's orders. For nearly two more years, about twice a week, he passed on classified information to the blond chef and such was the simplicity of the arrangement neither he, nor Jean Duprè, were ever suspected of covert activity. Indeed, as the months slipped by, Duprè became more blasé and Mike was half-convinced he was doing very little wrong. He felt immune from detection and as long as Duprè, if that was his real name, carried out his part of the contract he was on safe ground. How Duprè passed on messages to Moscow was none of Mike's concern. The searches and checks in and out of NATO Headquarter building were rigorous and thorough. All secret information they transacted was handled in the mess and Mike suspected the daily deliveries of meat, fresh fruit and vegetables were a major factor in Duprè's scheme for onward transmission of information.

In January 1971 Major General Sir Geoffrey Baxter was due for replacement by a naval vice admiral. Regulations required him to submit an annual confidential report on his subordinates to the appropriate branch of the Services in Whitehall. He was also duty-bound to show his report to the individual concerned and Mike was astounded to read General Baxter's précis: 'Though Wing Commander Townsend's outlook and operational ability is exceptional and of the highest standard I have reservations about his social activities and, in particular, his propensity for alcoholic consumption in private'. Mike was fuming and rushed post-haste to face his commander, fully aware of General Baxters' antipathy to strong drink.

"General Baxter, sir, I'm extremely concerned about your summary in my confidential report."

"I understand, wing commander. The report will only be seen by your senior commodore at MoD. In that respect it will go no further and I have stressed you are not dependent on drink and I have not seen any detrimental effects on your ability to carry out your duties. I was made aware of your monthly mess bill for privately consumed alcohol and it is way over the top."

The obvious source of a 'leak' was the naval commander who was acting president of the mess committee and openly envious of Mike's closeness to the general. Thank goodness he had not made assertions about improper contact with Pierre Duprè! Mike backed down rapidly. "I've had slight marital problems of late and I'm probably taking a few more tots than usual. I'll soon put that to rights, sir."

General Baxter's face lightened up in a broad smile. "That's the spirit, Michael. It's good news if only for the sake of Sir Charles and Vanessa and be sure to make a good impression on the naval vice-admiral who'll succeed me next month."

In May 1971, in the middle of the third year of Mike's tour of duty, a fresh face appeared at NATO with appointment of an RAF telecommunications officer. Squadron Leader Timothy Cosbey had volunteered for the RAF straight from Hounslow Grammar School in 1962. He was commissioned as a navigator at Cranwell College a year later and, for seven years, crewed Vulcan long-range bombers. Grounded in 1970 due to a persistent middle ear infection he was promoted squadron leader and posted to NATO where Mike Townsend became his immediate superior officer. Unmarried, shy and diffident, the Townsends took an immediate liking to the tall, lanky, bespectacled young man with a serious outlook on life. Encouraged by the Townsends Timothy, who had a flat in the British compound at Evere, spent most of his off duty hours in their company and Vanessa devoted more and more of her time to her apartment in Brussels. Unable to have a family of her own Timothy Cosbey filled a void in her otherwise sterile existence and, within a short time, they became practically inseparable. Soon recognised as a technological whizkid by NATO commanders, Timothy's expertise was in great demand at the Satellite and Telecommunications Centre. Even amongst the staff, access to this complex was strictly limited to senior officers and its records and files were highly sensitive in nature. Squadron Leader Cosbey was in his element amongst a mountain of transducers, high-frequency radios and a console of complicated satellite and radar screens. The one man he trusted implicitly was Wing Commander Townsend who had free access to the nerve centre and, for his own purposes, made a point of spending a couple of hours each day in Timothy's complex wonderworld.

Timothy turned up in the mess extremely late for lunch one day. The canteen was completely deserted and the dining tables had all been cleared. Monsieur Duprè appeared through the kitchen door.

"Yes, Squadron Leader Cosbey, what can I get you? The kitchen staff are all off duty."

"I'm terribly sorry, Jean, I'm late. Anything will do".

"I can knock you up a plate of *coq au vin* followed by my own *crème brulle*. Will that do for you, sir?

"That'll be fine Monsieur Duprè. *Merci boucoup.*"

The blond-haired chef retreated to his kitchen to reappear three minutes later with a tray laden with dishes and cutlery. As he lifted a hot dinner plate off the tray a flimsy white sheet of paper, which had adhered to the bottom of the plate, floated elegantly on to Timothy's lap. He immediately recognised it was torn off a NATO memo pad and showed a set of figures and details of a nuclear missile site in Western Siberia which had only been discovered by satellite photography the previous day. Jean Duprè reacted rapidly. He grabbed the gravy-stained paper, crushed it in the palm of his hand, and blurted out a flustered explanation, "*Pardon monsieur!* The kitchen staff have not washed up properly after lunch. I will have a word with them tonight. The paper is tomorrows' order form and I will write out another immediately. *Excusez moi s'il vous plait?*" and he beat a hasty retreat into his kitchen. Timothy slowly ate his lunch and ruminated over the incident. He knew full well the significance of the coded message and figures he had seen fleetingly displayed on his lap and after lunch went immediately to Mike Townsend's office explaining in detail what happened in the mess and Jean Duprè's uncanny response.

Mike smiled indulgently but, inwardly, he was on the point of panicking. "You're quite sure the message on the paper was a copy of this mornings' transcript?"

"Yes. I'm absolutely certain, Mike."

Mike knew the truth as he himself had passed on the flimsy sheet to Duprè earlier in the lunch hour. How had the idiot been so careless as to leave such an incriminating message lying about? He would have to act quickly to prevent a catastrophe. "Very well, Timothy, leave it with me. I'll look into it and sort things out."

It took two days for Mike to concoct a watertight story, "I've carried out a full investigation in this matter. The chef has been employed here for six years and is clean as a whistle. He recalls the incident in the mess but he knows nothing about a memo. He thought it was his own order form and showed me a copy of a duplicate he had drafted. Unfortunately the original was binned and has, by now, gone through the incinerator. He apologises to you for acting so rudely but he was furious with the kitchen staff and his main concern is that you are annoyed about eating off a dirty plate."

Mike poured himself a glass of orange juice. Timothy was still perplexed, "But how did the highly secret memo get to the kitchen?"

"I can't explain it. I have checked on all personnel on duty in the satellite complex during the twenty four hours in question. The only possible explanation is that the memo went out of the satellite room stuck to the bottom of a tray. The lads on night shift drink a lot of coffee from the mess canteen."

Timothy knew full well the story was implausible. The duty night shift were strictly forbidden to bring food or drink into the telecommunications and satellite complex. Mike interrupted his thoughts, "The important thing is not to take matters further and start a witch hunt. The higher-ups are very sensitive about this sort of thing and, as no harm's been done, we'll sweep it under the carpet and forget it happened. Is that alright with you, Timothy?"

"Yes, of course, Michael as long as there are no comebacks."

Mike could not afford to let matters rest. He warned Pierre Duprè of the danger of being too careless and hinted that information would not be forthcoming for a few weeks. Duprè became truculent and insolent and Mike was forced, under threat of exposure, to re-start passing on classified information at irregular intervals to the blond-headed agent.

Wing Commander Townsend was again driven to desperation and it came as a tremendous relief in March when he heard he was being posted with immediate effect to the Ministry of Defence in Whitehall. Such an appointment was frequently a prelude to promotion but his chances remained remote as he had only been a wing commander for three years. Vanessa moved in to Belvoir Hall and Mike rented a small flatlet in Knightsbridge. For a whole year at MoD (Air) he was not allocated an office or a secretary and he stood around kicking his heels. He was not gainfully employed and, in his own opinion, he was merely a glorified tea boy and gofer. He spent his working days devising schemes to avoid bumping into Sir Charles Lampton, ably aided and abetted by Tony Widgeon, the commodore's hot favourite and a certain candidate for early promotion to group captain. Mercifully, at the end of the first week in May 1973, Mike was informed he was getting his own command and being sent for three years to a British airbase in the Maldives. There was some urgency about the posting and he was expected in Gan in the first week in June. The authorities made it clear that due to its inhospitable location and climatic conditions, Gan was an 'unaccompanied' posting. When Mike broke the news to Vanessa she was not unduly perturbed but her irascible father did not see eye to eye with RAF regulations.

"The place for a military wench is by her husband's side in the front line. It's good for morale and the top brass look out for that sort of thing. I'll see if I can pull a few strings."

Vanessa prayed fervently her father would not succeed in 'fixing' things and Mike also hoped the brigadier's intervention would not bear fruit. From what he had heard Gan was no place for the fairer sex and ordinary airmen and non-commissioned officers were usually only sent there for a nine month stint at a time. It was regarded by most as a punishment posting or a posting to Hell. In the event, and despite his powerful contacts, the brigadier failed to get MoD to change their policy on the 'unaccompanied' ruling. Vanessa feigned disappointment and so did Mike. A compromise was reached which partially satisfied Brigadier Sir Charles Willoughby. Vanessa would join Mike in Gan for a month annually during the three year tenure of his overseas posting in the Maldives.

Chapter Five

Gan and Baros

THE MALDIVES REPUBLIC is an archipelago comprised of nineteen atolls and over two thousand volcanic coral islands, nestling in the Indian Ocean, 450 miles to the west of Sri Lanka and a similar distance form the southern tip of India. The microcosmic land masses are spread over an area of 600 miles, straddling the equator from 4° north to 1° south, and are 80 miles across at their widest point. None of the atolls are more than 12 feet above sea level and only 220 islands are inhabited. The Maldivian word atoll *describes ring-shaped coral formations enclosing a lagoon. Originating from volcanic eruptions the islands were formed in a string of crescentic, heart-shaped, or nearly round rings which from the air appear as pale, yellow-blue daubs of paint splashed across a broader canvas of the deep, azure-blue Indian Ocean. The similarity to a string of perfectly-formed opalescent pearls is striking.*

Nowadays the population of the Maldives is 250,000. As a result of their position on the maritime trade routes between Europe and the East the atolls, over the centuries, have been settled by a wide variety of ethnic groups, mainly from India and Sri Lanka, but Malaysian, Indonesian, Arabian, African and European settlers have also made the island paradise their home. Almost exclusively Sunni Muslim since the 12th century the inhabitants speak divehi, *a patois liberally spiced with Arabic. A Sultanate for centuries and a British protectorate since 1887, the Maldives gained independence in 1965 when it became a republic with Ibrahim Nassir as its first president. The independence agreement allowed Britain to maintain a strategic airbase on Gan, the southernmost island in the Maldivian archipelago. Gan was finally evacuated by the British on March 29th 1976, officially designated the Republic's Independence Day.*

At the southern end of Addu Atoll and 1° below the equator, Gan was appropriated by the British for military use in 1941. Twelve hundred natives were evacuated and resettled at Maamendhoo. Designed as a 'safe fleet' anchorage and known as port T, a short airstrip was constructed on the island and used for photo reconnaissance, air/sea rescue and meteorological sorties by Liberator Vs of 160 squadron. In addition Sunderland flying boats used the lagoon as a staging harbour. At the end of the war the RAF left and the evicted inhabitants returned to Gan. In the early 50's Sri Lanka withdrew the facility of its military air station at Colombo and Britain's vital air link with the Far East was threatened. Gan was selected as a staging base and its inhabitants were again forcibly ejected in 1956, this time to Feydhoo, a small township on Addu Atoll. 5001 Airfield Construction Squadron and Costains, a civil engineering firm, moved in and lengthened the eastwest runway to 3,000 yards. A 400ft jetty was constructed on the south shore of the island to bring in fuel supplies and heavy equipment. A causeway connecting Gan and Feydhoo was extended and strengthened and Nissen hut accommodation and barrack facilities for 500 personnel was provided on the north shore of the lagoon. At Hithadhoo, on Addu Atoll and some 22 kilometers west of the airfield, radar and a telecommunication mast were installed to service the airbase.

Gan station became operational in August 1957. Three ferry boats, Faith, Hope and Charity, brought civilian employees each day from Hithadhoo while the work force from Feydhoo came across the causeway on foot or on bicycles. There was a permanently-manned guardhouse at the Gan end of the causeway. In a dominating position on the north side of the runway a brick-built, two storey control tower with a panelled, perspex observation cupola housed the airfield's control and short range telecommunication equipment. The officers and sergeants messes and quarters were in Nissen type accommodation at waters edge on the south lagoon. The airmen's billets, some hutted but mainly permanent tented accommodation, were located to the north of the runway as was the NAAFI and recreation hall. Both ends of the runway were expanded into flat concrete

platforms wide enough to allow large planes to turn about for take off.
Two fuel storage tanks and an electricity power plant were installed
about a hundred yards from the jetty and a large metal-framed canvas
hangar at the eastern end of the runway was used by engineers and
also acted as the base's motor pool. Officers' billets, messes and
administrative buildings covered about half the ground area to the
south of the airstrip whilst on the north side, behind the control tower,
an enterprising officer had designed a nine-hole golf course complete
with sand bunkers and hard-baked sand and clay greens.

Throughout the 1960s some 7,000 passengers a month, mainly
service personnel and their families flying to and from the Far East,
were catered for at Gan and transit facilities for both passengers and
aircraft was provided. In addition to a steady flow of Hermes transport
and VC 10 passenger planes, front line aircraft frequently used the
base for refuelling and, in the late 60's, Gan became a Victor tanker
supply station for Lightnings and Phantoms. It was also a rescue co-
ordination centre for 1125 Marine Craft Unit and a brace of
Shackletons were used for air/sea rescue missions in the Indian
Ocean. As 1974 approached Gan's usefulness as a staging base
declined rapidly and the volume of air traffic diminished apace. When
the time came to hand Gan back to the Maldivians, on March 29th
1976, the airbase had become a ghost station and a forlorn image of
its glorious heyday in the sixties.

Bathed in perspiration Gan's medical officer, Squadron Leader
Aneurin Clement Ernest Garvey, sat uncomfortably behind his desk in
the medical center. Located on the southern side of the airstrip and
about 40 yards from the officers mess, the medical centre consisted of
a thatch-roofed Nissen hut partitioned into a sizeable waiting room, a
small office and consulting room and a sparsely-equipped treatment
and operating theatre. It was mid-June 1974 and the heat and intense
humidity were overpowering. A *hulhangu,* a south-westerly tropical
monsoon, brought relief from time to time when fierce winds and
torrential rain tore across the island and caused devastation – leaking
roofs, uprooted trees and dislodgment of untethered tents and
moveable equipment. There had not been a *hulhangu* for a fortnight
and a fresh outburst from nature's climatic cauldron was due any day.
Wiping his brow with a handkerchief and readjusting his horn-rimmed

glasses, Squadron Leader Clement Garvey concentrated his gaze on a journal on his desk. That morning a plane had brought in current issues of the Lancet and British Medical Journal but the volume he held in his perspiring hands, and which consumed his attention, was a quarterly issue of the Journal of Respiratory Physiology.

Squadron Leader Clement Garvey was an enigma in more than one sense. In the first place he should never have become a practicing doctor. His brilliance in his pre-clinical studies were rewarded by gold medals in physiology and biochemistry and a BSc honours degree. But once his theoretical training was complete and he was let loose on the wards of Queen Elizabeth Hospital in Birmingham, the rot set in. He lacked a bedside manner and avoided touching and examining patients like the plague, eventually struggling to qualify BSc MB BCh in May 1966. A year later he volunteered for the RAF and, on the strength of his BSc, he was accepted for training in aviation medicine. This was an unwise career move as he was completely unsuited to regimentation and pathologically incapable of carrying out commands and orders from his superiors. In addition he disliked the brouhaha of mess life and relationships with his fellow officers and he showed little pride in wearing the Queen's uniform. Shunned by his peers he was a complete outsider and dismissed as an intellectual boffin. For his first two years in the Service he was one of the station MO's at Manston where his lack of enthusiasm for the job brought him into recurrent conflict with his superiors. After a string of undutiful postings spread over a period of two years, he was finally promoted squadron leader and posted to Gan in April 1971. The Gan posting was regarded as a well-deserved punishment by his fellow officers.

The second part of Dr Clem's enigmatous background lay in his upbringing. The only son of a Scottish shop-steward at Guest Keen and Nettlefolds, he was born in a slum area of Birmingham in 1944. His father, a conscientious objector and an ardent left-winger, insisted on naming his son after the labour stalwarts of the day – Aneurin Bevan, Ernest Bevin and Clement Attlee, Britain's first post-war premier. Young Clement was destined to follow in his father's footsteps but two quirks of fate combined to steer him towards a career in medicine. In 1959 his father was killed in an accident at work and pressure from his headmaster encouraged young Clement to enter medical school where he was mainly remembered for his ultra-militant chairmanship of the students union which generated the wrath of the medical school council. Far from being a punishment the Gan posting played into Squadron Leader Garvey's hands. When he arrived at Gan the commanding officer, one Wing Commander Gilpin, was critical of the MO's dress but, within a month, standards were relaxed and Dr Clem became a familiar figure strolling around the base in an open-necked shirt and a pair of faded blue shorts. And when Wing Commander Gilpin was replaced by Mike Townsend in June 1973 the MO was allowed to continue in his inimitable way. The new 'boss' had been around for nearly a year and a tenuous affinity developed between the two men. Of differing backgrounds and culture, both men were hooked on underwater exploration and the clear, blue waters of the Maldives were idyllic hunting grounds – lagoon after lagoon of dazzling multicoloured tropical fish and mile upon mile of unspoilt coral reef with its unique piscine and crustacean denizens.

Dr Clem's reading was interrupted when a batch of twelve Gurkhas arrived for their booster TAB inoculations. A company of the 3rd battalion Royal Gurkha Rifles had been manning the base defences for nearly a year and were due to rejoin their regiment having completed their normal tour of duty. Permanent staff, engineers, aircraft maintenance crews and radar and telecommunication officers, sometimes remained on the base for two or three years and the MO had already completed nearly two years of his tour of duty. Syringe in hand, Dr Clem approached the line of soldiers. Under the watchful eye of their sergeant the impassive-faced Gurkhas stood rigidly to attention, their left arms bared and ready to receive the doctor's needle. Anxious to get back to his journal, Dr Clem wielded his syringe with gusto plunging his needle into the deltoid muscle of the first man. 'Next' he bellowed and before he could refill his syringe the next in line was ready and waiting and so on until he called 'next' and found himself looking into the clear, blue eyes of his station commander who had bared his left arm and joined the tail end of the queue. Mike Townsend was smiling and his pale-blue eyes twinkled in amusement.

"Do you want a jab sir?" the MO asked.

"Can't say I do Squadron Leader Garvey. If I'm due for one go ahead."

"I can't tell for certain without looking up your medical records."

"Don't bother Doc. Shove it in anyway. I feel like an injection to liven me up. There's a monsoon about. I can feel it in my bones."

"Yes sir! A *hulhangu's* on the way, thank God. I'm melting into a blob of lard in this joint. Here we go" and, without further ado, he jabbed the needle viciously into Mike's upper arm.

"Ow! That hurt like hell you quack," Mike remonstrated.

"The Gurkhas don't complain sir," Dr Clem replied as he swabbed the oozing puncture wound with a gauze square soaked in alcohol.

"No," Mike replied, "they've got skins like pachyderms. They're tough little men prepared to die for Queen and country."

"I don't know about that," the doctor replied, "one of them fainted when I jabbed him a couple of days ago."

"Yes, I know Clem. I'm not surprised the way you stick your needles in! He was in front of his company commander this morning. The poor fellow was given seven days detention for fainting on parade."

Dr Clem grimaced, "That's totally out of order. I'll have a word with his company commander. By the way, you won't catch me dying for the Queen. The Royals are abusing their privileges and the money they get every year would be better spent on Birmingham's unemployed."

"I know your political convictions Clem. In any case you're not likely to become involved in any shooting of a hostile nature!"

The CO's face relaxed in a wide grin, "I'm not here to discuss world politics or to have a jab for that matter. How are you getting on with our scuba equipment?"

For about two months the MO had been designing a diving apparatus suitable for exploration in the deeper waters off Gan's precipitous, ocean-facing coral reef. Adequate for the lagoon, ordinary snorkelling equipment only allowed a diver to remain at depth for ninety seconds though local Maldivians were able to stay under for three or four minutes without surfacing. With the help of the recently-departed naval engineers of 1125 Marine Craft Unit Dr Clem had perfected a mouthpiece with a non-returnable respiratory valve controlled by pressure from an oxygen cylinder strapped to the diver's back. As yet the new device was untried and untested in the waters off Gan's coral reef. Squadron Leader Garvey produced an anesthetic mask and a series of rubber tubes from a cupboard and proceeded to assemble the contraption under Mike's watchful gaze.

"We'll have to nick a few oxygen cylinders from one of the aircraft passing through. According to my calculations one cylinder should be sufficient for at least 20 minutes submerged."

Mike gave the matter a few seconds serious consideration. "That will have to do for a start. We'll test the equipment in the lagoon on Wednesday. If it works I'll take it along with me to Male at the weekend. I have an appointment at the Maldivian Transport Ministry on Saturday. How about coming along with me and sharing in the fun? I'm told there are a couple of super islands for snorkelling off Male."

"That will be fine by me, Mike," Dr Clem replied, "let's hope the monsoon has passed through by the weekend."

Even as they spoke the wind was freshening from the south and by nightfall a full-blown *hulhangu* had well and truly arrived. For two days, Gan was awash with lashing rainstorms and sea spray and the airstrip was out of action. Dr Clems' homemade scuba equipment could not be tested in time but the two officers were able to leave for Male in a two seater, single-engined seaplane on Friday morning.

When Wing Commander Paul Gilpin departed for Blighty in June 1973 he left Gan in perfect working order for the incoming station commander. On average about six planes a day made use of Gan's staging facilities. The majority were Hermes transporters carrying freight, military equipment and supplies to and from the Far East. Most of the planes simply took on fuel and were away again within the hour. More often than not passenger-carrying VC10s stayed on the ground for a few hours to allow their passengers to use NAAFI facilities and have a cooked meal and a wash and brush up. Rarely, if aircraft needed maintenance, passengers were accommodated in the 'Blue Lagoon Hotel', a modest two-storey brick building near the causeway. About two or three times a month strategic bombers and spy-planes landed for refuelling before continuing on their transglobal flights. In addition, twice a month, a Royal Fleet Auxilliary supply tanker berthed off the jetty replenishing aviation fuel storage tanks and bringing in essential supplies for the messes and the NAAFI. The RFA sailors frequently used Gan for a trip ashore to the NAAFI, or to visit one of the messes, returning to their ship at night.

To cater for passengers and to service their planes Mike Townsend had a staff of 350 airmen, swollen daily by an influx of about 80 or 90 Maldivian employees who came to Gan by ferry from Hithadhoo, or bicycled across the causeway from Feydhoo, and worked on the base as cooks, waiters, cleaners and labourers. There were no airwomen or female civilians on Gan. For this reason, and because of the intense heat and humidity and despite its tropical paradise image, Gan was regarded by RAF servicemen as a 'posting to Hell'. The number of long-serving officers in the mess at any given time fluctuated between eight and eleven of whom four were semi-permanent appointments – a squadron leader engineer, a senior signals officer, a wing commander quartermaster and Squadron Leader Clement Garvey, the station medical officer. When Mike Townsend arrived Gan had a permanent padre but within a few months he had been repatriated and the base's spiritual needs were catered for by an occasional service conducted by a padre in transit. The airfield was serviced by a satellite radar and radio transmitting station at Hithadhoo on the main atoll and some 22 kilometers west of the airbase and manned by a signals officer and six airmen twenty four hours a day. The airfield had two motorcycles, half a dozen jeeps and station waggons and heavy equipment and the fire trailer were transported around in a cohort of three-tonners. For access to the nearest islands in the atoll two *dhonis* were berthed at the jetty and a sturdy *masdhoni*, a type of fishing smack, was available to the marine craft unit for combined air/sea rescue operations. When they completed their contract in 1956 Costains, the civilian contractors, left two single-engined, two-seater seaplanes at anchorage at Hithadhoo and qualified pilots from Gan had access to these planes for inter-island hopping.

"Males' coming up at 11 o'clock," Dr Clem announced excitedly. Mike had already located Male but he allowed the navigating medical officer to be the first to spot the township. The Merlin-powered, twin-seater seaplane had behaved impeccably during their two and a half hour flight from Gan. They proceeded northwards at 3,000 feet, navigating by compass and dead-reckoning, skirting alongside Graf Alif Atoll and flying directly over Laamu, Meenu and Vaaru Atolls. While over Vaaru Mike spotted Male in the heat haze ahead but it was twelve minutes later before Dr Clem excitedly pointed towards the township when they were still eight minutes or more flying time away from their destination. In theory Mike should not have been flying without a co-pilot as Queens Regulations forbade a base commander to risk his life unnecessarily. But Mad Mike was an exception to all man-made rules. When he arrived at Gan he had taken one of the light seaplanes up on a training flight. It was a challenge to his aviatory skills and he compared the experience to flying a Tiger Moth trainer atop a fixed undercarriage and packed with half a ton of lead. After two hairy hours in the air he got the hang of it and thereafter one of the seaplanes became the CO's personal run-about. His favourite trip was 60 miles north of Gan to the smallest uninhabited atoll in the archipelago. Gnaviyani lay on the equator and maintained a prodigious bird life and was infested with crows. And now, with the medical officer in the co-pilot seat, he was on the longest flight he had undertaken since arriving at Gan. An MoD memo had requested him to pay a visit to the Maldivian Transport Ministry to advise on development of an airport for tourism. Perhaps he would have been wiser to bring along the chief engineer with him but, at tomorrow's meeting, he would present Dr Clem as an expert in airfield construction. He glanced sideways at the doctor and raised his voice to overcome the noisy reverberation from the Merlin engine, "Yes Clem, you're dead right. That's our target. I'll do one strafe over the harbour to see if we can land in the lagoon. If not I'll put her down outside the harbour entrance."

Mike brought the seaplane slowly down from 3,000 feet and skimmed over Male's harbour at house-top level. They clearly saw the startled black faces looking upwards from the packed streets below and the inner harbour chock-a-block with fishing dhonis bringing their catches to a thriving, late-morning fish market.

"No chance of putting her down inside the harbour. I'll take her out to sea and put her down near the lighthouse. Here goes! Hang on tight!"

Mike banked in a wide curve, fighting the controls to counteract the weight of the floats, and then, gracefully, the seaplane hit the sea and aquaplaned for a hundred yards to come to a stop about fifty yards from the inner harbour entrance. Mike grinned, "We made it Doc!"

"Yes," the relieved medical officer replied, "I thought you were going to wrap her around that bloody lighthouse!"

They burst out laughing.

Within minutes of the seaplane coming to a standstill a dhoni, flying a Maldivian flag and displaying a green pennant on its mast, came chugging towards them. Mike removed his flying goggles and slid open the perspex cockpit window. "That official-looking chap, standing at the sharp end, looks like a VIP."

The dhoni hove-to beside the stationary seaplane and a barefooted man of medium height, dressed in a short, brown-coloured *lungi* and a cut-away jacket with silver buttons, stood in the prow. On his head he wore a black fez, reminiscent of a flattened, inverted flower pot and adorned with his badge of office, a solid gold anchor. As the dhoni drew alongside the man pressed his hands together finger tip to finger tip in front of his chest and bent his head slightly forwards, "*Assalaamu alaikum*. Welcome to Male. I am Ibrahim Farheed the harbourmaster."

Mike responded, "We are the British officers you have been expecting. We have a meeting tomorrow with your transport minister. I am Wing Commander Townsend and my companion is Squadron Leader Garvey."

The harbourmaster again inclined his head forwards in a token of respect. "We'll tow your plane to a berth in the harbour and get you ashore as quickly as possible."

Maldivian seamen are expert at manoeuvering their curiously-beaked boats and, though they had never been asked to tow a seaplane before, they quickly worked out the correct attachments for the tow ropes. Within a few minutes the light seaplane, with its human cargo, was safely berthed in the inner harbour. Once their plane was secured Mike and Dr Clem clambered on to the seaplane's floats and were assisted on to the harbourmaster's dhoni which conveyed them across the inner harbour and tied up at a pier directly opposite a bustling fish market.

Ibrahim Farheed led them across a busy road and straight into the market which was preparing for its daily, mid-afternoon sale. A steady stream of porters and fishermen jostled and pushed their way across the road carrying their catch to market. The white-tiled floor of the open-ended, high-ceilinged building was covered with neatly arranged rows of recently-gutted, medium-sized bonito and tuna, each fish almost an exact replica of its neighbour. In one corner four giant sailfish were on display and in another four men, ankle deep in entrails and blood, were gutting the fish and preparing them for sale. Farheed proudly announced that all the fish were caught with handlines adding, "Nets are forbidden in the Maldives."

Mike and Dr Clem were very impressed with the efficiency and cleanliness of the enterprise and made comments to this effect. Farheed pushed out his chest and smiled, "I thank you sirs. You see, as well as being the harbourmaster, I am also controller of the fish market."

Farheed's talents were limitless. Apart from his two declared appointments he was a member of the Maldivian parliament, the Majlis, and had a vested interest in Hotel Alia where Mike and Dr Clem spent their first night on Male. And when, the following day, their meeting at the ministry was over Farheed arranged a courtesy visit to Baros which was, not surprisingly, one of three islands north-west of Male franchised by President Ibrahim Nassir to Farheed for development as holiday resorts. Evidently Mr Farheed had a finger in every pie in the Maldivian infrastructure.

"Welcome to my humble office."

Farheed had taken them into a dark, dingy, downstairs room in a two-storey building next door to the fish market. Natural light filtered into the interior through a grime-covered, smoked-glass window. The floor space was taken up by a long trestle table covered with sheets of paper and cardboard files and one wall supported a rickety ladder of shelves festooned by more files and stacks of manila envelopes. The visitors were introduced to Abdul, a large, corpulent, sweaty office manager dressed in a grubby, once white, *jellabah*. The office was unbearably hot and stank of decaying fish. The overhead, defunct, electric fan hung by a frayed cable from its bracket in the ceiling. Farheed sensed his visitor's discomfiture and hastened to explain, "This is my humble workplace. My official office is in the building next to the Citizens Majlis where you will meet the minister tomorrow. Arrangements for your visit are as follows – you will sleep tonight in a suite at Hotel Alia and I will personally escort you to the meeting at the Ministry tomorrow morning. Afterwards you may wish to come here and I will conduct you to our island resort at Baros where you may stay as long as you wish. I am honoured to be at your disposal for this important visit and President Nassir wishes you to have everything you need whilst you are his guests on Male."

Mike stammered a condescending 'thank you' and winked at Dr Clem who was clutching a handkerchief to his nose pretending he was developing hayfever. Farheed sensed his increasing unease.

"Abdul! Send for the porters to carry our guests' luggage to the hotel."

Abdul shuffled to the grime-spattered doorway and clapped his hands twice. As if by magic two thin, athletic, smiling men of indiscriminate age, something between 16 and 36, appeared and picked up the valises. Without further ado they scurried down the wide, sand-covered Boduthakurufaanu boundary road and past the fish market and customs wharf with Mike and Dr Clem hurrying along about 20 yards in their wake. After three quarters of a mile the guides took a sharp left turn up an alleyway, the Haveeree Higun, and stopped outside Hotel Alia.

The hotel had seen better days. It was a two-storeyed, grey building situated in an angle between Haveeree Higun and an unnamed alley. The upper floor bedrooms were surrounded by a wide balcony and verandah which was of little advantage as a sea view was completely obscured by an engineering works and a bottling factory. A balding, tubby manager in a clean white shirt and pin-striped trousers met them at the top of the steps and led them into a darkened entrance vestibule. Their upstairs suite consisted of two sparsely-furnished, inter-communicating bedrooms, each with its own bathroom. An electrically operated ceiling fan provided ventilation and both rooms had access, through frosted glass doors, to the communal verandah.

"Not quite the Ritz," Mike commented, "but it will do for one night."

Clem grimaced. "The manager bloke insists this is the best hotel in Male. If that's true I'd like to see the worst one!"

The outlook from the verandah was uninspiring – residential houses across the alley on one side and the noisy bottling factory across Haveeree Higun. Within an hour, showered, shaved and changed they sat on the verandah clutching their gin and tonics. Knowing the strict prohibition regulations of a predominantly Muslim country Mike had come prepared and brought along ample supplies of gin and whisky and they proceeded to make a sizeable incursion into their alcohol supplies. That night they ate in a typical Maldivian fish restaurant on Chandhani Magu. The choice was fish, or fish, and more fish to follow. They started with fish balls, *gulha*, followed by *garudhiya,* a fish stew faintly reminiscent of a French bouillabaisse and rounded off with *hanaakurimas*, a dry fish curry served with coconut flavoured rice. As dictated by custom only the right hand was used for eating and the left hand was deemed unclean and only used for toiletry and other bodily functions.

On the following morning at precisely 10 o'clock Farheed, accompanied by two porters, met the officers on the steps of the Alia. For the purpose of the meeting Mike and Clem were dressed in their light blue service uniforms with medals. They started out in line with Farheed, elegantly turned out in his national costume, the *libras,* striding out ahead at a brisk pace and Mike and Clem marching abreast some ten paces behind him. Valises on their shoulders, the white-turbaned porters brought up the rear. Mike's sense of humour soon got the better of him. "This is a bit like passing-out parade at Cranwell. All we need is a fiddler or a flautist to lead us and we could be a cavalcade. No! We're not mounted, so we can't be a cavalcade. I think we should call ourselves a pedacade. Is there such a word in the Oxford English Dictionary?"

"I dunno sir," the recalcitrant MO replied and, forgetting his antipathy to all things military, he squared his shoulders and fell in step beside his commanding officer.

"Let's show these chaps the Royal Air Force can march in time with the best regiments of Her Majesty's Foot Guards."

Mike smiled at the unexpected patriotic outburst from a rabid anti-establishmentarian and wondered if Dr Clem had completely sobered up after their alcoholic excesses of the previous night.

Their route to the meeting started down the western extension of Boduthakurufaanu Magu to the fish market and then along the eastern limb of the same avenue towards the Citizen's Majlis. As they proceeded down the road it soon became evident to the Britishers that Farheed had pre-orchestrated the walk. Between the Alia and the customs wharf numerous ancient lorries and pick-ups were parked and

Mike recognised at least three converted wartime station waggons. Their drivers, who brought vegetables, fruit and firewood to market, stood sullenly beside their trucks looking on in wonder at the 'pedacade' and two or three of the out-of-town artisans bowed in cynical deference. As they approached the vegetable market the number of people and bicycles on the road increased and traders and porters pulling handcarts pushed their way aggressively through the bustling throng which swelled into a crowd outside a mosque. Like Moses parting the waters of the Red Sea Farheed plunged steadily onwards as a pathway cleared in front of him. Murmurings of subservience and fervent *alaikum's* were eloquent testimony to the importance of the man who was leading the British officers and the reverence the common people felt for Farheed. He in turn bathed in the adulation showered on him. The final accolade came outside the fish market. Abdul had gathered about twenty porters on the steps and they bowed and 'alaikoumed' in unison and burst forth into a tirade of premeditated, feverish hand-clapping. Farheed was almost reduced to tears. He managed a wan smile and raised his arms heavenwards, silently thanking Allah for making the people of Male such devout and loyal subjects. Undoubtedly, with such support he was destined for higher things: a ministerial post in the Majlis? perhaps minister of the soon to be created department of tourism? and, possibly, even the presidency itself?

They were well down the eastern limb of Boduthakurufaanu Magu, opposite the Atoll Administration Building, when Farheed's bubble burst. Dr Clem suddenly shouted 'stop'. Farheed pulled up as if he had been shot in the back. For a couple of minutes Dr Clem had been muttering under his breath and threatening to 'Put a spoke in this chap's wheel. He's showing off like a randy peacock'. Mike sternly rebuked him, conscious of the sensitivity of the situation. But Dr Clem with a bee in his bonnet was not to be denied. 'Stop,' he shouted once more and the harbourmaster pulled up abruptly registering dismay at the untimely incursion into his valedictory parade. Dr Clem was pointing a finger at the Atoll Administration Building and spoke over his shoulder to Mike, "There you are sir! I told you there were crows on Male."

His finger pointed at a row of six carrion crows perched in line on a telegraph wire outside the Atoll building. Farheed scornfully interjected, "What's so unusual about crows, squadron leader?"

"We don't have any on Gan," Dr Clem explained and, without allowing the harbourmaster to comment, he continued, "and I've got a theory about that. I think crows have a special brain centre which dictates they mustn't live, and breed, south of the equator. Gan is only 1° below that line but that's enough. What do you think Wing Commander Townsend?"

Mike did not reply. Farheed flashed a sickly, insincere smile. "That's very interesting squadron leader. We must push on." Turning on his heel, he walked rapidly past the coastguards headquarters and the Citizens Majlis and, at twenty minutes to eleven, the party arrived on the second floor of the Ministry for Foreign Affairs where the Department of Transport had its offices. They were ushered into a reception room overlooking the sea and Ibrahim Farheed abruptly took his leave. The Minister's male secretary was attentive and courteous and reassured Mike they would be seen promptly at 11 o'clock. An offer of a cold drink was gratefully accepted and during the secretary's temporary absence Mike turned on Dr Clem, "What the hell was all that business about crows?"

Clem grinned sheepishly, "I wanted to take Mr Farheed down a peg or two. He was getting on my nerves. I'm convinced my theory about crows and the equator holds water."

"Bullshit," Mike retorted, "have you ever seen a crow's brain? It's about the size of a peanut. How the hell can anyone identify an equatorial centre inside such a small skull? Besides . . ." and then the secretary returned and the conversation centralized around Maldives' changeable weather and the climatic difference between Male and Gan.

At precisely 11 o'clock the secretary's buzzer flashed green and Mike and Dr Clem were ushered into an adjoining office where a man in his mid-thirties sat behind a polished teak desk. He rose to greet them. He was tall for a Maldivian and tastefully dressed in a dark blue suit with a stiff white collar and a flamboyant, striped MCC maroon and royal blue, 'egg and tomato', necktie not recognized as the colours of the prestigious Marylebone Cricket Club by his British visitors. He was a handsome man with sleek black hair, greying at the temples, and he wore gold-framed spectacles. His handshake was firm and his welcoming smile warm and disarming. "I am Maumoon Abdul Gayoom, permanent secretary to the transport department with special responsibility for tourism. My Minister regrets he has been called away and is unable to be with us. I hope Ibrahim Farheed is looking after your needs?"

Mike Townsend was taken in by the warmth of the reception and replied with alacrity, "Yes, thank you Mr Gayoom. We are being well catered for."

Dr Clem wriggled uneasily in his seat. Introductions over the British officers were again offered, and accepted, tumblers of refreshing ice cold lime juice. Mr Gayoom wasted no time coming to the point. "My government has come to the conclusion that the future for the Maldives lies in tourism. Very soon we shall have a Ministry of Tourism. Our traditional sources of income, such as coconut palm products and the fishing industry, are declining. In 1972 various members of the Majlis, Ibrahim Farheed was one of them, were granted franchises by President Nassir to develop certain island resorts. Four resorts are now operating and are receiving guests. Our main difficulty is access for tourists and only two routes are available to them. They come to the Maldives by sea or they fly in. The sea route is used by visitors from Sri Lanka and southern India but the numbers arriving by air are disappointing. My government has come to realise the answer lies in air travel from further afield."

Secretary Gayoom paused to sip his lime cordial. "We have a small airfield on this atoll, south of here, suitable only for light aircraft carrying up to twenty passengers. Our resorts could take ten times that number each week. My minister has been in contact with Westminster for over a year asking for help to extend our existing runway to accommodate larger planes but little progress has been achieved so far. The Maldivian Government requests we be allowed to use your airfield at Gan to fly in customers from Europe, the Middle East and South Africa. We would use light planes to ferry passengers from Gan to Male and your airbase would only be used as a landing strip. There will be no onus on you to arrange accommodation or recreation facilities for ongoing tourists. I would be obliged if you will pass on this request to your government and we are hopeful for an answer in the affirmative. The matter is urgent as our economy is precariously poised and our best hope of survival as a nation, is a dramatic increase in tourism which, at the present time, only your air force base at Gan can provide. Will you help us?"

Mike was caught off balance. He thought he had been invited to Male to discuss extension of the existing civilian airstrip. But here was an honest, concerned man asking for partial use of Gan for tourism.

"Mr Gayoom. Thank you for stating your case so candidly. I have to point out that I am Gan's station commander and cannot speak for the Ministry in London. Off the record, and as far as I am concerned, your request is reasonable. But we do have sensitive flights in and out of Gan from time to time and the presence on the base of nationals other than British is a tricky issue. I will forward your request urgently to London and give you support in principle."

Secretary Gayoom smiled appreciatively. "My government will be grateful for any help you can offer. And what does Squadron Leader Garvey think about it all?"

Dr Clem was about to offer an opinion when Mike interjected, "The squadron leader came along to advise on development of Male's airstrip and his expertise will not now be required."

"That's very true wing commander. He must be a versatile man. He wears the insignia of a medical officer but he must be doubly qualified as an engineer and a doctor, an interesting combination!"

Gayoom made the last statement with a mischievous glint in his eye. Mike wondered how the minister's private secretary had such intimate knowledge of RAF insignia. Mike Townsend had not done his homework and had not bargained on coming up against such a polished politician. Though born in Male, Maumoon Gayoom was educated in a British school in Ceylon where he developed an all-consuming passion for cricket. He graduated in Islamic studies and law at the University of Cairo and followed on with postgraduate studies in English at the American University in the same city. Abdul Maumoon Gayoom was nobody's fool and he had quickly seen through Mike and his errant companion. But his innate sense of fair play disbarred him from taking advantage of the British officer's naivety. It just wouldn't be cricket!

"I hear Mr Farheed is taking you to our jewel in the crown later today. Baros resort is truly breathtaking. Please enjoy your stay and if there's anything I can do you only have to ask."

They shook hands warmly and the meeting was over.

As they strolled up the road towards the fish market Mike had misgivings about Dr Clem's behaviour on their march through Male which might sour their relationship with Mr Farheed. And so it transpired. Fat Abdul accompanied them on the one hour dhoni trip across to Baros. According to Abdul, Mr Farheed had been called away to an urgent conference in the Citizens Majlis and the sweating stand-in kept stressing and repeating the important nature of Mr Farheed's business with the council. The constant repetition nearly drove Dr Clem to distraction. He whispered to Mike, "I can't stand this man's whining. If he doesn't stop soon I'll shove him overboard."

Mike smiled indulgently and had to admit to himself that Abdul was an insufferable bore and Mr Farheed's antics earlier in the day had also nearly driven him around the bend.

Baros had been in full view for 40 minutes before the dhoni tied up to a rickety, wooden jetty and Abdul and his two charges clambered ashore. The party were met at the end of the jetty by a smiling manager and four bearers who jostled with each other for the honour of carrying the visitors' luggage to their adjoining cabins. The vaulted, thatch-roofed, wooden cabins were set back some 20 yards from a sandy lagoon beach protected from sea breezes by a screen of tropical foliage, coconut palms, screwpines, breadfruit and casuarina trees and an abundance of wild frangipani, hibiscus, bougainvillea, poinsettia and a fragrant pink rose of the polyantha family. The latrines and showers were in a separate hut at the back of each unit. Baros had recruited its first visitors in October 1973, a year after Karumba and Bandos. Seventy five separate cabin units were planned for the resort but when Mike and Dr Clem arrived only a dozen had been commissioned. The communal centre for social gatherings and messing was an open-ended thatch-roofed grand hall in the middle of the island with a primitive lean-to cookhouse and an open barbecue area set to one side. The manager had his own chalet at the back of the mess hall and his all-male staff lived in ramshackle 'long houses' behind his residence. None of the cabins were ventilated and, after dark, light was provided by spluttering kerosene lamps suspended from the ceiling. The cookhouse had three wood-burning stoves and sandalwood chippings were used for barbecuing. There were no domestic animals on Baros and, consequently, no indigenous sources of meat or dairy produce. Tea, flour, dried milk, chickens and eggs were imported daily from Male. In common with all other islands comprising the atoll the staple diet was fish garnered from abundant stocks of mackerel, sailfish, bonito and skipjack tuna in the waters off the island. Baros had two fishing dhonis at sea most days and one *masdhoni* was used for deep-sea trawling. Wherever man settles rodents usually follow and Baros had its own resident population of rats, largely kept under control by non-venomous snakes. Multi-coloured lizards and geckoes abounded and centipedes and scorpions were common denizens in the subtropical forest. Bird life was abundant. Seagulls, terns, herons and the common crow nested on the island and flocks of migrating birds frequently made use of Baros as a staging post. At dusk fruit-bats, also called flying foxes, came in from neighbouring islands to feed but the irresistible attraction of this subtropical island paradise lay in the waters in the lagoon and along the perpendicular face of its flourishing coral reef.

After unpacking Mike knocked on Dr Clem's cabin door. "Let's take a stroll around the island before the light fades."

"Okay. I'll be with you in a minute. I'm just going out the back to the latrine."

Walking at a leisurely pace, it took them fourteen minutes to circumnavigate Baros and most of the time, and much to Mike's displeasure, Dr Clem offered a dissertation on human hygiene and the process of collection and disposal of human excreta. He admitted the visit to the latrine had stimulated his thoughts and he had missed his vocation. "I should have become a shithouse wallah instead of a practicing doctor. There's money in number twos!"

As they strolled along the perimeter path he warmed to his subject. "They've got the same problem here with waste disposal as we have on Gan. They've only got three feet of subsoil before they hit water and they can't put in cisterns or cess-pits. The stuff is collected in trays and dumped, untreated, out at sea. In time the water will become polluted, especially if they have an increase in visitors. Untreated sewerage is a killer in salt water. Mark my words, they'll have a problem in five or six years time."

Mike was getting impatient and tried to change the subject but Dr Clem had the bit between his teeth and would have none of it.

"And what about the dhonis?" he asked, rhetorically.

"I'll tell you about the dhonis. Someone reckoned there are about a thousand at sea each day in the Maldives. I'm told the fishermen wait until they're on the water before they perform their daily ablutions. On the small two-man fishing dhonis they crap by hanging on to a stern platform and pushing their bottoms over the back of the boat. On a masdhoni there's a cubicle overhanging the sea at the stern and the sailors defaecate through a hole in the deck. There are twelve to fourteen potential customers on each masdhoni and, between all of them, that's a hell of a lot of waste deposited in the sea each day. Opening their bowels regularly is as much a religion with the fishermen as praying four or five times a day and, if they fail to do so, they lose credibility in the sight of Allah. That's something to think about Mike."

They were on the last hundred yards of their walk and Mike had had enough. All the talk about latrines and disposal of human excreta was exasperating. He had enjoyed the walk, the flora and the fauna, but not Clem's lecturing.

"For God's sake, Clem, put a sock in it! We're here to enjoy ourselves."

Dr Clem was crestfallen at his companion's rebuke. He sulked. "I thought you would be interested, sir."

"I am," Mike lied glibly, "but there's a time and place for everything and now is not the time to discuss management of Maldivian sewerage."

They continued in silence to the cookhouse where the cooks were preparing an evening meal. One sat on a low stool, a *huni gondi*, grating slivers of coconut and another was kneading flour, coconut juice and salt to make *roshi*, a flat bread pancake baked on a griddle. The third chef tended two large boiling pots, one for rice and the other a clear fish soup called *garudhiya* containing large chunks of tuna. This was to be the supper served after prayers and within an hour of sunset. The guests were summoned to the dining hall by a booming gong struck five times at five second intervals. After the meal and three large gins and tonic, Mike and Dr Clem were in bed by 9.00 pm.

Mike Townsend woke at 5.00 am to the sound of the dawn chorus.

Slipping on a pair of shorts he pushed his way through the foliage screen on to the deserted lagoon beach. In the early morning light the sight that greeted his squinting eyes was breathtaking. About forty yards to his left, standing on one leg, a blue heron was fishing for his breakfast. The keen-eyed bird appeared to be stalking an oil slick which on closer inspection turned out to be a conglomerate mass of hundreds of thousands of golden-eyed herring parr, weaving and wafting in unison in the clear, blue water of the lagoon. Around the edges of the school there were six, two foot long, black-tipped reef sharks cruising nonchalantly. Suddenly the sharks made a lightning strike into the middle of the piscine mass causing panic and havoc and many of the minnow-like parr jumped clear of the water and landed on the beach. As soon as the predators withdrew the school reformed into a solid phalanx and continued their synchronised wafting movements in the tidal current. Mike watched mesmerized. The sharks' forays continued at irregular intervals but, strangely, their attacks were singularly unproductive and they withdrew to deeper water to regroup and plan their next assault. Mike ran up the beach to fetch Dr Clem to witness this unique phenomenon of nature's 'safety in numbers' ploy. In response to Mike's call the short-tempered, bleary-eyed, doctor appeared at his cabin door, "What the hell's up at this unearthly hour?"

Without his thick, horn-rimmed glasses, and with his bushy eyebrows almost meeting in the midline above his aquiline nose, he looked like a predatory hawk.

"You must come and see what's going on in the water just off the beach. I've never seen anything like it," Mike responded.

Dr Clem reluctantly pulled on a pair of shorts and followed Mike down to the lagoon edge. His peevishness disappeared like an early morning mist at sunrise when he saw nature's premier aquatic predators in action. Mike spoke in an awestricken whisper. "The antics of these sharks remind me of the one and only daylight raid I flew with an American heavy bomber squadron out of Lakenheath in Norfolk in 1944. It was a 120 strong Flying Fortress raid on Dortmund and the Messerschmitts came at us when we were over northern France. The ME 110's selected one plane at the periphery of the armada and came at it from three different directions at once and the Americans lost four Fortresses in that raid. The German pilots had learned the lesson to concentrate their attention on one bomber at a time and it worked in their favour."

They stood watching the 'show' for two hours and were late for *mas huni*, a breakfast consisting of slices of rolled roshi bread garnished with coconut, onions, chilli and lime juice. Afterwards it was back to the lagoon and the golden-eye herring 'slick' and hundreds of multi-coloured tropical fish. At a few points in the lagoon the coral reef was breached and the snorkellers were able to reach the ocean side of the reef where the depth of water suddenly plummeted from six to thirty or forty feet. A snorkel only allowed about seventy seconds underwater, hardly sufficient for deep exploration. But Mike and Dr Clem saw a sufficient variety of large and exotic fish to be convinced that a return to Baros with their scuba equipment was a 'must'.

The three day break on Baros passed far too quickly. Promises were made to the manager of an early return for further underwater exploration. The reception from Mr Farheed in Male was cool but polite. He supervised their safe departure but warned that, if they did return, they would have to do so in an unmarked plane. Technically RAF roundels on the sides and wings of their seaplane constituted a military target. On his return to Gan Mike did two things – he arranged for the seaplane's roundels to be masked with strips of white cloth and he sent a full report of his meeting with Mr Gayoom to MoD (Air) in London. His report stimulated little interest at headquarters. The Maldivian Government's intention of securing Gan for civilian air traffic and tourism was well-recognised by the Ministry of Defence and completely out of the question. Gan was a military base and the arrival of non-British nationals on sovereign territory could not be contemplated. Final return of Gan to the Maldivian's was a thorny problem awaiting a political solution. Wing Commander Mike Townsend had been sent to Male as a placebo and his detailed report was noted and filed and it still remains, in obscurity, gathering dust in the bowels of the Ministry of Defence in Whitehall.

Back at Gan a letter had arrived from Vanessa announcing her intention of paying Mike a visit in November or December. 'Daddy' was on the mend and the brigadier insisted the place for a service wife in peacetime was at her husband's side. Mike had been away from England for over a year and, in the brigadier's opinion, "You can't expect a full-blooded officer to keep on the rails forever when he's far from home and his loved ones. Temptations are too great and he needs his wife's steadying hand."

Mike realised that Vanessa was serious when she wrote she would be sacrificing her attendance at the Boxing Day meet of the Lincolnshire Border Hunt. Pressure from Daddy, and her innate Girl Guide spirit, had convinced her she should join Mike and that she should 'give it a go'. Mike groaned. He was certain Vanessa would not fit into the scene on Gan but he couldn't say 'no' without making it patently clear that he did not want Vanessa by his side. He wrote back grudgingly admitting he was delighted with the news and he looked forward to their reunion in November or December. By that time they would have been apart for eighteen celibate months.

Chapter Six

Vanessa *v* Sonitha

DURING THE WEEK FOLLOWING MIKE TOWNSEND'S return from Baros Dr Clem was laid low with a tummy bug. In his underpants, and sweating profusely, the medical officer lay supine on his bunk. His face was flushed and one hand rested on the right side of his lower abdomen. His deep set, predatory eyes looked up anxiously at his commanding officer.

"What's wrong with you Doc? You look a little peaky."

"I've got a bellyache. It started last night after our mess dinner. I vomited during sick parade this morning and skipped lunch. I've been lying here all day and the pain is getting worse. It's like a knife stabbing me in the guts."

Mike's face lit up with a beaming smile, "I don't suppose its anything to do with the booze we consumed last night?"

The mess night had been a wilder dining-in session than usual.

"No sir. I think it might be my appendix."

"Well, Clem, you're the medical officer so you tell me."

Dr Clem's flushed face screwed up in concentration, "I haven't seen an acute appendix since my student days. I've got a few of the symptoms. Apart from the belly pain my breath smells foul and I seem to remember halitosis is one symptom of appendicitis."

"Okay Doc," Mike replied, "what's to be done about it?"

"I'm sure it will keep till the morning. In any case I might be wrong and the bloody pain will go away overnight. I'm constipated, which is quite unusual for me, and I've taken a big dose of laxative."

"Okay Clem. Corporal Hobart will sit with you tonight and we'll review the situation first thing in the morning. Is there anything you need?"

"Yes please, Mike. Ask Reki to bring me a crate of soda or tonic water. My mouth feels like the inside of a parrot's cage!"

"Cheerio old chap! Keep your pecker up! I'll look in later."

When Mike dropped in around midnight Dr Clem was peacefully asleep and the vigilant medical corporal sat in a comfortable chair in one corner of the billet.

"How's the patient, Corporal Hobart?" Mike whispered.

"He was sick twice after drinking two bottles of tonic water and he's been asleep since nine o'clock. His temperature's settling and he looks more comfortable. I think he's over the worst, sir."

"Very well, corporal, keep an eye on him. We'll review the situation in the morning."

Mike reappeared at 8.00 am to find Dr Clem had taken a turn for the worse and Corporal Hobart was full of concern and anxiety, omitting to mention he had fallen asleep for four hours during the night. He whispered, "Squadron Leader Garvey's temperature is down but he doesn't look too good sir."

Mike approached the still figure on the bed and could see for himself the MO was in serious trouble. Gone was the healthy, pyrexial flush of the night before and Clem's face was ashen and his brow soaked in a cold sweat. The corners of his nostrils flared in and out with each shallow breath and his anxious eyes were dull and lustreless. At Mike's approach Clem tried to sit up but fell back on the bed and groaned.

"How's it this morning Clem?" Townsend asked.

The sickly medical officer managed a faint grin, "Not so good sir. I've been puzzling on and off all night about the signs of appendicitis and it came to me in a flash this morning – rebound tenderness. I definitely had it last night but its gone this morning. My belly feels quite comfortable and the colic has settled. I think the tonic water did the trick and that was without gin! I feel nauseated all the time. I think you'd better take steps to get me out of here."

"Right," Mike decided, "we'll casevac you to Colombo. I'll start the ball rolling right away."

As chance would have it a replacement medical officer for Changi

Hospital in Singapore was in transit on the first plane to touch down at Gan that morning. Fresh-faced and fresh out of Guy's medical school, the young flight lieutenant had a look at Dr Clem and had no hesitation in pronouncing the medical squadron leader had a roaring appendicitis and maybe peritonitis and, in his newly-acquired opinion, needed urgent surgical attention. He was relieved to find the facilities in the medical centre woefully inadequate for any form of major surgery. Having only performed one appendicectomy during his medical training he was not about to practice his fledgeling skills on a squadron leader and a medical colleague to boot. He agreed with alacrity that urgent evacuation to Colombo was the only practical solution. Mike saw Clem off an hour later in a VC 10 and, squeezing gently, briefly held his cold hand, "Good luck Clem old pal."

The medical officer managed a wan smile. "During the time I've been on Gan I never imagined I would be the first to make use of a blood waggon. I'll be back Mike and we'll perfect our scuba gear. So long, sir, and thanks for everything."

The VC10 took off eastwards towards Sri Lanka and Mike Townsend had a sinking foreboding that he would not be seeing the cranky medical officer again. There was no way of escaping the realisation that Squadron Leader Aneurin Clement Ernest Garvey's number was probably up.

Gan. 3rd December 1974

Vanessa Townsend and two leather-bound luggage trunks arrived in Gan on the first plane from Bahrain on a Thursday morning in December. By coincidence the same plane brought Squadron Leader Clement Garvey back to Gan to resume his post as station medical officer. After a two hour operation and a turbulent recovery in a military hospital in Colombo Dr Clem was flown home to convalesce at RAF Hospital, Nocton Hall, near Cranwell. He slowly recovered and was a candidate for discharge from the Service on medical grounds but a dearth of qualified doctors volunteering for military service saved his bacon and he was reassigned to Gan. During his five month absence, between June and December 1974, five locum medical officers passed through the station. They lasted for only a few weeks and, in one instance, a few days. The younger ones were full of ideas for improving medical services but came up against higher authority and their schemes floundered. Two, of higher rank, were content with treating their posting as a holiday in the sun and one MO became so enthused with availability of cheap alcohol that he spent most of his waking hours drinking in the officers' mess. Mike Townsend sent the drunken doctor packing when he failed to attend to a Ghurka rifleman who had broken his ankle. But now that Dr Clem was returning to duty all was well.

At 7.30 am on a cloudless, sunny morning Wing Commander Mike Townsend sat in a station waggon at the end of the runway awaiting arrival of the first plane in, a VC10 en route from Bahrain to Hong Kong via Singapore. The sun was already climbing high into the sky to the east and the air temperature was approaching the low eighties. As soon as the four turbojet engines were switched off the ground staff wheeled steps up to the exit door in the belly of the plane where a staff sergeant crewman appeared to supervise disembarkation of his charges. He had forty-nine passengers aboard, five in the officers section including one complaining lady who thankfully was stepping off at Gan and forty-four other ranks with wives and children, all bound for a three year tour of duty in Hong Kong. The sergeant adhered strictly to protocol, allowing the women and children to debus first, closely followed by the haughty lady from the officer class section. The sergeant saluted Vanessa and murmured his best wishes as she emerged into the sunshine at the top of the steps. Vanessa arrogantly ignored him. As soon as Mike saw his wife he knew she was in a foul mood. For one thing she was inappropriately dressed for the thirty two hour flight from Brize Norton and she wore a full-length woollen dress and a suede overcoat with a wide-brimmed, floral, straw hat rammed firmly on her head. Suspended from her left wrist she carried a large, brown, leather handbag with a fox and hounds motif emblazoned on its front panel. Vanessa descended the steps slowly protesting at the jostling and pushing of the women and children around her. Mike took a step forwards, saluted, and gave his wife a peck on her cheek, "How was your flight, darling?"

Vanessa's clear blue eyes were ablaze with anger, "Don't ask Michael. It was horrendous! Get me out of this hot sun before I faint."

Mike ushered her into the back seat of the waiting station waggon and barked an order to the driver, "Take us to my quarter, Warlow."

He then turned his attention to Vanessa. "What went wrong on the flight, darling?"

"Everything!" Vanessa exclaimed, "I was in a first class cabin with four male officers. We were only separated from the other ranks by a flimsy curtain and the noise from the children at the back was intolerable. The loo arrangements were ghastly and I had to share with the other rank's wives. The five hour hop from Brize Norton to Cyprus was not too bad. A squadron leader sitting on my left and a Black Watch major in front of him were drinking all the way. I accepted one 'g and t' from them just to be sociable. We all got off the plane at Akrotiri where they replenished their stock of gin and whisky in the NAAFI. I thought alcohol was strictly forbidden on military flights?"

"Yes," Mike replied, "its an MoD instruction."

The station waggon was approaching Mike's married quarter. Vanessa bit her lip to contain her tears. "But the worst part was the seven hour flight from Bahrain to Gan. The Black Watch major passed out and the squadron leader turned his attention to me. For an hour he fiddled with a calculator on his lap and then he started babbling about disposal of human excreta from aeroplanes. He had worked it out that the passengers on our flight would discharge x amount of waste material into the atmosphere during a 24 hour flight. This figure multiplied by the number of people, say twenty thousand, in the air all over the world at any given time, and assuming they all used the toilet once during this period, would produce ten thousand pounds of excreta. His conclusion was that in 200 years our atmosphere and the ozone layer would be replaced by 'you know what' as it had nowhere to go. I was interested at first but when he kept repeating his theory, and rechecking his figures on his calculator, I pretended to be asleep. He then woke up the Black Watch major and they started singing bawdy rugby and medical student songs. What a horrid man! Thank God he and the Scottish major are going onwards to Hong Kong."

The station waggon pulled up outside the CO's bungalow.

"Vanessa! Was this man on the plane wearing thick, horn-rimmed glasses and did he have black, bushy eyebrows?"

"Yes," Vanessa replied.

Mike allowed himself a faint smirk, "Then, my darling, he's not going on to Hong Kong. He's my medical officer, Squadron Leader Clement Garvey, and he's getting off right here in Gan. Well, here we are. This is your home from home."

Vanessa looked with disdain at the pokey bungalow which served as the commanding officer's quarter.

"Can two people actually sleep in this ghastly little shoebox?" Vanessa asked, whereupon she pronounced herself utterly exhausted by her long journey and flung herself, fully clothed, on to one of the twin beds. Mike removed her shoes, adjusted the mosquito net and turned on the ceiling fan. He then made a beeline for the officers' mess.

Dr Clem and his recently-found Black Watch friend were propping up the bar clutching large tumblers of iced gin and tonic. Clem made an effort to stand to attention and introduced his drinking partner. "This is Major Iain McCulloch of the Black Watch. He's on his way to join his regiment in Hong Kong. The VC 10 takes off in twenty minutes so we're having a quick snifter before he leaves," and, with a mischievous wink, he added, "Did you know sir, alcoholic drinks are not allowed on the old crate? Will you join us sir?"

Mike angled a withering glance at his MO and answered acidly, "It's eight o'clock in the morning squadron leader. When you've finished your drink, and Major McCulloch is on his way, I will see you in my office."

About an hour later Dr Clem staggered into Mike's office. Swaying on his feet he attempted to apologise for his inebriated state. "I'm afraid, sir, we had a bit of a session on the plane after we left Bahrain. There was one lady and three young subalterns with us in the officer's section. I tried my best to humour the female but she would have none of it. I expect, by now, she's back on the plane with poor Iain McCulloch who'll have to put with her tantrums all the way to Hong Kong."

"Squadron Leader Garvey that lady was my wife and she's staying right here on Gan for a few weeks."

The medical officer was dumbfounded and started stammering an apology. Mike interrupted him, "Squadron Leader Garvey, this is what you'll do. You will retire to your quarter for the rest of the day. Tell your orderly you suffer with air sickness and jet lag. Tomorrow morning you will start work at 6.30 am sick parade. And you'll have to ease off on this drinking business. I do not wish to go through the palaver of cas-evacuating you again. That will be all."

Dr Clem departed, head bowed and deflated. Mike felt irrationally sorry for him. A bachelor with tenuous family ties, his recent illness had obviously taken a lot out of him. He had lost two stones in weight and his face was haggard and drawn. His sunken, dark-brown eyes behind thick-rimmed glasses, bushy black eyebrows, an aquiline pointed nose and thin bloodless lips, made him look like a startled barn owl. Mike was genuinely concerned about his friend's drinking habits. They always enjoyed a couple of sundowners before dinner and an occasional binge on dining-in nights and, perhaps, they overdid it on occasion. After all there was very little else to do on Gan in the evening and with NAAFI Gordons gin at nine shillings a bottle there was every incentive to push the boat out. Mike wondered if Clem's serious illness had affected his personality and driven him to the bottle in a big way. Time would tell but it was comforting to have the old reprobate back in the fold again.

Vanessa slept solidly for eight hours and when she awoke the whingeing began, "Can't you do something about these beds? The mattress is lumpy and can't you get rid of my mosquito net? It's claustrophobic. When I went to the outside loo an hour ago there were creepy crawlies on the wall. I won't go in there again until they're removed. And will you please get rid of the smell of disinfectant?"

Mike sighed and thought 'here we go again'.

"I'll get the mattress changed right away. We can't get rid of the nets because this island is infested with mosquitos. The loos can't be changed and need a disinfectant. Water is at a premium for washing and showering and flush toilets are not practical. And those little guys on the loo walls are lizards and on our side. They eat mosquitos. If we got rid of them a new batch would turn up at the drop of a hat. You must learn to love them, darling."

"Don't patronise me!" Vanessa retorted, "I think they're horrid! And don't keep calling me 'darling'. My proper name is Vanessa and not Van or Vanny. You should know that by now."

Mike was exasperated. He had envisaged some difficulties in making his wife comfortable on Gan but to start complaining after only eight hours on the ground was a bit much. But worse was to come and Vanessa's whingeing knew no bounds. She did not approve of the officers' mess where, all day long, someone was propping up the bar and celebrating some inconsequential event or other. She insisted on having her meals brought to Mike's quarter by a mess steward and refused to join in mess dining-in nights. She got her way with the lizards in the loo only for a fresh crop to take up residence overnight. The first night she slept without a mosquito net she was bitten all over her face and neck and, to make matters worse, one of the bites went septic and had to be lanced by 'that horrid medical officer'. Vanessa's attire did not help her cause. She had brought ten full length, couturier-designed woollen dresses in her luggage, eminently suitable for cocktail parties in Britain but completely unsuited for the hot, humid Maldivian climate. Her wardrobe did not include a pair of shorts or a bathing costume. She objected to the airmen strolling around the base in shorts with their sweaty torsos and brown knees exposed to the unrelenting sun. Even her own husband walked about topless when not on duty.

"Can't you do something to make these men cover up? I can't stand looking at their revolting bare flesh. After all, Michael, you are the commanding officer."

Mike simply shrugged his shoulders knowing full well he could not enforce an order which required his men to wear shirts when they were working in temperatures of over 100° Farenheit. In some of the buildings and messes it was a different matter where all officers and airmen had to be suitably clothed. The exception was Dr Clem who was prone to drop into the officers mess, or the NAAFI, for a quick snifter mid-morning and whose dress left a lot to be desired. And then there was the matter of Vanessa's diet. She abhorred curries and spicy dishes. Locally caught fish, mainly bonito and tuna, did not please her palate and, as most cooked Maldivian dishes contain fish of some sort or another, traditional dishes were not acceptable. During her stay on Gan she lived on omlettes, boiled rice, canned peas and peaches and bowls of corn flakes.

One night Mike took Vanessa to the sergeants' mess for a social evening and a game of housey-housey, She did not enjoy herself and complained, "All those drunken sergeants leering at me and trying to get me interested in the game – legs-eleven, clickety-click and all that rubbish. And that awful medical officer knocking back the gins and calling the sergeants by their christian names – revolting! I shall not be going there again or to the officers' mess."

"But they are only trying to be sociable, darling."

"Please don't 'darling' me, Michael. I don't like it and I want to go home to Daddy" and she bit her lower lip to hold back her tears. The next day Mike took her around the nine-hole golf course but Vanessa performed dismally. Her hand-eye coordination was so poor she failed to knock a ball off the tee. Exhausted by her efforts, and a bath of perspiration in her thick woollen dress, she retired to Mike's quarter where she found another cause for complaint. The water supply to the base was strictly controlled and most days of the week there was a complete shut down for four hours in the afternoon. Vanessa stood under the shower and turned on the taps. Three spurts of rust-coloured water sprayed her skin and then a gurgle and a rush of air in the shower head confirmed that the cistern was dry. Vanessa threw herself on to the bed and burst into tears, "I hate this ghastly place. It's horrid! I want to go home."

She had only been on Gan for ten days. That night Mike concluded that something had to be done about the situation. He suggested they should go away to Baros for a few days and described the island's idyllic beauty, stressing they would be alone and away from it all. Vanessa reacted favourably. "Anything to get away from this repugnant place. What shall I wear for the trip, Michael?"

There was no answer to that. It would have to be one of the twelve impractical dresses she had brought from England. Mike gallantly replied, "Any dress that goes with your beautiful straw hat, darling."

And, for once, Vanessa did not castigate Mike for using the noun of endearment.

Friday was mess dining-in night and Mike attended without Vanessa. As always he sat at the head of the table with Dr Clem seated on his right.

"How's your good lady, sir? I saw her hitting hell out of a Dunlop 65 on the golf course yesterday."

"She's fine but still tired after her flight from the UK. It's taken her over a week to get acclimatised. We might pop up to Baros for the weekend."

Dr Clem grinned, "Take my advice as a doctor, for what its worth.

A few days on Baros will do you both a power of good. Recharge the batteries, so to speak, just like Victorian gentry going to Cannes or Antibes. If you could leave it a week I'll have our scuba kit in working order. I brought back two custom-built, non-returnable valves from the UK."

Mike ignored the broad hint from Dr Clem that he should go with them. "No, I can't wait a week," he replied, "we'll be off to Baros in the morning."

Later on Mike and Dr Clem sat together at the dining table while the younger officers were in a back room playing darts and semi-violent mess games which usually ended in one or other getting drenched in beer or having to down a yard of ale in ten seconds flat. Dr Clem was tipsy and in a melancholic mood. "I nearly died after my appendix operation in Colombo. At the time I was really dodgy my brain was lucidly clear. I remember thinking how lucky I had been to get to medical school from the slums of Birmingham and to enlist in the Royal Air Force and then to get posted to Gan and treated as an equal by yourself and other members of our officers' mess. When I was convalescing at Nocton Hall I went to see my mother and was appalled at what's happening in Brum. The whole place in inundated with Indian and Pakistani immigrants and around my mother's flat they're living twenty or thirty to one house. They're nearly all existing on state benefits and the local Brummies are no better. It filled me with disgust and, as a dedicated socialist, I could envisage Beveridge and Aneurin Bevan turning in their graves. And this open immigration policy, condoned by Harold Wilson and Jim Callaghan, is paid from our taxes. When Wilson devalued in 1968 and said 'the value of the pound in your pocket remains the same' I believed him, but he was lying through his teeth. I went to see my bank manager and was amazed at the amount of tax deducted from my salary by the Callaghan government, up to sixty per cent on my monthly income and most of it goes to pay those lazy bastards on the dole and sponging off the welfare state."

The medical officer paused and took a generous gulp of his port wine. Mike was about to interrupt but Dr Clem obviously wanted to get something off his chest.

"I called to see my surgical chief at Queen Elizabeth Hospital for an opinion on my tummy problems. He told me that a private gastrectomy operation paid him one hundred and fifty guineas but, by the time the tax boys had sorted him out, he only received twenty one pounds. I ask you? Who in his right mind takes the risk of performing a life or death operation and only get twenty one quid out of it at the end of the day? So I sat down and thought long and hard and came to the conclusion that Labour has gone down the wrong road. I like this new fellow Heath. He's taking us into the European Common Market and I think it will be good for Britain. I had three days in London before I flew out of Brize Norton. On Sunday morning I took a bus trip to the see the sights and at the Tower I had a sense of history and the greatness of Britain. Outside Buckingham Palace I saw the changing of the guard. It was there and then I realised the Monarchy is as integral a part of British life as sausage and mash and fish and chips and my views about the Royals changed. I now believe they are doing a good job and worth every penny they receive. So you see, Michael, I'm now prepared to die in Her Majesty's service. That's the oath we pledged when we joined the Royal Air Force," and then, rather sheepishly, he added, "I'm probably a Tory voter too. Do you understand what I'm saying?"

Michael could not believe his ears. Even in the desperate days of the night sorties over Germany he had never admitted to himself that he was prepared to sacrifice his life for King and Country. But here was Dr Clem, a rabid left winger, turning his back on his socialist heritage and furthermore revising his attitude towards the monarchy. He wondered if Clem's illness had affected his mind and, in the nature of things, a recent convert is more devoted to the cause than someone born into it. Mike smiled, sipped his port, and raised his glass to the perplexed medical officer, "Welcome to the fold Clement. All you've told me makes perfect sense."

But it didn't.

The seaplane was hardly clear of the water when Mike realised that the 'honeymoon' trip to Baros was, perhaps, not a good idea after all. When she saw the seaplane Vanessa exclaimed, "It's too small to take both of us! And is it safe?"

"Yes. These little aircraft are the safest in the world."

Vanessa had to be coaxed off the jetty at Hithadhoo into the passenger seat. All the space behind the pilot was taken up by one of Vanessa's trunks containing five dresses, one for dining each evening and Mike was beginning to regret his over-enthusiastic description of Baros resorts' facilities. For himself he only brought along a spare shirt, a pair of shorts, bathing trunks and snorkelling equipment. As soon as the Merlin engine burst into life Vanessa's whingeing started above the reverberations, "I can't stand this noise. Can't you turn the engine down a bit?"

Mike pretended not to hear and kept revving for take-off. Eyes tightly shut, Vanessa sat mumbling an incoherent prayer and she remained in this state until they reached the plane's cruising height of 3,000 feet and Mike was able to ease back on the throttle. She opened her eyes ten minutes into the flight, when they were over Graf Alif Atoll, and relaxed at the sight of the perfectly-rounded, verdant-green islands and yellow sandy beaches surrounded by pale blue lagoons and set in an azure-blue ocean vastness. By the time they came in to land on the sea off Male she was almost human again but, as the little plane hit the water, panic returned and she screamed aloud. Transfer by dhoni across the busy inner harbour produced a few grumbles and, once ashore, she sniffed the air and plunged her face into a perfumed handkerchief, "What's that ghastly fishy smell? I can't stand it."

"That's coming from a fish market across the road, Vanessa. It's their busy time at the moment. Do you wish to have a look?"

"Not if you give me a thousand pounds. Let's get away from here."

"I'll pop across to Mr Farheeds' office and order a taxi. Just wait here a moment."

Mike crossed the road leaving Vanessa and her leather-bound trunk standing at the quayside hemmed in by bustling market porters.

Since Mike's last visit six months earlier Mr Farheed's office had undergone a transformation. It now had a large plate-glass window and a freshly painted door with a sign, 'Farheed Travel', on a wooden board above the entrance. The interior of the little office was light and airy and two walls were covered by neatly arranged wooden filing cabinets. A mahogany desk had replaced the old trestle table and Fat Abdul had been supplanted by the most beautiful native woman Mike had ever seen. She was dressed in a pink *faaskun hendhun*, a long-sleeved silk dress with a wide, scalloped collar and reaching down to her ankles. On her head she wore a sequined *pallu*, or headscarf, of matching colour. The dress was eye-catching and the facial beauty of the woman was overwhelming: large brown eyes set wide apart and a generous red-lipped mouth, partly open in a welcoming smile to reveal two rows of perfectly set, pearly-white teeth. This was a distinct improvement on sweaty Abdul! The beautiful apparition rose to her feet, "*Assalaamu alaikum*. I am Sonitha Farheed. Can I help you sir?"

Her English was perfect. Mike stood transfixed and the woman kept smiling. With an effort he pulled himself together, "I was here in June with a friend and we spent three days on Baros. Mr Farheed looked after us. My wife and I came in by seaplane an hour ago and we wish to spend a few days on Baros. Will this be possible?"

"Of course, sir. I will arrange for your transfer tomorrow. Mr Farheed is my father and he is now First Secretary to the new Ministry of Tourism. I run this office and Hotel Alia. I have nothing to do with the market next door" and, pretending disgust, she pinched her nose and giggled. Mike guffawed. Sonitha turned towards her filing cabinets, "What is your name please?"

"Michael Townsend."

"Abdul was fat and lazy but he kept good files. Ah! here we are! On June 10th Wing Commander Michael Townsend and Squadron Leader Clement Garvey stayed one night at the Alia and three days on Baros, guests of the President and Mr Gayoom. I will make the same arrangements for you and Mrs Townsend and I will personally escort you to Baros tomorrow."

"Thank you Miss Farheed. Would you be kind enough to order a taxi to take us to the Alia?"

Back at the dockside Vanessa was fuming, "Where in God's name have you been? You left me standing here on my own in this horrible heat jostled about by these natives carrying smelly fish across to that stinking market."

"I'm sorry Vanessa but I've been arranging our accommodation and there's a taxi on the way."

When it arrived the rickety old cab, a converted wartime jeep with two seats strapped on to an elevated platform, was uncomfortable and not to Vanessa's liking. Neither was the Alia Hotel. Their room was unbearably hot, the electric fan only worked sporadically, the beds were lumpy and the shower only emitted a trickle of tepid, rusty-brown water in irregular spurts. The evening meal was a fiasco. Maldivian restaurants specialise in fish dishes and vegetable curries. Vanessa, dressed in one of her elegant gowns, made do with a bowl of rice and two hard boiled eggs. Back in their room in the Alia she tossed and turned under the mosquito net canopy and Mike, stripped to the waist, sat chain smoking on the balcony overlooking the bottling factory. He was gasping for a gin and tonic but, recognising Vanessa's antipathy to alcohol, he had not brought any supplies with him. A bath of perspiration, he eventually fell asleep in a wicker chair and dreamt about Sonitha. He awoke, stiff-limbed, just before daybreak and went to lie down beside Vanessa. After a disturbed night she was now snoring sibilantly in a deep sleep of utter exhaustion and despair.

Mike and Vanessa were at the fish market pier by 8'o'clock. The harbour and market were not busy and the larger masdhonis usually brought their catches in at around 11 o'clock and, from that time until mid-afternoon, bedlam ensued as they discharged their cargos. A Maldivian crewman placed Vanessa's trunk in a dhoni and they were all awaiting Sonitha's arrival. Mike spotted her when she was still a hundred yards away and his heart missed a beat. For the sea-journey Sonitha wore a bright blue *salwar*, or pantaloons, and a matching embroidered silk *kamiz*. Her long black tresses were gathered into an oiled and perfumed bun at the nape of her neck and, on her head, she wore a white, woven bonnet held in place with mother of pearl hair-grips. She looked stunning and walked with the assurance of a woman who knew it. A radiant smile of recognition and welcome beamed like a beacon as she reached the waiting couple, "*Assalaamu alaikum* wing commander."

"Good morning, Sonitha. *Alaikum salam*. You look stunning this morning."

The radiant smile broadened as Mike introduced her to Vanessa.

"*Assalaamu alaikum Memsahib* Townsend. Welcome to Male."

Vanessa stiffened and was taken aback by the girls' perfect English. She bowed her head in recognition of the Maldivian woman's greeting and her straw hat fell into the flotsam near the harbour wall. The hat was quickly recovered by the crewman but not before it was sodden in fish-smelling brine.

"What will I wear Michael? I can't put this foul-smelling rag back on my head."

Sonitha came to the rescue. She crossed the road to her office and returned with a blue headscarf, a traditional Maldivian *pallu*.

"For you, *Memsahib*, with my compliments."

The dhoni carefully made its way out of the inner harbour. Mike and Vanessa were seated one either side of the leather trunk and the captain, a boyish-looking man of thirty, took the tiller. Arms akimbo, the crewman lookout boy stood at the prow of the dhoni and Sonitha sat at his side clutching her knees under her chin and staring fixedly ahead as the diesel-driven boat chugged its way, at a leisurely pace, towards the island resort of Baros.

Born in 1953, the only daughter of Ibrahim Farheed a Citizen's Majlis member and harbourmaster, Sonitha had a carefree, tomboyish childhood. A privileged child, she was brought up as a strict Muslim. By virtue of her father's wealth and position, at 12 years of age, she was sent to a British-run Catholic boarding school in Colombo where she remained for six years. At the boarding school Sonitha was exposed to 'western ways' but, by and large, kept true to her faith. So as not to appear different to other girls she relented in her dress code and wore jeans on casual occasions and a one-piece bathing costume in the swimming pool. But though temptations were persistently present, she never experimented with smoking, drugs or alcohol. For her last two years in Colombo Sonitha attended a Ladies Business College and by the time she eventually came home to Male she spoke English and French fluently. A call for her to return home came in July 1974 when her father was appointed first secretary to the newly created Ministry of Tourism. Wishing to keep his business interests within the family he made a younger brother harbourmaster and manager of the fish market and gave his only daughter the responsibility of running Hotel Alia and the three resort islands franchised to him by the Maldivian President. At the age of twenty one Sonitha Farheed had taken up her appointment on 1st September 1974 and was nearly four months into her new job when the Townsends arrived and booked a few days on Baros.

Throughout the hour-long journey Mike gazed fixedly at Sonitha's back. The forward curvature of her spine caused the hem of her *kamiz* to ride upwards exposing two inches of olive-brown skin above the firmly-buttocked *salwar*. The girdle of exposed skin fascinated and, in a strange way, sexually excited Mike and his imagination ran riot. He began to mentally undress the desirable woman and his concentration was so intense he only half-heard Vanessa's whispered question, "Why is that woman coming across with us?"

Annoyed at having his lascivious reverie interrupted Mike snapped back tersely, "Sonitha has every right to be on this boat. Her father owns the island and she's the tourist agent for Baros."

Vanessa retorted, "At least the hussy could cover up properly. I find that exposed skin revolting."

Mike winced, shrugged his shoulders and sank back into his previous preoccupation with Sonitha. And a few minutes later Vanessa again interrupted his concentration, "Are we safe in this boat, Michael? Why is that man at the front waving his arms about? We seem to be zig-zagging a lot."

"We are in the hands of the best sailors in the world, Vanessa. The man at the prow is a lookout. The waters around here are shallow and coral reefs change their shape from day to day. These boys are experts. Look to your right at two o'clock. That's Baros coming up."

Vanessa gazed towards their destination and Mike's attention was again rivetted on Sonitha's tantalising midriff. Twenty minutes later his reverie was again interrupted. "I don't like wearing this headscarf. Gracie Fields and the wartime factory workers used to wear them. It's a bit common and my straw hat is still wet and smelly. Do you think I should I take the scarf off before we reach the island?"

Mike took a quick glance at Vanessa. Her delicately-chiselled, peaches-and-cream complexion was beautifully complimented by the multicoloured headscarf. For a few seconds he compared Vanessa's classic facial beauty with Sonitha's Asiatic features and mentally registered a draw. But when his mind wandered to their feminine contours and sex appeal it was no contest. Sonitha won hands down. He came to earth with an involuntary bump. "Please yourself, Vanessa. You look superb in the silk headscarf. I would wear it if I were you."

The compliment from her husband did the trick. When they landed on the jetty at Baros she wore the blue silk *pallu* and carried the offending straw hat at arms length.

Sonitha stayed only an hour on the island before returning to Male. She introduced the Townsends to the resort manager, a Mr Mohammed Saeed, who saw them settled into their cabin and Vanessa announced her approval of their accommodation. Set in a coconut grove at the lagoon's edge, their cabin was spacious and airy and the furniture and fittings were constructed from burnished sandalwood. But her enthusiasm waned perceptibly when she visited the outside toilet and shower. Both cubicles were occupied by a family of geckoes. Their fearsome-looking jaws, darting eyes and erratic, rapid movements, combined to produce a predictable reaction. She screamed and came running into the cabin. "Michael, Michael, come and see the monsters on the walls in the loo."

"They're only geckoes, Vanessa. They're quite harmless and they won't touch you."

Vanessa pouted, "I'll go into the bushes to spend a penny."

Mike lost patience. "You'd better not, darling. There are snakes on the island."

Vanessa's eyes widened in horror.

"Snakes! Snakes!" she choked on the words.

"Yes," Mike replied digging the knife in deeper, "they need snakes to keep down the rat population."

"Rats!" Vanessa screamed, "Rats! I feel faint."

Mike smiled to himself. This was one round he won conclusively. Vanessa's lavatorial requirements were settled amicably. As she did not possess a pair of shorts, or a swimsuit, one of her Hardy Amies dresses was sacrificed and she waded fully-clothed into the lagoon. Even this method had its drawbacks when she learned later in the week that some of the larger fish in the lagoon were black-tipped reef shark, said to be completely harmless to humans. This knowledge did nothing to allay her fears of dunking in the lagoon to answer a call of nature.

Vanessa's other persistent bone of contention was the food served in the central big hall. Meals were cooked, or barbecued, in the nearby cookhouse and guests were expected to sit cross-legged on the wooden floor and eat with their right hands without the use of knives, forks or spoons. When the gong sounded for lunch on their first day the menu consisted of a Maldivian fish stew, roshi bread, curried vegetables and boiled rice. The dinner menu was practically the same and, for three days, there was little variation. The other twelve guests were Asians and the food suited them well but none of the dishes were to Vanessa's liking. She survived on boiled rice, coconut flavoured roshi and hard-boiled eggs specially brought across from Male for the Memsahib. Coconut juice was plentiful and refreshing but clean, unadulterated drinking water was at a premium. Mike spent most of his daylight hours snorkelling in the lagoon and on the reef and he soon developed a snorkeller's tan – a pale, white chest and abdomen and a deep bronze colour to the back of his neck, torso and calves. In her own way Vanessa, despite the endemic discomforts and lacklustre diet, enjoyed herself and while Mike was out snorkelling she sat in the shade of a palm tree reading romantic novels.

After three days on Baros Sonitha came to fetch them in a dhoni. At the sight of her smiling face and flashing eyes Mike's interest was rekindled. He wondered what shape her body and legs might be underneath the coloured *kamiz* and bulbous *salwar*? She appeared to be a little flat-chested, just like Vanessa, but this appearance was deceptive. In common with unmarried girls of her age her well-formed breasts were bound and flattened against her chest wall by broad linen bands. In any case her female contours could not fail to be more alluring than Vanessa's angular body.

On the pier at Male Sonitha's father, elegantly turned out in a dark suit and white shirt, met their dhoni. He was particularly courteous to the Memsahib and Vanessa commented afterwards: 'What a nice man. For a local he's a perfect gentleman.' Ibrahim Farheed inquired about London's reaction to the Maldivian request to use Gan as a tourist airfield and Mike had to admit he had not received a reply to date. Whilst Farheed was helping Vanessa into the dhoni Mike had a brief moment to speak to Sonitha. He held her hand gently and probed deeply into the limpid pools of her dark-brown eyes, "Goodbye Sonitha. Thank you for everything. I shall come back one day on my own."

"Yes please, Sahib, come back soon. My heart will be happy to see you again. And please call me Soni. All the girls in my school in Colombo did. I like it better than Sonitha.'

Mike squeezed her hand affectionately and then let it go abruptly. "Good luck Soni."

He turned on his heel and joined Vanessa in the dhoni which took them out to the seaplane. During the return flight to Gan Vanessa, for once in a benevolent mood, slept all the way despite noisy reverberations from the seaplane's Merlin engine.

On the day of his return from Baros a cablegram from the director of overseas operations at MoD lay on Mike's desk. He slit open the envelope with trembling fingers,

From A.C. Sir C. Lampton. MoD
To Wing. Co. M. Townsend O.C. Gan
'Return UK with immediate effect. App. MoD 1200 hrs on 04.01.75.
Replacement OC will arrive Gan on 20.12.74.'

The implications of the order were twofold. He was either being relieved of his command and retired from the Air Force or he was in line for promotion and another posting in the UK. He preferred to think of the latter possibility. Group Captain Michael Townsend sounded just right and, in his view, completely justified. After all he had done a good job on Gan and had not blotted his copybook. With a light heart he rushed off to his quarter to tell Vanessa. She was thrilled with the news and responded with a question, "What's the date today Michael?"

"It's the sixteenth of December."

"Good," she replied, "if we get away in the next forty-eight hours we will be home in time for the Christmas hunt ball on the twenty-second. What shall I wear for the ball Michael?"

Mike had no interest in the hunt ball and was irritated to see that Vanessa was not over-enthusiastic about his possible promotion. But the good news did pay dividends. Vanessa was so pleased they were leaving Gan she allowed Mike to make love to her that night, not the customary brief encounter but for two prolonged sessions. On December 19th 1974 Wing Commander Townsend and his wife left Gan station on a VC10 flight, staging at Bahrain and Cyprus, and bound for Brize Norton in the UK.

Chapter Seven

Two Trips to Baros

WING COMMANDER MIKE TOWNSEND came in early to the officers mess for a ritual sundowner session. Dr Clem and a young naval sublieutenant off an RFA supply ship were already propping up the bar, hands cupped around their Maxwell specials. At the approach of the commanding officer they slipped off their high barstools and stood to attention until Mike reached the counter.

"What will it be sir?" Clem asked deferentially.

"The usual please Ruskin," Mike ordered and watched as the barman expertly measured four fingers of gin into a cutglass tumbler and added coconut juice and three drops of angostura bitters.

"Cheers!" Mike exclaimed and downed most of his drink in one gulp. The gin-based cocktail was a Gan speciality concocted by a popular CO of the early 60s, one Wing Commander Constable Maxwell, and a sure way of relaxing the officers when they congregated in the mess before dinner to review the day's events which were never discussed at the dining table. As the months slipped by the time for a sundowner session gradually crept into the afternoon and Dr Clem and his naval friend had been drinking since teatime.

Clem introduced the naval officer, "This is Sublieutenant James Falkirk off Royal Fleet Auxilliary, Lyness. His Captain is coming ashore to join us for dinner later," and, lamely, he added, "I've been entertaining James and showing him around the station. This is his first visit ashore on Gan."

"You could not be in better hands Mr Falkirk. Our sawbones knows every nook and cranny on Gan and is a specialist on the layout of the officers' mess."

Clem blushed and the sublieutenant looked uncomfortable. A few seconds' awkward silence was broken by Dr Clem, "I was telling young Falkirk about our snorkelling trip to Baros last year. When are we going again sir?"

Mike glared at the MO and threw back the rest of his drink. "There's too much to be done at the moment. Baros will have to wait. I'll see you at dinner."

He turned on his heel and marched out of the mess. Clem looked after his departing commanding officer with concern, "I wonder what's up with the old man? He's usually very chirpy on sundowner parade. Still, he's got a lot on his plate at the moment. Drink up James! Two more Maxwell specials please, Ruskin, and make them doublers."

Mike was a worried man. Since returning from UK leave in January he had been working long hours on the complicated logistics of dismantling the airbase and, at the same time, maintaining a service for incoming planes and transit passengers. An inventory of all moveable equipment, down to the last knife, fork and spoon in the NAAFI, had been undertaken by the quartermaster and Staff Sergeant Jack Fussell. They had drawn up evacuation schedules, starting with non-essential equipment and stores and, as departure day approached, working up to important machinery and transport. The petroleum storage tanks, the electricity power station, the desalination plant and the telecommunications mast at Hithadhoo would be left in situ for the incoming Maldivians. Earlier in the week he had received a signal from MoD indicating the hand-over date would be in March 1976 which gave him nine months to finalise his evacuation plans. The inevitability of closure was now a depressing fact. Mike himself was responsible for all personnel under his command and, only two days ago, a signal arrived ordering deployment of his Ghurka defence company to Dehli in early August. The volume of air traffic on Gan was diminishing to a trickle and most of the larger transporters and VC10's were rerouting to the British/American base at Diego Garcia, 450 miles to the south. Every day brought in movement orders for one or other of his airmen. Mike was also responsible for laying off civilian-employed Maldivians, a distasteful task as he was severing their sole source of income and many had been faithful and loyal servants for 20 years, or more, and had forsaken their traditional livelihood as fishermen and seafarers. The cut-backs were beginning to bite and overshadowing all else was a persistent niggle that one day soon he would be receiving orders from Moscow. These background worries paled into insignificance when he read a personal letter which was delivered to his quarter while he was dressing for dinner. Penned in his own handwriting the memo was from Tony Widgeon. With trembling fingers Mike slit open the blue, flimsy envelope and read the airmail.

Group Captain Anthony Widgeon
MoD (Air)
Whitehall
London

17th June 1975

My dear Mike,

Long time, no hear! Wonders never cease! I got my promotion last week. Old Lampton is stepping off next year and they've pushed me up the ladder. Thank God you weren't around as I wouldn't have stood a chance! Ce la vie! My money is still on you getting a big gong before I do. So make a good job of Gan. The handover has been scheduled for March and you'll get official confirmation of the exact date shortly. Contacted Van last week. She's very down in the mouth and her father is pretty sick and demanding. She did tell me about the happy time you spent together in Male and Baros last December. Which brings me to a coincidence and my reason for writing to you personally. You met my brother-in-law, Bobby Davidson, at the wine bar in Firth Street on your last home leave. He's now 2iC of a minesweeping flotilla and they hope to dock in Male for a courtesy visit during the first week in July. He would love to meet you for a chat and he's mad keen on snorkelling. I know he'd appreciate it if you could pop up to Male and show him the delights of Baros. Please do me this favour and I'll owe you one.

With best wishes to you and your command in paradise,
Yours aye,
Tony

Mike screwed the letter into a ball and threw it on the floor. He resented Tony Widgeon's promotion but his main worry was a reference to a visit from the mysterious 'Bobby' and the fact that Tony was a go-between for the Russian secret service. The letter was not a polite request to go to meet 'Bobby' but a direct order from Moscow. He had hoped that, after over six months' silence, his Russian connections had forgotten about him. Battling with his conscience he lay fully clothed on his bed and fell into a deep, troubled sleep. He missed dinner. He was woken at 0600 hours next morning by Rekitutha, his Maldivian orderly, who brought him a cup of tea. The fastidious Reki had retrieved the crinkled blue-paper ball from the corner of the bedroom and, whilst ironing a drill shirt, he also flattened the creases in the crumpled air-mail letter. Before going to the mess for breakfast Mike burnt the letter and disposed of the ashes in an Elsan toilet. By the time he reached the mess he had made up his mind. He had no alternative but to go to Baros and confront the Russian agent.

Baros, first week July, 1975
Mike flew alone to Baros on the tail end of a south-westerly *hulhangu*. He was full of forebroding and wondered if there was any way out of his dilemma. Tony's letter really upset the apple cart. Day in and day out he had wrestled with his conscience and had misgivings and mood changes about the 'contract' he had so foolishly embraced all those years ago at the LSE. And now his bosses were calling his bluff and using Vanessa as a trump card and what depressed him most was the realisation that Tony Widgeon was in cahoots with the foreign agents. Consequently he was not in the best of humour before he flew up to Male and was rude and assertive in preventing the irrepressible Dr Clem forcing his company on him. In the end he had to insist on spending a week away on his own to recharge his batteries and for solitary relaxation At the back of his mind there was also an off-chance of seeing Sonitha again.

As the little seaplane, urged onwards by a strong tail wind, approached Male his melancholia lifted a little at the thought of seeing the Maldivian beauty but, even in this hope, he was thwarted. The tourist office next to the fish market was closed and displayed a notice 'On Vacation'. He haggled with two dhonimen who were reluctant to take him across to Baros and maintained the place was shut and the landing jetty had been washed away by a monsoon. Mike upped the ante and a few extra *rufiya* changed their minds but the fishermen insisted on taking a masdhoni, better able to negotiate rough seas and stabler than an ordinary inshore dhoni.

The jetty at Baros had suffered in the storm. The resort was officially closed but the manager and his skeleton staff made Mike comfortable in an undamaged cabin. Snorkelling off the reef was dangerous and, even in the normally placid lagoon, visibility was restricted by sand-clouds generated by pounding waves. For three days the turbulence continued. Mike's disappointment at his inability to snorkel was overshadowed by elation at the thought that, due to the inclement weather, his contact might not be able to keep the assignation. The mysterious 'Bobby Davidson' would presumably come in by ship and during a monsoon few large vessels took the chance of getting stranded on a Maldivian coral reef. Mike thanked God for the *hulhangu* and prayed that this one had a longer 'tail' than usual. On the fourth day the squalls abated and snorkelling became possible. With only two more days to go on Baros Mike would have fulfilled his part of the bargain and then, on his fifth day, the Russian agent appeared.

Once the high winds settled a constant stream of dhonis carrying workmen and repair materials came across from Male. Mike spent his time in the water, only joining the workers at mealtimes. He was the only guest on the island and, in view of the chaos, he was left to fend for himself which suited Mike down to the ground. Towards the evening of the fifth day Mike had come off the reef into the lagoon when he saw the squat figure of a man, wearing a grubby, white 'I love Male' T-shirt, wading out from the sandy beach towards him. The man made no effort to swim and, as he splashed his way nearer, Mike could make out he was an European but definitely not the Bobby Davidson whom he was expecting to meet. The visitor had a thick black stubble on his chin, close-cropped, crinkly hair, two deep-set dark, malevolent eyes and a broad, spatulate nose with cavernous nostrils. He lost little time in addressing Mike in guttural, broken English, "You are Townsend?"

Mike removed his swimming goggles and nodded.

"Me, I am Bobby and I have a message."

The man was outwardly concentrating and making every effort to get his message across word-perfect. "You are to allow an Antonov transport plane to land on your airbase at Gan. You will arrange to refuel the plane and you must stop your soldiers entering the plane. The plane will be on the ground for only a short time and, once it takes off, your task is over. You will not inform London about the plane landing and until four hours after it has departed. You will receive further instructions. Is it clear to you Townsend?"

Mike looked blankly at the secret agent. His mind was in a dither but he could see no way of backing down. He lowered his head and whispered a muted 'yes'. The Russian scooped up two handfulls of water and doused his sweaty, close-cropped scalp. He grunted a few unintelligible words, turned and pushed his way ashore and, within a minute, he was off the beach and out of sight amongst the palm trees. Five minutes later Mike heard a dhoni phutt-phutting its way out of Baros's lagoon. Mike was relieved. The demands from Moscow were not too onerous and all he had to do was to facilitate onward passage of a Russian plane taken short on fuel. He did not know when the plane might land and he did not know if the plane was a fighting machine or carried passengers. It did not matter. As CO of Gan he would be seen to be acting on humanitarian grounds, aiding an aircraft in distress. The more he thought about it the rosier the picture became and a great weight was lifted off his shoulders. That night he celebrated and consumed a bottle of whisky in the privacy of his own cabin. He decided to spend another two days on Baros to allow the Russians to get clear of Male and he could then return to Gan with a light heart.

On the afternoon following the secret agent's departure Mike, suffering from a hangover, was snorkelling on the reef some fifty metres outside the lagoon. He was ascending for air when he caught a glimpse of a large, reddish object moving at pace in the depths of the reef some thirty metres below him. He continued his ascent and, after gulping a few lungfulls of air, he looked around. There was an empty dhoni anchored off the reef some sixty metres to his right but otherwise the sea was clear of vessels. The flashing red 'fish' intrigued him. He waited patiently on the surface to regain his breath and, fixing his vizor firmly over the upper half of his face, looked down into the water. From the depths a person dressed in red came hurtling upwards, becoming larger by the second as it approached the surface. Suddenly a mop of black hair emerged about a yard away from him. The head took in an enormous gulp of air and turned to face Mike. Sonitha's beautiful face broke into a welcoming smile, *"Assalaamu alaikum* Mike. How are you?"

Mike was unable to resist the temptation. He tore off his mask and kissed Sonitha on the lips, a brine-flavoured kiss which only lasted a few seconds. Sonitha broke away and, gesturing Mike to follow, she swam with easy strokes across to the moored dhoni.

"Sonitha! I did not expect to see you."

Sonitha laughed. She sat cross-legged in the well of the dhoni, her wet silk *kamis* and *salwar* clinging seductively to her curvaceous body. She was full of the joy of reunion.

"I had to go to Cochin to a tourism conference and the monsoon delayed my return. I'm sorry to see what the *hulhangu* has done to Baros but we'll soon have the place in shape again. What are you doing here Mike without the Memsahib?"

"I came to see you Soni," he lied with a flashing smile.

They looked deeply into each others' eyes. Sunset was about an hour away and the golden orb was low on the horizon.

"I have to be back in Baros before dark. I'll come across again tomorrow."

"Yes please Soni. We can swim in the morning but I have to leave for Gan in the afternoon. You're an expert swimmer Soni."

She smiled wistfully, "When I was young I was a, how do you say it, tomgirl – or is it tomboy? I used to dive for coral with the local boys and I can stay down for three minutes. And in Colombo, I was the school swimming and diving champion for three years running."

"I don't believe you can stay underwater for three minutes, Soni!"

She pretended to be insulted.

"Wait till tomorrow Sahib Townsend and I will show you."

She broke into a mischievous cackle, revealing her ivory white teeth. Mike was mesmerized. He sat and stared at her with a reverential surge of unfettered adoration.

On the following day things did not go as planned. Sonitha was unable to get away and they met on the inner harbour pier as Mike was about to board a dhoni which would carry him to his seaplane. Warned off by her father, Sonitha was slightly formal but she still smiled. "Well, Mr Townsend, you are leaving me again?"

"Yes, Sonitha, I have to go but I will be back."

"Is that a promise?"

"Yes Soni."

They touched hands briefly, a subtle, intimate gesture. Soni was falling in love with the English officer old enough to be her father. It was absurd. He was 28 years older than she and yet she could not help herself. Her father's warnings of a liaison with a person of a different faith went largely unheeded. But would he return to Baros? Soni feared her provocative actions on the reef might frighten Mike away. She placed her hands firmly together, fingertip to fingertip, bowed her head and solemnly wished Mike a safe journey back to Gan.

The Ghurka infantry company was redeployed and left Gan in mid-September 1975. The void was filled by recruiting airmen to guard the base and this meant extra duties, much resented and carried out with lack of enthusiasm and purpose by the airmen. The base was literally crumbling to bits and non-essential catering duties and mess waiting were delegated to employed civilians. Rekitutha became the officers' mess steward and continued in his position as catering manager to the NAAFI. Standards deteriorated and Gan became a stagnant backwater waiting for the inevitable hatchet to fall and final closure. Every week an 'essential' officer or NCO was posted home or eastwards to Singapore or Hong Kong. Promised replacements never materialised or, if they did, were raw recruits. By mid-October 1975 Mike's command was reduced to six officers and 200, largely untrained, other ranks. Matters came to a head during the second week in October when the senior operational signals officer and two of his staff were recalled to the UK. By this time dismantling the telecommunication and radar equipment at Hithadhoo had become a priority. Mike put in an urgent request for suitable replacements and, in late November, Squadron Leader Timothy Cosbey and three signallers arrived on temporary attachment. The same plane brought in Warrant Officer William Williams DSO. Well-known in Cranwell, and a feared drill sergeant instructor for many years, he came to Gan with the specific task of boosting morale amongst the airmen and preparing the base for the grand hand-over ceremony in March 1976.

By November 1975 air traffic through Gan was reduced to one plane every other day and most of the flights took away a few of Mike's ground staff. For a change, at 0830 hours on November 20th, a VC10 brought in reinforcements in the shape of Squadron Leader Timothy Cosbey, a signals corporal and two airmen operators and Warrant Officer William Williams DSO. The radiant sun was already sending its skinpiercing rays earthwards as the base commander waited at the end of the runway for their arrival. The squadron leader came down the steps, smiled at Mike, and saluted. "Christ, sir, is it as hot as this all the time?"

Timothy Cosbey had been uprooted at short notice from the frosty autumnal climate of a Lincolnshire flying station. Mike smiled ruefully. "It's hot now, Timothy, but give it a couple of hours and you'll really feel the heat!"

Immaculately turned out despite the trials of a long, confined flight, Warrant Officer Williams sprang to attention and gave Mike an exaggerated salute. "Warrant Hofficer Williams reporting for duty, sir."

"Glad to have you aboard Mr Williams. There's plenty of work awaiting you."

The WO twirled the tips of his pencil-thin moustache. "'Ave no fear, sir. I'll 'ave the airmen in good working h'order and we'll 'ave a first class drill squad for the 'and-over. Leave it to me, sir."

Mike smiled. The warrant officer's enthusiasm was infectious but he had a big job on his hands. 'Rather you than me' Mike thought as he escorted the new arrivals to the waiting station waggon.

Warrant Officer William Williams, known as Willie Squared or Silly Billy to the squaddies at Cranwell, was an archetypal RAF non-commissioned officer. A native of the South Wales mining valleys, he enlisted in the RAF Regiment in 1947 and immediately saw active service during the Berlin airlift. He transferred to the 'proper' RAF in 1953 and worked his way through the ranks. For the past six years he had been a drill sergeant at Cranwell College where he was remembered with varying degrees of affection by the officer cadets and he became an acknowledged expert on ceremonial drill. Willie Squared was a short, dapper man with jet black, dyed and brylcreemed hair and deepset, penetrating black eyes. Eschewing a typical RAF handlebar he had cultivated a pencil-thin grey moustache modelled on a regimental sergeant-major of Her Majesty's Foot Guards. Ramrod stiff and carrying a measuring stick under his arm, his shrill, high-pitched commands had reverberated around Cranwell's parade grounds for half a decade. After twenty-two years service in the 'proper' RAF he was coming to the end of his career and the Gan posting was his swansong. WO William Williams DSO intended leaving his mark on the god-forsaken island and he started right away. As they were driving off the runway and approaching the NAAFI building he ordered the driver to stop the station waggon.

"Hey you there! Where do you think you're going dressed like that? And get your 'air cut."

The shambling figure making his way towards the NAAFI pulled up in surprise. Mike, on the verge of bursting into laughter, contained himself with difficulty. "Mr Williams that's Squadron Leader Garvey our medical officer."

"I'm sorry, sir, I couldn't see 'is badges of rank."

"That's not surprising. He hardly ever wears them and even on his mess kit they've faded badly in the sun."

Mike introduced the new arrivals to the MO who took an immediate dislike to both of them. He could not stand the bullying arrogance of the pumped-up little warrant officer and the quietly-spoken signaller seemed much too friendly with his CO and might prove a threat to his special relationship with Mike. Later on Dr Clem discovered that Tim Cosbey was an abstemious drinker and, for all intents and purposes, practically teetotal. This confirmed his first impression that the signals officer was an intellectual wimp and not 'one of the boys'.

Within three weeks of his arrival WO Willie Squared had transformed the standard of dress and discipline on the base. Other ranks were down to one hundred and twenty in number and the Maldivian workforce had been cut back from eighty to a couple of dozen. On his first parade, compulsory for all airmen and NCOs below the rank of sergeant, he laid down the ground rules. "Discipline 'ere is lax and the standard of dress h'is diabolical. From now on this is what will 'appen. Everyone will get a regulation 'aircut. There will be no h'excuses, not even a chitty from the MO. You will wear a clean shirt every day and the punkah wallahs will do your laundry. Regulation blue shorts with razor-sharp pleats will be worn to one inch above the knee and white socks to one inch below the knee. Your boots will be polished so as I can see my face in 'em. Your belts will be blancoed twice a week and I want your belt buckles and cap badges shining bright. The only men h'exempted are the cooks and fitters who will wear blue dungarees. All personnel on duty after sundown will wear regulation issue trousers and drill shirts and you will not be let into your mess, or the NAAFI, if not properly dressed. Is that clear?"

For a week after the parade the station barber had a steady stream of customers and the standard of dress improved almost overnight. Enforcing discipline was not so easy. There was no facility for imprisonment on Gan and the only sanction was confinement to barracks which, in practical terms, meant the miscreant was banned from the NAAFI. His mates, however, were always more than ready to smuggle cigarettes and alcohol to his quarter and the results of infringing Silly Billy's orders were never severely punitive. The officers, with the exception of Dr Clem, took a greater pride in their turnout. The MO became openly recalcitrant and regularly announced his favourite pastime was 'baiting Silly Billy'. The new WO did one thing to please Dr Clem's social conscience. Appalled by the variety and quality of dress of some of the employed Maldivians he ordered the quartermaster to issue them with standard white linen shirts, blue, knee-length, kilt-like skirts and light-blue service-issue plimsols. The uniform was completed with a regulation forage cap and three of the more senior employees, two corporals and a sergeant, were issued with red chevrons to sew on their sleeves. Mike Townsend agreed to the new innovations but was none too pleased to learn that Silly Billy had promoted his own servant, Mohammed Rekitutha, and made him sergeant in charge of the Maldivian employees.

Mohammed Rekitutha was born on Gan island in 1935. His father was a fisherman, one of many in a community of 1200 souls who were all forcibly evicted to Mammendhoo in 1940 to make way for an RAF base on the island. After the end of the war, in 1946, Rekitutha's family returned to Gan. Practically illiterate, the 12 year old became a deckhand on a masdhoni operating off the Maldives in the South Indian Ocean. The British Air Force returned to Gan in 1956 and the residents were again ejected and rehoused in Feydhoo. Richard Costain, the civil engineers, and an RAF construction unit employed 2000 local labourers to extend the runway and rebuild a causeway to connect Gan with Feydhoo and a coral extension track to Hithadhoo. Rekitutha, now 21 years old, was one of the first to volunteer his services. The airfield became operational in August 1957 when the local workforce was drastically reduced. Commuting each day across the causeway Rekitutha found employment as a waiter in the officers mess and his reputation as an honest and trustworthy servant soon led to promotion. He became a cook in the sergeants mess and, later, head chef in the NAAFI where he produced fish and chips and apple pie and custard 'just like mother makes'. By the time Mike Townsend took over command, 38 year old Reki, as he was popularly known, had been a civilian employee for 16 years and had become an institution on Gan. Everyone from the CO down to the newest erk knew Reki. Apart from his culinary expertise he arranged laundering and uniform repairs and became as essential a part of the airforce base as the commanding officer himself. The only thing he couldn't provide was female companionship. MoD instructions were inflexible – no females, apart from those in transit, were allowed to set foot on Gan. Reki had noted the difficulties his commanding officer's lady had created when she was in residence on Gan just before Christmas last year. He sympathised with the CO who had done his best to make the Memsahib comfortable and, when the CO's orderly was repatriated in June 1975, Reki volunteered to look after Wing Commander Townsend while still functioning as NAAFI chef and manager.

The arrival of WO William Williams upset everyone. He took Reki away from the NAAFI and from batting for the CO, gave him a white shirt with three red chevrons on his sleeve and placed him in an office in charge of the Maldivian workers on the station. The 'mad' fellow, the airmen called him Silly Billy but not to his face, was now teaching Reki's cadre to march and salute. Reki was inordinately proud of his chevrons and enjoyed the daily drill parades. His little squad were adapting better to discipline on the parade ground than the conscript airmen which pleased Silly Billy as it showed the 'regulars' how it should be done. Reki's only regret on his promotion was the loss of privilege of looking after the CO and he held Wing Commander Townsend in high esteem.

All commissioned and non-commissioned officers on the base, duty personnel exempted, had to attend the CO's monthly conference held in the NAAFI dining hall at 1100 hrs on 18th December 1975. Reki provided tea, coffee and biscuits. The commanding officer opened the batting. "The hand-over date is officially confirmed for 29th March. Further details of the hand-over ceremony will be issued in due course."

Mike paused and scanned the room. He was pleased with the turnout of his officers and senior NCOs. Despite his autocratic manner WO Williams had certainly spruced up the station. The only nigger in the woodpile was the medical officer who sat in the front row in a frayed, sweat-sodden drill shirt and rumpled blue shorts. Mike made a mental note to have a word with Dr Clem after the conference.

"We are up to date with our evacuation schedules. Christmas is nearly upon us and we can all take a well-earned rest over the holiday. Taking it in turns, everyone on the base will have four days local leave between now and the New Year."

There was a general murmur of approval broken by the dapper warrant officer who sprang to his feet. "Permission to speak, sir?"

"Yes, Mr Williams, what is it?"

"There's a lot of work to be done on the parade ground. At present the Maldivain section is drilling better than our lads."

"You'll have plenty of time to smooth off the rough edges in the New Year Mr Williams. My order stands. All our cooks and servants are Muslims and they will certainly not be celebrating Christmas."

Mike scanned his notes.

"We will now hear details of the evacuation schedules and arrangements for the hand-over ceremony".

A wing commander engineer predicted all maintenance machinery, heavy tools and equipment would be in transit by mid-February. It was agreed that the power station, the ineffective desalination plant and near-empty fuel storage tanks would be handed over to the Maldivian government. A transport and flights squadron leader reported that, apart from two station waggons, three jeeps and four three-tonners, all vehicles would be off the station by 1st March. One of the Hithadhoo seaplanes would be taken aboard a supply ship in January and the second, at the CO's request, would be kept in readiness for local emergencies. Squadron Leader Tim Cosbey announced that the radar station at Hithadhoo was already dismantled and the short wave transmitter would be brought across for storage in the control tower on the airfield. The long-range transmitter at the Hithadhoo signals station would be left until the first week in March. When Hithadhoo was eventually evacuated the telecommunication mast and radar dishes would be left in situ for the incoming Maldivians. Mike then turned his attention to the medical officer.

"What are your plans for evacuating the medical centre and hospital Squadron Leader Garvey?"

Dr Clem had obviously not given the matter much thought. "I can pack everything in the medical centre into one handbag. We could be ready to move in ten minutes."

Mike smiled and rose to his feet. "That concludes the December conference. As you leave please pick up Mr Williams' schedule of parades for the next three months. Everyone on the station, including our Maldivian auxilliaries, are expected to turn out. There will be no exceptions. When we leave Gan we must go with our heads held high. That will be all gentlemen."

As they all rose to go Mike motioned to the medical officer to remain behind. Dr Clem thought he was about to be castigated for his flippant answers at the meeting but he was wrong.

"Clem, your standard of dress is appalling. You'll have to tidy yourself up and try and look like an officer. You can't go on handover parade looking like a tramp."

Dr Clem exploded, "Bugger the parade. I'm a medical officer and exempt from that kind of bullshit."

Mike's hackles rose. "You are not exempt from this one Squadron Leader Garvey. As long as you are wearing the Queen's uniform you will parade with the rest of us. You will obey the rules as set out in Mr Williams' schedules and that's an order."

"Bugger Silly Billy and his rules," the red-faced MO retorted.

Mike relaxed and defused the confrontation with a smile, "You may wish to do that, Clem, but I don't recommend it!"

They both burst out laughing.

Vanessa's letters were always full of doom and gloom. Daddy was persistently sick, or poorly, but his mysterious and serious illness did not prevent him riding to hounds or struggling along to regimental dinners. And when it wasn't Daddy Vanessa was equally concerned about the well-being of Belvoir Hall's pack of hounds and the family's horses. She knew the hounds by name and could recite their peccadilloes. And then there were the horses and horsey gossip about fetlocks and stridor and, though each letter was signed 'From your ever-loving Vanessa', Mike felt her insincerity bouncing off the pages. Sonitha lurked in the background of his mind like a guardian angel. Her radiant beauty and smiling face was everywhere and the memory of her curvaceous body, covered by a form-clinging pink sari, always produced a surging feeling in his groins such as he had not experienced since his lecherous days at the LSE. He was dying to see her again. As station commander he would have to be at Gan to celebrate Christmas with his airmen. There were six days to go before Christmas Eve and time enough to get to Male and back. On the spur of the moment he decided to go that day and, for respectability and much to Dr Clems' displeasure, he invited Tim Cosbey to accompany him. The medical officer was now more than convinced that the studious, humourless, telecommunications officer had ousted him from his position as CO's favourite and confidant. 'Tit for tat' thought the irrascible doctor, 'two can play at that game.' He cancelled his appointment with the station barber and decided not to ask Reki to mend and darn his tattered uniforms.

In retrospect Mike's four day break on Baros was not a success. Timothy developed a keen interest in Sonitha. She came to meet the dhoni at the fishermans' pier and, as usual, she flashed a broad welcoming smile as Mike made introductions. Tim's eyes were firmly glued to her face during the hour long trip across to Baros. Sonitha flirted openly with him but her passionate glances were reserved for Mike and Tim was quick to notice the obvious bond between them. Sonitha came across to Baros every day and spent most of her time in the company of the two officers. She always left the resort an hour before sunset, in time for prayers, and reappeared mid-morning the following day. On the first day the trio snorkelled in the lagoon. Tim was a poor swimmer and uncomfortable when his face was fully submerged in salt water. He avoided going out of his depth in the lagoon and there was no question of enticing him out on the reef. When Sonitha left at the end of their first day together Mike escorted her to the jetty.

"I'm sorry I brought Tim with me, Soni. I didn't know he couldn't swim."

"Don't worry Michael. He's a very nice young man and I like him. The two of us will go out to the reef together tomorrow."

Mike took her hand and gave it a gentle squeeze. In full view of the resort village, the jetty was no place for a public exhibition of their love for each other. Mike let go of her hand and whispered, "Until tomorrow, Soni."

When Mike got back to his cabin Tim was shaving in the ablution cubicle. His back was lobster-red and sore but he was as happy as a sandboy, "What a superb looking woman. I've never seen such beauty close up before. And her English is perfect."

Mike went on the defensive and decided to underplay his hand. "Yes, Soni's an attractive young lady. She looked after Vanessa and myself when we were here last year. Did you know she's the agent for this resort and her father owns it? She's very bright and helpful."

"She's got a crush on you, Mike" Tim replied.

"Whatever gives you that idea? I'm old enough to be her father!"

"I've seen the way she looks at you Mike."

Mike smiled, "I can't help it if I'm so handsome the native wenches find me irresistible! I wouldn't mind being her sugar daddy!"

Sugar daddy or not, Tim could not help but notice the electrifying exchanges between Mike and Soni. On the second day, when they were out on the reef together, Tim was certain they were making intimate physical contact as they surfaced for air and frequent kisses were exchanged. And when they parted in the evening there were long, lingering looks between the two and surreptitous, non-accidental touching of hands. After four days in their company Tim was convinced they were lovers. He felt like a schoolboy on the touchline watching a game of football but not allowed to strip off and get on the playing field. His experience of the opposite sex was very limited but he felt he could make a go of it with the delectable Soni. The main obstacle in his way was Mike and Mike was his commanding officer and Vanessa's husband. As they would say in Germany: 'Soni ist strangsten verboten'. Perhaps at another time, and in another place, Soni and he could make a go of it.

Mike and Soni were approaching the jetty in a dhoni after their last dive on the reef. Mike held Soni's hands in his own. "I will come back and see you again Soni and next time I'll definitely be alone."

"Yes please Michael. When will that be?"

"It depends on the work at Gan. We'll be very busy in January. I'll try to make it in the second week in February and I'll come for a whole week."

"That will be fine Michael. I shall count the days till we meet again."

She sighed longingly and it took all their willpower not to fall into a lovers' embrace. The dhoni was rapidly approaching the jetty where Tim was waiting to greet them. Mike released Soni's hand and, when they tied up to the pier, there was a respectable distance between the two lovers in the dhoni.

Chapter Eight

Brezhnev's *dacha*
11th and 12th November, 1975

LEONID ILYICH BREZHNEV was well pleased with his weekend's work. He had gathered together President Kosygin, four veteran Politburo members, Vladimirovich Andropov of State Security and three senior commanders of the Soviet armed forces. Secrecy was assured. The meeting place was Brezhnev's twelve-bedroomed, lakeside *dacha* four kilometres south of Podalsk and sixty kilometres from Moscow. A thin blanket of premature wintry snow covered the countryside and his visitors were transported from Podalsk railway station to his *dacha* in a fleet of horse-drawn *troikas*. For two days the planning sessions had dominated their lives and now, on Sunday evening, Leonid Brezhnev was about to summarise the outcome of their deliberations and to present their recommendations to President Kosygin. Before they gathered in the reception lounge Brezhnev insisted the delegates must watch a 1972 American gangster movie, the Godfather, starring Al Pacino and Marlon Brando. Everyone knew that Brezhnev was a film addict and frequently sat through two or more movies into the early hours of the morning. President Alexei Nikolayovitch had made a feeble protest but was reluctantly persuaded to sit through the three hour showing and now, in his sumptuous lounge and with his guests clutching tumblers of vodka, Brezhnev proposed a toast to the USSR promptly followed by another to President Alexei Nikolayovitch Kosygin. He then led the group into a palatial dining room with two long tables groaning under the weight of a sumptuous banquet complete with a selection of expensive wines and spirits from the decadent West.

Standing five foot seven in his stockinged feet the sixty-eight year old, round-faced, beetle-browed chairman of the Soviet Politburo glanced at his seated comrades as a faint flicker of a smile crossed his Slavic countenance. He coughed to clear his throat and addressed the committee in a gravelley baritone.

"Comrade President and comrades. We have had a successful weekend and I thank you for your constructive cooperation. As a result Operation Gan has emerged and will further embarrass the Western Block. Let me reconstruct the ideological basis of our agreement on strategic arms limitation with American President Nixon. In 1968, when I became chairman of the Politburo, negotiations were started which led to signing a SALT 1 treaty in Moscow in May 1972. We then began our second round of SALT negotiations which are still ongoing. As we all know President Nixon got into trouble with the Watergate affair but was again re-elected to the White House by the stupid Americans in November 1972. The Watergate trial opened in Washington in January 1973 and by April, Nixon's chief advisers had resigned en bloc. The press were calling him Tricky Dicky and the president's credibility was now in question. But he held on to office for a further twelve months finally, on threat of impeachment, resigning last July. In his second term of office America's foreign policy suffered and we have made little progress with SALT 2. Nixon was easy to do business with but his successor, Gerald Ford, is completely different. He has no insight into the problems of international politics and some Americans say he is so dumb and stupid he can't chew gum and hit a golf ball at the same time! We've given Ford every chance to come and meet us but so far he's keeping his distance. Britain also has difficulties with its leader. Prime Minister Heath was stubborn and unbending and a hard man in negotiation. He took Britain into the European Economic Market in 1973 but this year Harold Wilson and his Labour Party were returned to power. All our sources suggest Wilson is a sick man. He ducks and dodges and evades important decisions. The two major western powers are, at the present time, in disarray and poorly led and this is an opportune moment to drive a wedge between America and Britain and consequently to break up NATO. Which brings me to the point of the film. We all saw that in reality America is governed by the Mafia. I admire their methods. In a dispute they get at the bosses by bumping off junior members of the family. Comrades, we must do the same. The western powers' Achilles heel is oil. America has its own oil wells but is not self-sufficient and Britain is getting some oil from the North Sea but is still seventy per cent dependent on the Gulf States and, in particular, Kuwait. Our plan envisages threatening Britain's major oil depots with our strategic missiles and, at the same time, interfering with their supply lines from the Gulf. The plan to achieve this objective will be outlined by Comrade General Nikolayovitch Koniev."

Brezhnev sat down heavily in his chair. President Kosygin, seated on his right and apparently asleep, nodded his head in approval. He looked across at a heavily-built general with an array of campaign ribbons and glittering medals, "Comrade Leonid Ilyich has outlined the political advantages of our proposed action. Tell me of your strategic plans Comrade General."

General Koniev, Commander of Soviet Strategic Arms, took a deep breath, "Five targets have been selected on mainland Britain which are well within reach of our new long range SS20 missiles based in Poland and the Ukraine. They are oil refineries and depots at Gravesend, the Humber, the Solent, Merseyside and Milford Haven in the south west. These refineries have been accurately targeted and, to advertise our intention to attack, I am assured by Comrade Yuri Vladimirovich that the exact location of at least sixteen of our SS-20 bases are known to the West. Increased activity in and around our missile bases will create panic in NATO and divert attention away from our main thrust which has been proposed by Comrade Admiral Sergei Gorshkov. A T-class submarine will carry a neutron bomb from Vladivostok to Gan, a British air base in the Maldives. Comrade Yuri Vladimirovich assures me that a long range bomber can safely drop in at Gan to refuel and pick up the bomb and the senior commander on the base is known to be on our payroll The ultimate target will either be the Kuwait oilfields and refineries or Port Suez at the southern end of the Suez Canal. On balance we have selected Port Suez which will put the canal out of action and, after the attack, the strike bomber will proceed to Libya where Colonel Moammar al-Gadhafi will cooperate with any action on our part so long as it disrupts the Western Alliance."

President Alexei Nikolayovitch was the first to respond and his reaction was unexpectedly vitriolic.

"An excellent plan Comrade General. We need an attack on a target remote from Europe which will shock the world and remind them the great USSR is still a potent force in global politics. And we would only be using limited nuclear power against a pro-British Arab state with the threat of more to follow from our land-based SS20s. I am informed that our recently tested neutron bomb has limited capabilities."

A neutron is an electrically inactive elementary particle of the baryon family having the same molecular mass as a proton. It is stable when bound within an atomic nucleus and, when released as a free particle, has a lifetime of only 15 to 16 minutes. The bomb developed in the USA produces millions of high-energy neutrons with limited blast and long term radioactivity. The Russian version of the neutron bomb has the same radioactive potential but an enhanced blasting capability which produced absolute ground-level destruction for a six mile radius around the point of explosion. This was the nuclear weapon which President Kosygin wanted used in the Suez strike. General Koniev's face reddened and he looked askance at Admiral Gorshkov whose expression registered unease.

"But, Comrade President, we will not be arming the neutron bomb or using active nuclear warheads."

"On the contrary, Comrade General, there is no advantage in carrying an uncharged nuclear bomb half way around the world. I order you to ensure the bomb can be used offensively if needs be. Do you not agree Leonid Ilyich?"

Brezhnev had never seen his normally docile President in such an agitated state. Perhaps his life-long comrade was getting a little senile and protective of his presidential authority. But he was only three years older than himself. Over the past two years Kosygin had been leaning more and more heavily on Brezhnev and was President in name only. The real power behind the Politburo and the Kremlin was Leonid Ilyich Brezhnev. For the past few years he had longed to shake up and divide the western powers and this was a golden opportunity, too good to miss. He placed his hand gently on the President's forearm, "Absolutely Alexei Nikolayovitch. I am in full agreement.

Our instruction to Comrade General Koniev and Comrade Admiral Sergei Gorshkov is to prepare detailed operational plans for urgent implementation. Comrade Yuri Vladimirovich will keep us informed of the Western Powers' reaction during the build up to the attack. The military are to await authorization from President Kosygin and myself before an attack is launched. Finally, I must warn everyone present, the outcome of our work this weekend must remain an absolute secret."

The meeting broke up in a flurry of congratulatory handshakes and bear hugs, and the delegates departed in a fleet of government limousines leaving Leonid Brezhnev comfortably seated in front of a blazing log fire. Eschewing western culture he partook liberally from a bottle of twelve year old Black Label whisky. In a mellow mood he retired to the library and sat alone watching another replay of the Godfather. The plot continued to entertain and, as he quietly fell asleep, he silently thanked the Hollywood film makers for showing him the way to deal with the decadent, capitalistic Western Powers.

Chapter Nine

Ihuru Vladivostok London

"KEEP LOOKING STRAIGHT AHEAD MICHAEL. I'm unfamiliar with these waters and there are hidden reefs about. We must not founder before we reach Ihuru!"

Mike stood at the prow of the overladen dhoni, scanning the sea ahead, looking for submerged coral projections in the alternating patches of deep blue and light green water. The dhoni was about a mile off the uninhabited island of Vabbinfarhoo and about four miles north of Baros. There were still some three miles of treacherous, reef-laden sea to negotiate before they reached Ihuru. The temptation to look over his shoulder at the gorgeous helmswoman was overwhelming. He marvelled at Soni's versatility. At home in the water, both on the surface and in the depths of a reef, she now proved herself an expert helmswoman responding instinctively to his hand signals as they zig-zagged their way towards Ihurus' jetty. He felt his chest tighten in anticipation and managed a quick glance over his shoulder. Soni was hunched over the tiller, her pink headscarf fluttering in the breeze and her dusky face wreathed in a heart-warming smile. He winked slyly and gave her a 'thumbs up' sign. "Chocks away my darling. Angels at two o'clock."

The RAF wartime jargon meant nothing to Soni but she responded with a throaty chuckle and a delicate wave of her right hand.

Since returning to Gan for the Christmas celebrations Mike had Soni on his mind throughout his waking hours and in his dreams. Gone were the restrictions of age difference and a near-sterile marriage to Vanessa and the chivalrous morals of British society. He was completely and hopelessly in love. He foresaw the pitfalls ahead and at the end of the day he might come to earth with a bang. The business with the Russians was still a reality but, with each passing day, the chances of hearing from them receded. The month of January on Gan had been hectic and most of the heavy equipment had been loaded on cargo ships and transported to the UK. Tim Cosbey and his team had dismantled the powerful long-range transmitter and radar equipment at Hithadhoo and one seaplane had been taken away on an RFA supply ship. Tim was all for shutting down Hithadhoo completely but Mike, for his own selfish reasons, insisted on keeping the second seaplane at its mooring until final evacuation. This meant a corporal and three airmen were permanently on guard duty at the seaplane station, a cushy number which conferred immunity from Silly Billy's drill parades. At the end of January 1976 Mike decided he needed another break. Logically there was no reason for him to be away from Gan but the urge to see Soni again was overwhelming. Pleading an unexpected request to meet Maldivian officials to discuss arrangements for the handover ceremony he took off alone from Hithadhoo and flew north on the morning of 10th February, 1976.

Soni was at the quayside in Male to meet him. Within an hour she had closed her office, commandeered a dhoni and packed the craft with provisions, including two live chickens, a barrel of fresh water and a two-gallon can of kerosene. Offers from by-standing fishermen to take them across to Baros were turned down and Sonitha took the helm, ordering Mike to stand lookout at the ornate, curved bowsprit. They headed out to sea from the inner harbour and as soon as they were out of earshot, Soni explained, "We are not going to Baros this time and I will take you to Ihuru. My father is developing three resorts. Baros, you know and Vabbinfarhoo is uninhabited. We have started building on Ihuru but money is short. There are two caretaker families on the island and, at present, only four cabins are habitable and we shall have a cabin each. Ihuru is even more beautiful than Baros and I'm sure you will like the place."

"That sound's fine," Mike replied matter-of-factly, but inwardly he was seething with excitement at the thought of spending four or five carefree days on a semi-deserted tropical island with the most beautiful woman in the world. Not for a moment did he consider the risks he was taking. If London found out about his escapade he would be cashiered and dismissed from the service in disgrace, losing his pension rights. This thought only fleetingly crossed his mind. Wing Commander Mike Townsend was in love and love is blind. On Ihuru he entered into a liaison with Sonitha with his eyes wide open.

The reception committee on the newly-constructed jetty at Ihuru comprised two shabbily-dressed families: five males, three women and five children ranging in age from twelve years to a six month old, suckling baby. The inhabitants lived in three wooden shanties near the pier amidst a huge timber stockpile brought across from Male for cabin construction. A pathway alongside the lagoon had only recently been cleared and Mike's and Sonitha's adjacent cabins were at the very edge of the lagoon's sandy beach and some eighty yards from the jetty. When Mike called on Soni he found her at prayer, kneeling on a raffia mat on the sandy soil outside her cabin. Within a minute she sprang to her feet, rolled up her prayer mat, and dashed through the foliage screen into the lagoon where, fully clothed, she swam and frolicked in the surf. Whatever the circumstances Sonitha supplicated herself in prayer four times a day but, once her communion with Allah was over, her outgoing westernised personality reasserted itself and she behaved like any other emancipated woman.

At the end of their first day, before the light faded, Mike and Soni took a stroll around their small island paradise. Parts of the circular path were impassable and they detoured along the beach. Within ten minutes they were at the northernmost point on Ihuru where the lagoon was at its narrowest and the coral reef only some thirty yards away from the steeply-shelving, sandy beach. Driven by prevailing winds, a fairly strong current ran boldly through the enclosed channel. At that point Mike followed an overgrown pathway leading from the beach through the foliage screen and directly towards the centre of the forested island. He took hold of Sonitha's hand. "Let's have a look, Soni."

For once Sonitha was not smiling. She was perplexed and looked uncertain. In common with most Maldivians she was highly superstitious and believed in *dhevi*, the presence of a visible or sometimes invisible being, sometimes harmful and sometimes helpful and capable of moving unhindered across land and sea. She also believed in *fanditha*, a magic, pseudo-religious science intermingled with fertility rites and divination.

"No. You go Mike. There may be snakes in there."

Mike was insistent and dragged Sonitha behind him, pushing his way boldly through the thick undergrowth. Twenty yards from the beach they came across a stone-built structure almost totally encased in tendrils and concealed by a thick curtain of flowering hibiscus.

"What's this Soni?" Mike asked.

"I don't know. It's probably a Chinese temple. They were on these islands until the twelfth century. I don't like it Mike and I feel *fanditha* and evil spirits all around us. Let's go back to the beach."

She withdrew her hand from Mike's and ran back to the edge of the lagoon. Mike pressed forwards through the screen of clinging undergrowth into the dark interior of the temple and struck a match. The chamber had a twelve foot, high-domed roof lined by clusters of interlocking cobwebs and was just large enough to accommodate two dozen persons standing. On a raised plinth against the northeast wall was a pitted, stone figure of Buddha with three-quarters of its head missing and part of its torso lying in a pile of stone chippings on the raised altar. In one corner Mike was conscious of something moving and hissing. Suddenly he was in darkness again as his match flickered and went out. He stood there in awe consciously feeling the presence of an unseen being. Could it be *Dhevi* visiting the temple to vent its wrath on the Chinese heathens who had desecrated Ihuru all those years ago? Suddenly he felt cold and uncomfortable and a slight shiver ran down his spine. He quickly retraced his steps to join Sonitha on the beach.

By the time they got back to the jetty the sun had set and the villagers were gathered around a wood-burning fire with the evening's meal boiling merrily in a cauldron. The fishy smell from the cooking-pot confirmed that the dish of the day was *garudhiya*, a traditional tuna-fish stew served with chunks of *roshi* bread followed by a bowl of *hannakurinas,* a dry fish curry mixed with coconut-flavoured rice. Mike and Soni sat amongst the villagers and witnessed a bizarre ceremony. One of Sonitha's chickens was produced and unceremoniously beheaded by the headman. The bird was then released and staggered around for about ten seconds, spurts of blood gushing with diminishing force from its severed neck, until it fell to the ground near the open fire.

Clutching a second chicken in his hands the headman approached a young girl and, after decapitating the bird, he directed bright-red splurges of blood on to her thighs. The villagers clapped and hummed in unison. The dead birds were plucked and taken away and became the main meal for the following two days – a spicy chicken curry served with coconut-flavoured rice. Mike looked on in bewilderment.

"What on earth was all that about Soni?"

"The girl is nearly eleven years old and has not yet seen blood. The headman is using *fanditha* to call forth her blood. You see, Michael, if there is no blood coming from her body with each moon she cannot have children and a girl who is infertile will be of little use to the village. For one thing her dowry will be negligible. Maldivian men refuse to marry women who can't bear children."

"But Soni, she's only a girl, barely eleven years of age and there's plenty of time for her yet."

"I know, Michael. Most of our girls see blood at nine years of age and some are married by the time they're thirteen. Let's hope *fanditha* works for her."

And then, blushing, she added, "I saw blood when I was ten."

Mike fell silent. The hint was obvious. Soni was fertile and proud of the fact that she could bear children, his children, if the opportunity arose.

They retired early to their separate cabins on their first night on Ihuru. Mike slept fitfully and was up at the crack of dawn. He tossed and turned all night and, when awake, had vivid visions of the beautiful, nubile body that lay in the next cabin barely twenty paces away from his bed. He got up twice with the intention of crossing the threshold and throwing himself on to the bed to lay beside Sonitha. But on both occasions he lost his nerve and crept back under his mosquito net. And, unbeknown to Mike, Sonitha was also suffering the same pangs, longing for the handsome man with his infectious smile to take her in his arms. They breakfasted on a mild vegetable curry and coconut flavoured *roshi*. Both were bleary-eyed.

"How did you sleep Soni?"

"Very well, thank you, Michael," she lied.

Mike pursued the conversation. "It was very hot in my cabin. I had to open the door to let in a breeze off the lagoon."

Sonitha became flirtatious and smiled mischievously. "If I had known your door was open I would have paid you a call. I know how to keep someone cool."

"Now, now Soni, you're treading on dangerous ground. I sleep in the nude."

"It's funny you should mention that, Michael, so do I," and she lowered her head and blushed.

Mike and Sonitha slept together in Mike's cabin on the second night of their stay at Ihuru. They had spent most of the day on, in, or under the water and their kissing and cuddling intensified as the day wore on. After a chicken curry supper they sat for an hour after sunset listening to the sounds of the night: the throaty chirp of fruit bats feeding on wild berries and the frantic threshing of silver-bellied herring parr as they jumped clear of the water to avoid charges from the ever-vigilant, predatory reef shark. After a goodnight kiss at around nine o'clock, they retired to their respective cabins. Mike was not sure of the time, it was around eleven o'clock, when he woke abruptly from a deep sleep and had a sudden compulsion to move out to the balcony where he felt certain Sonitha would be waiting for him. And when he spoke to Sonitha on the following day she also confessed that her *dhevi* had guided her on to her own balcony in the certain knowledge Mike would be there. Their door latches clicked simultaneously. Mike was stark naked and Sonitha only wore a flimsy, silk kaftan. Their silhouettes were ghostly in the waning moonlight.

"Can I come across to your cabin Michael? I want to lay with you."

"Yes please, Soni darling."

Within seconds Sonitha was nestling her head against his bare chest and, locked in a passionate kiss, she guided Mike gently backwards into his cabin and on to the bed. She straddled Mike's pelvis and bent forward to kiss him on his lips. Her black tresses fell about his face which became engulfed in a cascade of delicately-perfumed, jasmine-scented hair. Mike inhaled deeply. This was paradise, a sensation he had never experienced even in his wilder, promiscuous days at the LSE. And then things began to happen in his nether regions over which he had little control. Sonitha massaged and teased his manhood and, when the time was right, she guided him inside her. He made love to Soni as he had never done before. She knew all the tricks of the trade and, at one stage, Mike wondered if she was a Kamasutra disciple. Finally, completely sated, they fell asleep in each others' arms. An hour or so before daybreak, at around four o'clock, Sonitha returned to her own cabin. At breakfast Soni was her normal cheerful self and made no reference to their lovemaking of the previous night and Mike wondered if it had all been a dream. The reality came to him quite quickly and their next four days on Ihuru were exact replicas of their second day on the island: sun-kissed hours on the beach and in the lagoon and torrid all-night lovemaking sessions in Mike's cabin save that, on the fourth night, curried chicken was not on the menu and they had do make do with boiled rice and a fish stew.

The time to leave came all too quickly and the villagers gathered at the jetty to see them off. The three women, in multi-coloured saris and with a hibiscus flower in their hair, stood in a group near the timber depot. The children ran around smiling, waving and self-consciously shouting 'goodbye' in English. The five men lined up at the pierhead, palms pressed together and heads bowed, murmuring their well-wishes in Maldivese. On the two hour journey back to Male Mike tried to make love to Soni. Strictly obeying the unwritten laws of her Muslim faith, that no male should cast an eye on a naked female body, she coyly refused to remove her *salwar*. 'What a contrary lover!' Mike thought. For four nights running she had laid down with him in darkness and performed sexual acts of ecstatic pleasure for himself and unbelievable complexity for her and yet, here out at sea and in complete isolation, she refused to remove her silk pantaloons to allow him access to the promised land. He quickly came to realise that Sunni Muslim women are forbidden to remove their clothing and expose their flesh in public in broad daylight.

About half a mile off Male's inner harbour they embraced and re-iterated their love vows.

"When my job on Gan is finished next month I will return to England and leave the Service. I will put my affairs in order at home and return here to be with you my darling."

"If you do, Michael, you will have to become a Sunni Muslim."

"I'll become a Buddhist, or anything you like, so long as I can be with you Soni."

She beamed one of her most radiant smiles. "I like it when you call me 'darling'. I promise I will wait for you."

"I love you Soni."

Back on Gan an unpleasant surprise awaited Mike. A personal air-mail letter from Tony Widgeon lay on his desk.

From Group Captain Anthony Widgeon DSO DFC

MoD (Air)   *Suite 48*
WHITEHALL   *The Athenaeum*
LONDON W.1   *Piccadilly*
                                                      LONDON W1

12th February 1976

My dear Mike,

I write to you about Van. I'm afraid she's cracking up and the old brigadier is driving her up the wall. We all do our best to cheer her up – cocktail parties and dinners, etc. The big concern is that the old rascal has been suspended from the Hunt for some misdemeanour or other. He apparently made his whipper-in cut off a fox's brush while the poor thing was still alive. He was spotted by a group of anti-bloodsports nutheads who are taking the old reprobate to court. The case comes up at Grantham Crown Court next week and, in the meantime, Vanessa and the old boy have been banned from riding to hounds. This, naturally, has upset Van. She knows you will be home at the end of March and for her sake it won't be a moment too soon. She needs you here. On 15th March I am joining Bobby Davidson and his wife at George V Hotel in Paris to celebrate their 25th wedding anniversary. I'm asking you in good time if you wish me to invite Vanessa along with me. A weekend away from Belvoir Hall will do her the world of good. I know she enjoyed her time in Paris when you were attached to Commandement du Nord and she could catch up with local gossip. I won't ask, however, if you don't think it's a good idea. So please check your diary and reply to the Athenaeum by return. I repeat, the date is March 15th. If we don't make contact in the meantime good luck with the handover on 29th March.

Yours aye, Tony

P.S. Be sure and let me know re 15th March.

132

So this was it. He was being ordered to fulfil his contract with his Russian masters on the Ides of March and Tony Widgeon was up to his neck in the filthy business. Tony had no interest whatsoever in Vanessa's well-being. In fact, since the wedding fiasco, they had hardly spoken more than one word to each other. Tony was using Vanessa as a pawn in the deadly game. Oblique references in the letter to comforting her were introduced to force Mike into acting to protect her. His own interest in his wife had declined rapidly since Sonitha came on the scene and his plans were to ditch Vanessa as soon as he was discharged from the Royal Air Force. Vanessa would receive his service pension and, with his lump sum gratuity, he intended returning to Male to his new love. But he was an officer in Her Majesty's armed forces and a gentleman and could not stand aside and see Vanessa, or her parents, suffer because of his misdemeanours. That would be a caddish trick and he was definitely not a cad. Prompted by three references to March 15th in Tony Widgeon's letter Mike penned a reply advising that Vanessa, in the present state of her mind and in the best interests of her health, should not under any circumstances go to Paris. He added that arrangements for handover were well in hand and on March 15th he would have a drink in the mess to celebrate Bobby Davidson's wedding anniversary. Once the letter was dispatched he sat down and looked up his calendar. There were twenty-six days to go before he might be called into action but as 15th March approached so his panic grew. Preparing for every eventuality, and in case he might have to make a quick getaway, he secretly stocked the seaplane at Hithadhoo with provisions and filled her tanks, and two reserve canisters, with gasoline. Then it was a question of counting the days as they went inexorably by and waiting for the wretched Russian plane to arrive. Time waits for no one. The Ides of March, the 15th day of the month in the Roman calendar, soon arrived.

MoD, London, January 1976

The first indication at MoD of mischief afoot came in January from aerial photographs supplied by long-range reconnaissance over Russian missile sites in Poland. There was evidence of heavy vehicular activity around the sites and, on two separate occasions, long range missiles were identified on carriers. Alarmingly the missiles had nuclear warheads attached. Despite the inclement weather the volume of traffic to the launching pads escalated throughout January and on 4th February Lampey and Widgey were summoned to a Defence Committee meeting at No 10 Downing Street presided over by the Prime Minister. Tony Widgeon recounted a similar alarm two years previously but the only difference this time was the Russians had developed a new long range weapon, carrying a heavier payload, and their SS20 missiles were fitted with activated warheads. When asked directly to summarize the significance of these actions by the Russians Air Commodore Lampton replied without conviction, "We believe this is merely a training exercise. We shall monitor Russian activity at the missile sites daily and increase the number of surveillance flights."

Prime Minister Wilson removed an unlit pipe from his mouth and turned his expressionless, flat-faced gaze towards the RAF duo. "Thank you air commodore. It sounds as if Ivan is sabre-rattling again. Keep me informed of further developments."

Vladivostok, February 1976
Naval intelligence in London became aware of some untoward activity at the Russian Pacific Fleet base at Vladivostok during the second week of February but saw no connection with the developing situation on the ground in Poland and the Ukraine. A flotilla of four T-class long-range nuclear submarines were known to operate out of Vladivostok. On 10th February 1976 two were in port and two were being tracked and under surveillance in Antarctic waters two hundred miles south of Cape Town. A week later, on 17th February, aerial photography revealed that a third submarine had slipped anchor and seemed to have disappeared into thin air. None of the routine nightly radio transmissions from the submarine had been picked up by surface vessels and SOSUS satellite detectors were drawing a blank.

February–March 1976
Marine Captain Uri Petrovski's T-class UK27 navigated a devious route northwards from Vladivostok across the partially-frozen Okhotsk sea

and then, after a broad lateral sweep southwards along the whole length of the central Pacific ocean, entered the Indian Ocean by passing through the Tasman straits between Australia and New Zealand. Once in the Indian Ocean UK27 proceeded northwards towards its goal, the Maldive islands, 450 miles southwest of the tip of the Indian subcontinent. Under instruction from Admiral Gorshkov UK27 had maintained strict radio silence throughout its twenty day voyage. By 14th March the nuclear submarine was in the South Indian Ocean 3 miles off Gan at Hithadhoo and had every reason to maintain radio silence. It carried a dangerous and valuable cargo. A 1,400lb limited-capacity neutron bomb was stashed in a lead-lined cabinet in its hold. In addition to its regular crew the submarine carried a section of twelve marine explosive experts and a nuclear physicist, one Alexei Uri Gagarin, present on board to supervise assembly and delivery of the submarine's lethal weapon.

No 10 Downing Street, 17th February 1976
Prime Minister Harold Wilson was on the red scrambler phone to the White House in Washington.

"Good evening Mr President. What do you make of the increase in missile base activity in Poland and the Ukraine? Our surveillance planes report the missiles have attached warheads."

There was a long, pregnant pause at the other end of the hotline. Harold Wilson could sense the president's brain clicking into gear.

"Yeah, Mr Prime Minister. Our own U2's are reporting the same thing and the armed missiles they have identified are pointing your way. My defence chiefs are of the opinion the problem is in your ball pen."

There was an even longer pause while both men mulled over the situation. There had never been a comfortable rapport between Harold Wilson and President Gerald Ford and they never became over-familiar during their transatlantic telephone conversations.

"Have you informed our NATO commanders?" the President asked, knowing full well the answer would be in the affirmative.

"Yes. They have been briefed by MoD and are fully aware of the developing crisis."

"This is an European matter and you'll have to work out a solution with NATO at your end. My Government are not prepared to get involved until we know the full extent of the crisis. What is your Defence Department's estimation of the current situation?"

Harold Wilson cringed at the thought that his American counterpart was again sitting on the fence and passing the buck. Had President Ford no sense of history? One of his illustrious predecessors, Harry S Truman, engineered the NATO alliance and coined a famous quote in 1945 – 'the buck stops here'. Wilson hoicked to clear his throat and prodded his upper lip with the mouthpiece of his unlit pipe.

"My advisers conclude that Brezhnev and Kosygin are sabre-rattling again. We'll monitor the situation daily and step up aerial surveillance. I'll keep you posted Mr President."

"Yeah, you do that Mr Prime Minister. Good afternoon to you."

There was an audible click as President Ford replaced the receiver. The click was also clearly heard at Andropov's telecommunication centre in Kiev. For three years the KGB had the capacity to unscramble transatlantic telephone conversations between No 10 Downing Street and the White House in Washington.

Chapter Ten

Operation Gan

15th-17th March 1976

THE IDES OF MARCH, the 15th, Moscow's designated day for action, was a long period of apprehension and foreboding for Mike Townsend. As the day wore on hopes that his Russian masters had forgotten him soared and he was determined not to arouse suspicion by varying his daily routine. Apart from being slightly more edgy than usual he showed little evidence of his internal turmoil. By the time he joined Tim Cosbey in the mess for an early sundowner session there was only an hour and half of daylight left and, after sunset, no self-respecting stranger would attempt to land a large plane on Gan. He had invited WO Williams to join him for a drink and clutching their Maxwell specials they were in earnest discussion about the finer points of military ceremonial when a mess steward interrupted their conversation. "There's a message for Squadron Leader Cosbey. He's wanted in control urgently."

Tim proferred his apologies and left. Mike froze and stiffened. This was it! It couldn't be anything else! His mind elsewhere, he kept chatting vacantly to WO Williams and it came as a relief when the steward reappeared and announced that Squadron Leader Cosbey needed Mike in the control tower.

"We've got a problem on our hands sir. There's a foreign airliner, AN 77, coming through on emergency, top priority, asking permission to land. Their English is atrocious and from what I gather they're short on fuel. She's about 300 miles north of us and about 50 minutes flying time away. I think she's Russian. How shall I reply?"

Tim took off his earphones. Mike looked duly concerned but he already knew his answer. "Is it a Mayday call Timothy?"

"Yes sir," Tim replied, "shall we give her the go-ahead to come in before it gets dark?"

Mike shrugged his shoulders. "We have no choice. Call them in."

Tim returned to his transmitter and reissued the Gan code sign. After three attempts, amidst a shower of ethereal crackling, a foreign-sounding voice, struggling valiantly with his English, came over the air requesting permission to land. The plane's estimated ETA at Gan would be 1755 hours. Mike summed up the situation. "The poor chap's in a panic and they're in real trouble. Did you know I studied Russian at LSE? I'm a bit rusty but I think I could have a stab at talking to them when they drop in."

"Had I better inform London we're expecting Russians?" Tim queried.

"No Tim," Mike responded, "let's wait until they touch down and we find out why they're in trouble."

"I've already been through to inform MoD we have a foreign plane in trouble on our patch. I didn't know at the time it was a Russian crate."

"What!" Mike exploded, "why in God's name did you do that?"

"It's Queen's Regs sir," Tim replied hurt and Mike's anger rapidly abated. The signals officer was quite correct. Regulations were regulations and there was nothing he could do to change matters.

In the rapidly waning light Mike and Tim watched the cumbersome Russian plane make a perfect landing at 1805 hours and come to a stop at the eastern end of the runway.

"I'm going across to sort out their problem. Hold your call to London until we know what's going on. I'll be back in a jiffy."

In the fading light Tim Cosbey watched from the cupola as Mike and WO Williams, with two armed airmen, approached the stationary plane whose silhouette was rapidly disappearing and blending with the encroaching darkness. By the time Mike's station waggon came to a halt two uniformed figures were just visible standing in the plane's fore-hatchway. One of them hailed Mike in broken English, "I wish to speak to your station commander."

"I am Wing Commander Townsend, officer commanding Gan," Mike replied.

"Come aboard please. My Captain wishes to speak to you."

Mike walked across to WO William's jeep. "I'm going aboard, Mr Williams, to find out what's up."

"Do you think that's wise sir? These blokes is in uniform and on sovereign territory. According to Queens Regulations we should h'arrest them and h'impound their plane."

"I understand all that Mr Williams. I'm going to see how we can help them on their way."

An airforce captain in a smart beige uniform welcomed Mike aboard. All passenger seats in the capacious forecabin had been removed and the space was taken up by a powerful transmitter, an engineers' station and rows of charts. The cabin stank of stale tobacco and unwashed bodies and was separated from the mid-section of the plane by a heavy, red damask curtain. There were five uniformed officers in the cabin. Embarrassed by his lack of English the captain, a fresh-faced, young-looking man with short-cropped blond hair and piercing blue eyes, flicked his fingers at a dark, swarthy hulk of a man with a pronounced six-o'clock shadow and deep-set, malevolent, black eyes. "Gorky!"

Dressed in a baggy, ill-fitting, light-blue uniform the man-mountain stepped forward. "You are Townsend?"

"Yes," Mike replied.

"Your instructions are to disarm all your officers and men and collect them into one building. Tomorrow you will arrange for our plane to be refuelled. Together with those men on the tarmac you will be kept on board as hostages and anyone interfering with our operation, or attempting to escape, will be shot on the spot. You will obey Captain Voroshov's and my orders at all times. Is that clear?"

Mike was crestfallen. Mowcows' original instruction had been to facilitate transit of a plane and now he was being ordered to hijack his own airfield. He looked around the cabin at the sullen Russian faces. There was no means of escape or turning back.

"Yes. It's quite clear comrade Gorky."

The unshaven giant smiled smugly when Mike used the appellation 'comrade'. "That's good, comrade, very good," and with an exaggerated gesture he placed his hand on a holster hanging loosely from a leather belt stretched around his corpulent abdomen. Mike descended from the plane and ordered WO Williams and the two airmen to leave their guns in the jeep and come aboard. As soon as they did so armed soldiers appeared from the rear cabin and ushered them through the red damask curtain to the back of the plane which was occupied by about twenty uniformed soldiers. WO Williams and his two companions were strapped into seats at the rear of the plane. As he passed his commanding officer in the forecabin Silly Billy failed to make direct eye contact with Mike who stood next to a large, scruffily-dressed goliath and averted his eyes, seemingly concentrating his attention on the transmitting panel.

Built in 1971 in Oleg Antonov's factory in Kiev, the four-engined turboprop AN 12 red 6 was adapted for long-range military surveillance. Its square fuselage tapered upwards towards the tail to form a cargo door. The plane's rear turret housed two 23mm NR cannon for defence and the navigator was located in a glass-framed cupola in the nose of the plane. The Antonov 12 was capable of carrying a ten-ton payload and had a range of nearly 3,000 miles at a cruising speed of 380 mph. The Antonov on the runway at Gan had been further modified to carry up to thirty military personnel and their equipment and was fitted with a bomb-bay and two reserve fuel tanks midships. Two four-wheel drive, ten-man troop carriers were stowed in the hold underneath the plane's main cabin. An 12 red 6 had taken off from Baku on the Caspian Sea and, heading south eastwards across northern Iran, it veered south to fly over Afghanistan and western Pakistan to reach the Arabian Sea. The rest of the eight hour, 2,800 mile, flight was along India's western seaboard towards the Maldives. The plane was manned by a flight captain and eight aircrew. There was one political officer, Comrade Gorky, on the flight deck and the rear cabin was occupied by a twenty strong spetcnaz section, one lieutenant and nineteen other ranks.

The next stage of the operation was conducted with efficiency and military precision and executed in near-total darkness. The plane's rear cargo door was lowered and the troop carriers driven on to the runway. Mike, Gorky and the spetcnaz lieutenant commandeered two three-tonners and an extra station waggon from the motor pool and made their way to the causeway where Mike advanced alone and ordered the guard commander and three airmen to discard their firearms and board the three-tonner. The disarmed British guards were replaced by armed spetcnaz. The convoy then travelled around the perimeter fence picking up airmen from two guard platforms. The next port of call was the control tower where the duty airmen were replaced by Russian telegraphists and two spetcnaz were left on guard outside the building. Systematically the airmen's quarters and the sergeants and officers messes were emptied and, with one exception, all RAF personnel and Maldavian employees were packed into the main hall of the NAAFI and placed under guard. By 8.00 pm on the Ides of March, Gan station was securely in Russian hands.

Five officers including Dr Clem, sixty-four other ranks and fourteen Maldivian employees were packed into the NAAFI hall, each with his own story to tell. Unaware of the serious significance of the sudden invasion of his NAAFI, Reki was overjoyed with the increase in his clientele. Never before had the entire complement of Gan station been in his establishment at one and the same time. But for some reason, his customers were not hungry or thirsty. They sat around sullenly discussing events of the past couple of hours and wondering what it was all about. Squadron Leader Garvey voiced his opinion, "Unless I'm mistaken the bastards are Russkies. They've taken over our airfield, God only knows why! and they've got our commanding officer and Warrant Officer Williams hostage on the plane. We must try and find out what's going on. But no heroics. We are dealing with armed professionals and they probably mean business."

He paused and looked around the room. "By the way, has anyone seen Squadron Leader Cosbey?"

A corporal telegraphist spoke up, "He left control about an hour and a half ago and said he was coming across here."

"Well," replied the doctor, "he didn't make it. I wonder where he can be?"

The same thought was worrying Mike Townsend. In the rush and turmoil of the take-over operation he could not remember seeing Timothy Cosbey. He hoped he was safe and sound and, in any event, he had more serious matters to worry about than the wherabouts of his signal's officer.

At around 11.15 pm Mike Townsend and Gorky, flanked by two armed spetcnaz guards, turned up in the NAAFI. The airmen cheered when they saw their commanding officer. Mike raised his hand for silence while Gorky stood menacingly at his side and the guards, submachine guns at the ready, placed themselves on a raised dais behind them. Mike addressed the audience, "Officers and airmen of Gan. I have to inform you that a foreign agency has taken over our station for a few hours. In that time you will remain confined and under guard here in the NAAFI. Mr Gorky assures me that any attempt on your part to leave these premises will be resisted and you will run the risk of being shot. You are to obey his orders to the letter. Warrant Officer Williams and I are held hostage on their plane and if you attempt anything we shall suffer. I will be across again in the morning. In the meantime settle down for the night and use the NAAFI facilities. Good luck to you all."

The listeners were stupefied. Someone in the crowd exclaimed in a loud whisper, "That big bastard looks like a gorilla."

Gorky took out his pistol and roared "Silence! Silence!" and let off one round into the ceiling as a warning he meant business and understood English which immediately silenced the airmen. Outside the NAAFI Mike spoke to Rekitutha, "Reki, there are over twenty hungry men on the plane. Bring across two urns of tea and tuna sandwiches. A jeep and a driver will wait for you."

Half an hour later Reki carried platters of tuna sandwiches and two tea urns into the foredeck cabin. While he moved about dispensing mugs of tea he kept his eyes open. Commanding Officer Townsend and five foreign officers were sitting, or reclining, on canvas seats amidst a plethora of machinery and instrument panels. Reki carried the urns into the empty middle compartment and two guards insisted on taking the snacks into the rear cabin of the plane but he managed a quick glimpse towards the tail-end. There were about seven men dressed in field grey uniforms seated in bucket chairs and, towards the very rear of the plane, he saw WO Williams' brylcreemed head. Gorky ordered breakfast for the crew demanding tea, roshi bread and fish and chips. The Russian had evidently heard about Reki's special dishes. Apart from the spetcnazs on guard duty around the airfield and the duty officer on the plane the crew of Antonov 12 red 6 settled down for a night's sleep in preparation for the anticipated action on the following day.

Leonid Brezhnev convened an emergency meeting at his Kremlin office at noon, Moscow time, on 15th March. Vladimirovich Andropov and General Nikolayovitch Koniev were present and President Kosygin was expected but, as usual these days, he was late. Brezhnev quickly came to the point, "Comrades. We are here to re-examine our nuclear strategy against the West. Up to a point our plans have worked but Comrade Yuri Vladimirovich has come up with some disturbing news which may cause us to abort Operation Gan" and he turned to face Andropov, "Yuri Vladimirovich?"

"Thank you Comrade Leonid Ilyich. For months we have been hearing about America's newest nuclear weapon – the Pershing long-range missile. The USA has deployed over twenty Pershings to the European theatre and these are now threatening our major cities and military establishments. Let me remind you comrades – two Pershings would wipe out Moscow. Is that not so Comrade General?"

General Koniev nodded in agreement and spoke up, "We must stop playing war games now. We must withdraw our SS20 missiles immediately and stop the attack on the Suez target. If we don't Moscow, Leningrad and a few major cities may disappear in a cloud of nuclear dust. Twenty four hours ago Admiral Gorshkov advised me that submarine UK 27 is in position off the island of Gan in the Indian Ocean. The sub is carrying the 'hot potato'. The plane, an Antonov 12 carrying a twenty-man spetcnaz section, took off from Baku mid-morning and is well on the way to Gan. We should be able to stop the flight by alerting Petrovski's UK 27 submarine. For obvious reasons the plane is maintaining strict radio silence but I see no difficulties in aborting the attack so long as we act immediately."

Leonid Brezhnev was pondering his decision when the door burst open and President Kosygin strode into the room. He was in a foul mood and plainly a troubled man. His once-handsome face was drawn and haggard and his deep-set, dark brown eyes stared vacantly into space, "Tell me Leonid Ilyich what have you been planning behind my back?"

Brezhnev ignored the implied insult and brought the president up to date with their deliberations.

"Call it off? Over my dead body! Have you not heard of Russian roulette? We'll play them at their own game. The live missile threat goes on until I call it off. Is that clearly understood?" the irate president retorted. The three men in the office nodded their assent and Kosygin stood to leave.

"With your permission, Comrade President, I will convene another meeting in this room tonight. The situation needs careful monitoring," Brezhnev mumbled. The paranoid president glared at the Chairman of the Politburo. "Convene what you wish! I will not change my mind," and he strode out of the office.

At the evening meeting the sick president made his excuses and declined to attend. Under pressure from his colleagues Brezhnev made an immediate and painful decision to call off Russia's threatened attack. At the touch of a button General Koniev stood down the Russian nuclear missile bases in Poland and the Ukraine. By the time a decision to abort was made the Antonov 12 was on the ground in Gan and, from Vladivostok, Admiral Sergei Gorshkov was unable to make contact with UK27. He had himself ordered the submarine to use its powerful batteries to jam the airwaves around Gan during the time the Antonov 12 was on the ground and for four hours into its flight towards its target. Pandemonium broke loose when it was realized in Moscow that 'Operation Gan' could not be aborted and Brezhnev came in for attack from all sides. President Kosygin got out of it lightly by denying his involvement in the whole affair. For twenty four hours on either side of the Ides of March 1976, the Western Powers and the USSR were on the brink of a nuclear confrontation.

In London and Washington the news that the Soviets were withdrawing their missiles brought instant relief. President Ford legitimately claimed his rapid deployment of Pershings to Europe had saved the day and compared his achievement with President Kennedy's diplomacy during the Cuban crisis in 1962. Harold Wilson smirked and boasted his prediction that Ivan was only sabre-rattling had, once again, come true. In his heart of hearts he was fed up with the bickering and jousting across the Iron Curtain and sabre-rattling summed up most of the Soviets' actions. He secretly wished he had been inventive enough to have coined the Churchillian phrase himself.

144

About an hour after the big Russian plane landed Squadron Leader Tim Cosbey's suspicions that all was not well were aroused by an increase in vehicular activity around the plane, at the motor pool, and in the vicinity of the NAAFI which seemed to be the convergence point for most traffic. And when a jeep containing four persons pulled up outside the control tower, Tim decided to act. Pushing aside his spark's corporal he frantically tried to get through to MoD in London but all attempts were futile. The air waves were jammed. Smelling a rat he told 'sparks' to keep trying and announced he was going across to the officers' mess. But he was too late. There was only one set of stairs down from the observation cupola to the ground floor and a Russian officer, with two armed guards and Mike Townsend, were on the way up. He dived into a store room on the first floor which contained three large wooden crates housing Hithadhoo's dismantled short-range transmitter. Tim ducked in behind two of the boxes and lay, face down, flat on the floor. His hiding place was directly above the chart room and within a minute he heard conversation from the cupola above his head, mainly in Russian but occasionally Mike Townsend's voice broke through in English. After about five minutes footsteps came downstairs from the cupola and the door to his hiding place was thrown open and a powerful torchbeam scanned the room. Mike spoke up, "That's only a general storage room."

The footsteps retreated downstairs and Mikes' voice came through again, "Where is Squadron Leader Cosbey, corporal?"

"He went to the officers mess, or the NAAFI, just before you arrived sir."

A minute later a jeep drove off at high speed towards the plane leaving two Russian radio operators in the cupola and two spetcnazs guarding the entrance to the control building.

Tim took stock of his surroundings. The only source of light was a two foot square, glass-paned window which in daylight gave him an uninterrupted view of the whole length of the runway. The floor space was almost entirely covered by three crates. In the centre of the floor there was a 1ft circular hole covered with a makeshift perspex hood which protruded into the ceiling of the room below and had been abandoned long ago as a source of illumination for the wall charts in the map room. Tim locked the door from inside and took up a position at the window overlooking the airstrip. He had a long night's vigil ahead. Extraneous noises, the scraping of chairs and intermittent guttural conversation, came from the cupola above his head. One of the guards outside the building was chain-smoking and had an irritating cough. Tim kept his night binoculars steadfastly fixed on the end of the runway where the Russian plane was parked in darkness. He struggled to keep awake but dozed off at around one o'clock and by 2.00 am the entire station had settled down for a few hours uncomfortable sleep.

At daybreak on March 16th 1976, Gan station woke up to the most eventful day in its 35 year existence. Half an hour after first light, at about 0510 hours, three inflatable dinghies from UK 27 came ashore at the causeway. They brought with them ten Russian marines, two large crates and a portable hoist and a thin, pale, curious-looking man who wore metal-rimmed glasses and a parody for an uniform. Nothing matched, but faded badges of rank on his lapels indicated he was a high-ranking Russian intelligence officer. Alexei Uri Gagarin, named after his illustrious astronaut uncle, was overjoyed at his release from the claustrophobic submarine and could not stop talking and, in Mike Townsend, he had a ready listener. Furthermore, Uri was thrilled at the prospect of practicing his English and he proudly announced he graduated in nuclear physics at Leningrad University. Gorky, the belligerent political officer, did his best to silence the gregarious physicist but, asserting his seniority, Gagarin told him to shut up. Gagarin hinted that the containers now stored in the mid-section of the plane held nuclear material. This information upset Mike as he pondered on the ultimate destination of the lethal weapon but he was soon to discover the answer later that morning.

The fish and chips breakfast served aboard Antonov 12 was a resounding success. So much so that an order was put in for a repeat at supper time. During delivery Reki was quick to notice the newly-arrived 'officer' in the forecabin and two wooden crates and a hoist in the midcabin guarded by two armed soldiers in blue poloneck sweaters and slacks. When he returned to the NAAFI he reported his observations to Dr Clem.

"And how was the CO?" Dr Clem asked.

"He was very quiet and did not look at me."

146

"And did you see WO Williams or any of the airmen?"

"No sir," Reki replied, "they're at the back of the plane. The soldiers stopped me in the middle cabin where I saw the crates that look like coffins."

"I wonder what Ivan's up to?" Dr Clem mused.

Reki had no solution to the question but he thought it pertinent to add with a hint of pride, "They enjoyed my fish and chips. They want the same again for supper."

Cramped and stiff, Tim Cosbey woke with a start at daybreak and stretched his limbs. The plane was still in the same position at the end of the runway. Half an hour later, two wooden crates were delivered into the hold at the rear end of the belly of the Antonov 12. The CO's jeep and two strange-looking troop carriers were under guard on the runway near the plane. At around 0900 hours Gan's petroleum tender was towed up to the aeroplane and, for the next two hours, a shuttle service refuelled the thirsty monster. Throughout the morning there was some human activity around the plane and voices, the scraping of chairs and movement above his head, confirmed the Russians were still in the observation cupola. The armed guards at the entrance to the control building occasionally came into view as they strolled around in the early morning sunshine. At around midday a jeep carrying four men came to a shuddering halt outside the control building. Wing Commander Mike Townsend, a large, fat man in a scruffy blue uniform, a Russian pilot officer and a thin, bespectacled man in a nondescript grey denim jacket, came into the building and made straight for the map room directly below Tim's hiding place. By the time Tim got to the opaque perspex hatch in the floor the four visitors, smouldering cigarettes in their hands, were gathered around a wall map of Africa and the Indian Ocean. That morning, Alexei Uri Gagarin had brought sealed orders from Moscow commanding Capt Voroshov to attack Suez and, after delivery, to proceed across southern Egypt to a safe haven at Maradan in Libya. Viewed through the perpex hood their outlines were indistinct but, more pertinently, Tim heard every word clearly. Captain Sergei Voroshov was speaking and the big fellow on his right translated his words into English. "My Captain he says we must get to our target by 0630 hours tomorrow."

"Tell Captain Voroshov he must leave Gan by midnight to reach

147

Suez by daybreak. A direct flight is possible but, to avoid commercial traffic, your safest flight path will be a great circle track 253 true to the Seychelles and then track 322 true over the Horn of Africa and up the Red Sea."

Gorky translated Mike's planned flight path. The men in the room below behaved amicably and Mike Townsend was not apparently distressed or under pressure. On the contrary he seemed only too pleased to cooperate with the invaders. Gorky took a full minute to translate Mike's plan followed by a voluble discussion between the Russians. When Captain Voroshov understood he beamed and spoke rapidly, quickly translated by Gorky. "My Captain he say 'thank you' and he ask you to repeat the coordinates."

Mike obliged. "Track TWO FIVE THREE to Seychelles and then track THREE TWO TWO up the Red Sea" – duly recorded on a notepad by the Russian aviator. The men left as abruptly as they had arrived. Discarding their cigarettes on the ground outside the control tower they piled into a jeep and were driven away at speed. Tim noted that when they had travelled a few yards the big man they called Gorky held a pistol to Mike's head. At that moment he came to realise the gun-toting charade was performed in order to impress any onlookers and Mike Townsend was cooperating under direct threat from the hijackers. The Russian attackers were planning some sort of assault on Port Suez at daybreak on the following day, in nineteen hours time, and he had to pass on the message to London. The upstairs transmitter, guarded by the Russian soldiers, was being jammed, presumably by the plane. Crated and ready for transportation to the UK, he shared a room with the other serviceable transmitter. He had to somehow cut out the Antonov's jammer before the plane took off at midnight.

At around 2.00 pm Reki brought a meal to the two telegraphists manning the jammed transmitter in the cupola and the spectnaz outside the control tower. Carrying a metal tray and closely attended by an armed guard, he arrived in a station waggon. Tim moved to the door to listen and, wonder of wonders, the only sound from the outside landing was the gentle flip-flop of Reki's sandals. Holding his index finger tip to his lips he opened the door wide. Reki's sudden alarm quickly abated when he saw the squadron leader.

"What's happening Reki?" Tim whispered.

"Sahib Townsend and Mr Williams are on the plane. The medical officer and four officers and about sixty airmen are under guard in the NAAFI. I'm feeding the Russians. They like my fish and chips."

"You've been on the plane?" Tim asked.

"Yes, twice, and I'm taking supper across tonight."

"Right!" Tim responded, "have you seen a jammer on the plane?"

Reki looked puzzled. "I think so. There's a lot of panels and knobs in the cabin where Sahib Townsend and the Russian officers are sitting."

"Well," Tim replied, "their jammer is probably a bit like ours. It will have three coloured levers. The red one is usually up and the other two down. To stop jamming the red lever has to be reversed and, to fix things properly, broken off."

"I've seen the levers Sahib Cosbey."

"Okay Reki! You'd better get up to the cupola. Stop again on the way down if you can."

Reki handed Tim a flagon of plain water and a tuna sandwich and scurried upstairs. Tim gently closed the door and waited and, about three minutes later, Reki was on his way down. Tim again waylaid him, "Tell the officers in the NAAFI, and if you get a chance our commanding officer and Mr Williams, about the red lever. We must try and put their jammer out of action. Many lives depend upon it."

Reki stared vacantly at the squadron leader who wasn't sure the Maldivian had understood him clearly. But he underestimated Reki's intelligence. Reki was fully aware of the gravity of the situation and, in gratitude for all the British had done for him, he intended to carry out Squadron Leader Cosbey's instructions and have a go at the red lever should the opportunity arise.

Throughout the day a searing, tropical sun beat down relentlessly on Gan: a fierce persistent heat with temperatures at noon in the low hundreds. The crew of the Antonov and off duty spetcnaz were allowed out of their oven-hot cabins, a privilege denied Mike Townsend and WO Williams and the two airmen hostages. The NAAFI hall, with its incarcerated human occupants huddled in a bad-tempered, sweaty mass, was ineffectively ventilated by two enormous ceiling paddle fans. Throughout the night the prisoners had kept up a flow of facile conversation and banter but, by midday on the 16th, they were tired out and listless, barely able to string one sentence together. Realising the dangers of dehydration, Squadron Leader Garvey insisted each airman must drink a measured amount of water at hourly intervals. Luckily the NAAFI had a plentiful supply of bottled water, soft drinks and iced beer. Confined in the small storage cubicle with little ventilation, matters were much worse for Tim Cosbey. Apart from the flagon of water Reki had given him he had no other means of sustenance. Throughout the long, hot day he kept vigil on the Russian plane and envied the crew's ability to seek shade under the generous belly of the Antonov and under a clump of palm trees protecting one of the greens on the nearby golf course.

The Russians had ordered their fish and chips supper for 1830 hours. After cooking solidly for over an hour Reki and two mess waiters were laying out fried tuna steaks on trays when Gorky and two armed spetcnaz burst into the NAAFI.

"I want a doctor!"

Dr Clem reluctantly got to his feet. Gorky glared at him, "Come with me."

Dr Clem felt like digging his heels in but the menacing bully carried the whip hand. "I'll need to get my bag from the sick bay."

Dr Clem, carrying a Gladstone bag, was bundled into a station waggon and sat next to Reki with two armed guards crouching behind them. In his haste to get back to the plane Gorky had departed in another jeep. The guards prodded Reki with their gun barrels, poking fun at him in a strange Russian dialect. Peasant recruits from the Ukraine, they had never come across a really black man before. In common with most other natives of Southern India and Sri Lanka Reki was as black as the ace of spades.

"Take no notice of the bastards, Reki. They're pig ignorant," Dr Clem exclaimed.

"Thank you sir," Reki replied, "I have a message from Sahib Cosbey. The levers on a jammer in the plane have to be broken off. The red one is the important lever."

"Don't try anything funny on the plane. It's all very well for Squadron Leader Cosbey to give orders. He doesn't have to carry them out. Where is he by the way?"

The conversation between Reki and the medical officer began irritating the guards. Their rifle prods became more menacing until suddenly one shouted 'stop' which, apart from 'hello' and 'hands up', was the entire extent of his English vocabulary. The spetcnaz made it quite clear that conversation was at an end and silence prevailed in the station waggon for the rest of the journey.

At the foot of the ladder into the plane the shabbily-dressed political officer, pistol in hand, was waiting and ushered Dr Clem through the forecabin into the mid-section of the plane. There were four officers in the forecabin and, as he was hustled past his commanding officer, Dr Clem made eye-contact with Mike. The light was poor but he could have sworn there was a pleading look, a look begging forgiveness, in Mike's eyes. In the mid-section of the body of the plane three commandos, one holding a torch, stood around a blood-soaked wooden crate. Two men were supporting a comrade whose exposed left arm was lying on top of a crate with a rubber tourniquet around his biceps and an oozing, open wound on the front of his wrist. Blood clots and blood-soaked dressings lay on top of the crate. Gorky glowered at the injured spetcnaz. "This is doctor. He will fix." Turning toward Dr Clem, he barked, "He cut his hand on a glass bottle."

Squadron leader Garvey took a quick look at the injured wrist. At least three tendons were completely severed. The forearm was dusky-blue and the hand and finger tips almost black.

"Christ!" Clem exploded, "how long has this tourniquet been on?"

"About an hour," Gorky replied.

Dr Clem knew enough about circulatory physiology to realise that complete occlusion of blood supply for more than fifty minutes might result in gangrene and loss of a limb. He pushed Gorky aside and released the tourniquet. For an agonising twenty seconds nothing happened and then a weak spurt of arterial blood came pulsing out of the congealed mess on the soldier's wrist. With each heart beat the pulsation became stronger and twenty beats later a full flow of bright red blood, controlled by direct pressure over the wrist, gushed out of the open wound. The patient fainted and fell to the floor. Surgery was not one of Dr Clem's fortes but to the Russians he was their comrade's saviour. Ignoring the tendons he clipped and tied both ends of the severed radial artery and generally cleaned the wound. A dozen skin stitches completed the job and by that time the patient had regained consciousness, normal colour had returned to his hand. As he was binding the wrist Dr Clem noticed unusual markings on the side of one of the wooden crates. Though the lettering was in Russian there was no mistaking the bomb-shaped motif and the kilogram weight of the crate's contents. The medical officer paused to think, 'These boys are on their way to drop a bomb somewhere and it could be a nuclear bomb'. In Dr Clem's book conventional armaments were acceptable but for humanitarian and environmental reasons nuclear weapons were taboo. He pondered on Reki's words. Could Tim Cosbey be on to something? Would sabotaging the transmitter panel stop these blasted Russkies in their tracks? There was only one way to find out.

All the while Dr Clem was operating on the wounded Russian his mates, with callous disregard for their stricken comrade, wandered to and fro carrying plates of fish and chips and mugs of hot tea. Reki appeared briefly but was sent packing by Gorky. After he had finished dressing the injured limb Dr Clem packed his bloody instruments into the Gladstone bag and supervised removal of his patient to a row of seats in the rear cabin where about six interested spetcnaz gathered around their wounded comrade. The rear cabin was well-illuminated and, strapped in their seats at the very back, he caught a glimpse of Silly Billy and the two airmen hostages. He raised his hand in a brief salute and was quickly hustled away by Gorky who, once more wielding a pistol, was intent on getting the doctor and the Maldivian waiter off the plane.

Once through the red damask curtain and into the forecabin Dr Clem immediately realised something was seriously amiss. Mike Townsend was on his feet and shouting, "Stop it you bloody fool!"

Mike's anger was directed at Reki who was on his knees and hanging on with all his might to a red-handled lever on the transmitting panel. A black-headed lever had already been dislodged from its setting and lay on the floor. Gorky weighed up the situation in a flash. Pushing Clem aside he brought his pistol butt heavily down on the back of Reki's head. The Maldivian slid to the floor and lost his grip on the lever and Gorky and two of the plane's officers manhandled Reki's inert body towards the exit. Dr Clem stood rooted to the spot staring at the bent red lever and then at Mike Townsend standing four feet away and shaking his head. His commanding officer's gestures were like a red rag to a bull. Mike's shaking head indicated 'Don't do it' which incited Dr Clem to react oppositely. Seething with rage, and having seen the attack on Reki, Clem hurled his thirteen stones on to the red lever. There was a loud crack and the lever came away in his hand. He turned toward Mike with a satisfied grin expecting a word of praise from his commanding officer. "That's cooked their goose, Mike. While I'm at it I'll yank the third lever out."

Mike Townsend looked on scornfully as Gorky came surging back into the cabin. As the green-topped lever bent under Dr Clem's weight Gorky's gun-butt came crashing down with a sickening thud on the nape of his neck and he fell, stunned, to the floor. Mike looked on disinterestedly and, as they dragged the medical officer's inert body out of the forecabin, he muttered under his breath, "You bloody fool Clem. You never learnt to control your temper."

He felt no remorse at the treatment meted out to his friend and fellow officer and to Reki his one-time servant for, in his opinion, they deserved all they got.

A three-tonner carrying the semiconscious medical officer and Reki veered off the runway and across four hundred yards of scrubland to the centre of the golf course coming to a halt near the fifth green and about half a mile away from the Antonov. The two victims were slowly recovering consciousness and were helped out of the lorry and half-carried to the edge of a green. They were made to kneel in a sand bunker and, without further ceremony, Gorky shot them in turn through the back of the head. Death was instantaneous. The bodies were left in the bunker and the execution squad returned to the plane and carried on with their normal duties as if nothing had happened. On the plane flight engineers were frantically attempting to repair the damaged transmitter but to no avail. Ironically Reki and Dr Clem's sabotage had not stopped the jamming which was controlled all the while by the powerful ground-level jammer of the surfaced nuclear submarine. But they had irreparably damaged the Antonov's radio transmitter and the Russians' ability to receive messages from, and transmit messages to, the outside world.

Between supper and midnight on the March 16th the Antonov's crew were preoccupied with preparations for take off. At one stage

Captain Voroshov proposed calling off the attack and returning to Baku, concerned about his defective receiver and transmitter, but he was overruled by the bumptious political officer and by Alexei Gagarin. The innocent-looking technocrat carried a higher rank in the Party than either Gorky or Captain Voroshov. Furthermore, having spent a lifetime developing and perfecting the neutron bomb, Gagarin was not about to allow a minor technical hitch to interfere with his opportunity for observing the effectiveness of his lethal 'toy'.

At 2335 hours Wing Commander Townsend was conveyed by jeep to the causeway. Ten minutes later Warrant Officer Williams and the airmen hostages were taken away under guard and made to sit in a group in a coconut grove at the far eastern end of the runway. Only eight spetcnaz remained on the plane for take off at 2359 hours The other twelve, including their lieutenant, remained on the ground and assisted the marine commandos with laying charges and preparing for final evacuation. Guided by powerful searchlights in its nose the Antonov made a majestic take off westwards into the dark night. By 0130 hours the marines' task was complete and the airfield became a hive of vehicular activity as jeeps and station waggons brought the Russian commandos and marines to the causeway. The last group to be pulled out were the guards on the NAAFI and the control building and the two spectnaz' guarding WO Williams and the two airmen at the coconut grove on the golf course. All the vehicles on the airfield were sabotaged with delayed action stun grenades. Finally, the remaining spetcnaz and marines piled into three inflatable dinghies and disappeared in convoy into the dark night. The thirty two hour Russian occupation of Gan was over by 0220 hours on March 17th 1976.

Chapter Eleven

A Phantom strike

SQUADRON LEADER TIMOTHY COSBEY had been incarcerated in the small storage room at the airbase control building for over thirty hours. The Antonov 12 airplane took off just before midnight and, for the next two hours, jeeps and station waggons buzzed around the airfield eventually congregating at the causeway. At twenty minutes to two a jeep came to the control tower and took away the men in the cupola and the spectnaz guards. The vehicle had barely gone a couple of hundred yards when there were two loud bangs above his head The Russians had left their visiting cards – two delayed action stun grenades which blew in the transmitter's instrument panel and brought down the radio mast rendering them useless. Tim ran downstairs and dialled the NAAFI. An engineer flight sergeant answered the telephone. "Flight Sergeant Hanley speaking."

"Squadron Leader Cosbey here in the control tower. Are the commanding officer and Warrant Officer Williams with you?"

"No sir. We last saw the CO yesterday morning when he came in with the Russians. He told us WO Williams was with him and being held hostage on the plane. The Russian guards left the NAAFI about thirty minutes ago. We can't go after them as they took away our guns."

"That's all right sergeant. Get up here as quickly as you can and bring half a dozen men with you. Is the MO in the NAAFI?"

"No sir. He was with us until last evening when he was taken away at gunpoint to the plane. They also took Reki and plates of fish and chips. We haven't see either of them since."

"Thank you Hanley. Get across here at the double."

Upstairs in the cupola the smell of cordite hung in the air. The front panel of the transmitter had been shattered and the instrument was totally defunct. In the absence of the CO Tim Cosbey became the senior combatant officer on the station and his priority was to re-establish contact with the outside world and alert London about the lethal cargo on its way to Suez. By now the plane was over two hours into its deadly flight and in another five or six hours it would reach its target. Together with Sergeant Hanley and six airmen he began breaking into the storage crates and assembling the reserve short-range transmitter.

Within minutes two airmen, led by WO Williams, came rushing upstairs. The warrant officer had a sad tale to tell. After his release by the Russian guards he and the airmen dashed across to the control tower and on the way found Reki's and the medical officer's bodies in a sand bunker near the fifth green. The flustered warrant officer continued, "We saw Wing Commander Townsend twice. The Russkies brought him in at gunpoint. When 'e 'ad a chance 'e gave us a thumb's up sign. We was held at the back of the plane and couldn't see everything wot was going on at the front. Yesterday morning they brought on two wooden crates about the size of coffins and a pale, thin h'officer called Gagarin came aboard with some Russian marines. Gagarin is related to the famous Russian cosmonaut and I 'eard someone say 'e was a nuclear physicist. 'E was a very odd man and wouldn't stop talking. All the time we was on the plane there were six to eight armed spetcnaz commandos with us. I thought about escaping but we 'ad no chance."

"I understand Mr Williams. Now gather a few men and get down to the causeway to see what's happening."

Even as WO Williams was leaving the sharp, distinctive crump of exploding grenades was heard from the direction of the motor pool and the causeway. The departing marine demolition experts used delayed fuses to grenade the camshafts of all serviceable vehicles and, by the time the warrant officer reached the causeway, the spetcnaz and Russian marines had been gone for over half an hour.

In the control tower Tim and his helpers eventually assembled the transmitter and Sergeant Hanley rigged a temporary antenna aerial up a flagpole. When the radio transmitter went into action at 0250 hours the airwaves were still jammed and, by now, the Russian plane was well outside jamming range. Puzzled, Tim Cosbey turned to his wireless operator. "Who the hell is doing the jamming? Our transmitting range is limited but we should be able to get through to Diego Garcia once the jammer is lifted. I'm going across to the NAAFI to see if they're okay and for a wash and brush up. As soon as you get a clear signal get on to Diego Garcia on our emergency call sign. I wish to speak to Diego Garcia's officer commanding."

Once the naval marines and most of the spetcnaz off the plane were safely aboard, Captain Uri Petrovski took UK27 out to sea. As instructed by Vladivostok the jammer was released at 0320 hours and, thereafter Gan's air waves were clear. While still cruising on the surface the submarine received urgent instruction from Gorshkov's headquarters to abort the Antonov mission. Despite repeated and frantic attempts to contact the plane Captain Petrovski had to admit defeat and reported his failure to Vladivostok. The news was received with consternation and disbelief at Gorshkov's HQ and with alarm, verging on panic, in Moscow.

For the final hour of the Russian evacuation Mike Townsend stood on the causeway watching the darkened figures of the spetcnaz and marines congregating and loading on to the inflatable dinghies and disappearing stealthily across the water into the pitch dark. Twenty minutes later the ensuing silence was suddenly broken by the unmistakeable crump of exploding grenades in the motor pool at the eastern end of the runway and, much closer, near the end of the causeway. For himself Mike had salvaged a motor cycle which was propped against the causeway handrail. It was time to go. He mounted the bike and rode cautiously along the 22km causeway extension and dirt road to the dismantled radar base and seaplane anchorage at Hithadhoo.

Corporal Angus Forbes's duty stint at Hithadhoo was nearly over. He and two erks were due for relief on the following day and, after the radar and radio equimpment had been dismantled and removed,

Hithadhoo had become a ghost station. The only item of military value left was the CO's two-seater seaplane, anchored to a stubby jetty. A fervent highlander, Angus longed for the tall crags, fresh clean air and tranquil lochs of his native Aberdeenshire. He preferred the night shift when the temperature and humidity dropped a little after midnight and a cool, benevolent sea breeze came wafting in from the south. Still, there were only a dozen days to go before the RAF evacuated Gan. Angus had been unlucky. His posting was onwards to Hong Kong. He lit another fag and strolled along the jetty reflecting that Hong Kong would have more to offer than Gan. For one thing there would be Chinese lassies to relieve the boredom of service life. Gan might be an island paradise but it lacked one vital ingredient and that was female companionship. Angus had not had his oats for nine months and the frustration was beginning to show. Irritably, he threw his half-smoked cigarette into the sea and cursed under his breath.

Earlier, around midnight, a large plane with headlights ablaze had taken off from Gan flying directly overhead in a westerly direction. Angus reckoned it was the same plane as arrived in Gan at dusk the previous evening. Later, at around 0215 hours, he heard muted bangs coming from the direction of the airfield. Afterwards all was quiet until 0250 hours when he saw a headlight approaching along the dirt road from the causeway. He alerted his companions and, rifles at the ready, they stood together at the barrier which guarded the approach to the jetty. As a motor cycle skidded to a halt Corporal Forbes moved forwards with his loaded rifle held across his chest. "Halt! Who goes there?"

"At ease, Forbes. It's your commanding officer."

Acting on impulse Forbes sprang to attention and presented arms. Mike returned the salute and curtly barked an order, "We've had a spot of bother at the station. I'm flying down to Diego Garcia to raise the alarm. Get the seaplane off its mooring and ready for take off."

Corporal Forbes peered incredulously through the gloom. "You'll be waiting for first light sir?"

"No. I'll be taking off in ten minutes."

"It'll be dangerous in the dark sir."

"I know, Forbes, but I'm the only qualified pilot left on the station.

I'll just go and take a leak before we go down to the plane and you can cast me off."

Before he fired the engine Mike shouted at the three dimly-outlined airmen on the jetty, "When I'm safely up, Forbes, get on the motorcycle and report to Squadron Leader Cosbey or Warrant Officer Williams. Tell them I've taken off for Diego Garcia to raise the alarm. Stand clear lads! I'm starting the engine."

In total darkness the seaplane taxied slowly clear of the jetty. The three petrified airmen stood rooted to the spot. The engine revs increased rapidly as the small plane skimmed over the waves and then, in a matter of seconds, the engine noise began receding as the seaplane clawed its way southwards into the enveloping blackness. The airmen relaxed. Corporal Forbes lit another cigarette and, as the waves created by the departing plane came slapping against the jetty, Angus turned to his companions. "That was some take off lads. Very risky. Did you know the old man flew Lancasters in the last war? He's got a DFC and Bar." Grinding the stub of his cigarette under his boot, he continued, "I'm off on the bike to report to Squadron Leader Cosbey. I wonder what's happened at the airfield? I'll send a truck to pick you lads up at first light. We won't need guards at this place from now on."

Corporal Angus Forbes arrived at the control tower at around 0340 hours to find the place in utter chaos. Packed into the cupola were a dozen airmen gathered around a makeshift transmitter and Squadron Leader Cosbey, earphones on his head, shouting into a mouthpiece, "I don't care if he's had a bad day. Get Colonel Sheldon immediately. This is a priority one emergency."

Everyone waited patiently in silence broken by the new arrival, "Excuse me, sir, I have a report from Hithadhoo."

The signals officer waved him away but the corporal persisted and Tim took off his headphones. "Yes. What is it Forbes? Make it snappy!"

Forbes blurted out his message, "The commanding officer took off in his seaplane about forty minutes ago. He's flying to Diego Garcia to get help."

The assembled group barely had time to digest Angus's bombshell when an irate US air force colonel came on the air. "What's the trouble Gan? You do realise its nearly four in the morning?"

Tim Cosbey brushed aside the American's brusque remark. "This is top priority Colonel Sheldon. My commanding officer, Wing Commander Townsend, is on his way to you in a seaplane but he won't arrive for another three hours. I want you to transmit an urgent message to MoD London and to repeat the message every five minutes until you get a response. Message reads. *'Russian Antonov AN12 made emergency landing Gan at 1800hrs on 15th. Russian spetcnaz, repeat spetcnaz, and marines took over station and jammed our transmitter. Two fatal casualties – medical officer and a Maldivian employed national. Antonov took off at 2355 on 16th with suspected nuclear weapon aboard. Destination – Port Suez. Flight tracks – 253 true to Seychelles and 322 true up the Red Sea. Repeat – nuclear weapon aboard. ETA at Port Suez approx. 0600hrs local time. Gan CO on way to Diego Garcia. ETA at DG 0515hrs'.* Message ends."

Colonel Sheldon's reaction was instinctive. "Christ, squadron leader, this is a tricky one! The boys will have to get their skates on to stop the bomber. When London acknowledges I'll buzz you. We'll keep an eye open for your CO."

The weary squadron leader took off his earphones and rubbed his forehead. He was utterly exhausted.

"There's nothing more I can do here. Keep the line to Diego Garcia open. I'm going to my quarter to lie down but inform me immediately you hear from Colonel Sheldon," and, as an afterthought, he added, "Get Mr Williams to take out a party at first light and bring in the medical officer and Reki. He can lay out the bodies in the medical centre."

Group Captain Tony Widgeon made certain he was the senior duty officer at MoD on March 15th, 16th and 17th. In response to the mini-crisis created by deployment of Russian missiles in Poland and the Ukraine he volunteered to sleep 'over the shop' and used one of the duty rooms overnight. He dealt with the message from Gan at lunchtime on the 15th which reported an unidentified plane seeking permission for an emergency landing and, within an hour, the direct line to Gan had gone dead. He dismissed his junior officer's concern that something was amiss at Gan, explaining that interruption of radio transmissions from the Middle and Far East frequently occurred during the monsoon season. The group captain had no idea if monsoons were active in the Indian Ocean at that time of the year but he confidently assumed the young flight-lieutenant manning the transmitter was also ignorant of Maldivian climatic variations. He was happy to sit back all day on the 16th reassuring his staff that lack of telegraphic communication with Gan held no sinister implications. And all was calm and serene until 2045 hours on the 16th when a vital message arrived from the American/British airbase at Diego Garcia. As soon as he read the transcript Tony Widgeon realised that, on this occasion, his Russian masters meant business and their strike plane was only about four hours away from its target.

To save his own skin Tony Widgeon acted speedily. He convened a 'red alert' meeting at the Ministry of Defence and, within an hour, Air Commodore Sir Charles Lampton and Tony were presenting their information to the Defence Committee. Sir Charles stressed the gravity and urgency of the crisis adding they had about three hours leeway. When asked for a solution Air Commodore Lampton concluded the only feasible course of action was to shoot down the Russian bomber before it reached its target. The Committee agreed unanimously. The Prime Minister was informed and, without prevarication, gave his go ahead. The Defence Committee was nonplussed by the prime minister's instant blessing for an air strike with its potentially catastrophic political consequences but they were unaware that, a few minutes before hearing from the Defence Minister, Harold Wilson had also had a telephone conversation with Leonid Brezhnev in Moscow.

Leonid Brezhnev had had a harrowing time throughout March 16th. Though the ground missiles threatening the West had been removed, communication with the Antonov transport and submarine UK 27, which was doing the jamming, proved impossible. It came as a great relief when, at 11.00 pm Russian time, UK 27 broke radio silence and at last they had a potential means of contacting the Antonov. During the next hour it became evident that the aircraft and its lethal cargo was maintaining radio silence and was well on the way to its target. In an agony of indecision he consulted General Nikolayovitch Koniev who advised a fighter strike to eliminate the Antonov in mid-ocean. When asked where the fighter force might come from, the general had no simple answers. Though the Yemeni and Sudanese governments were communist sympathisers they were completely unreliable and likely to botch the whole enterprise. He could not procrastinate for much longer and world peace was dependent on his actions in the next twenty minutes. It was approaching 1.00 am in Russia and 10.00 pm in London. Leonid Ilyich did the unthinkable. He aborted Operation Gan and spoke, person to person, with Prime Minister Wilson at No 10 Downing Street. He knew he would be sacrificing the lives of the Antonov's crew but this was a price Russia had to pay for dabbling in war games and endangering world peace. Leonid Brezhnev requested the British to shoot the Antonov out of the sky. He gave his personal assurance there would be no Russian repercussions or claims of acts of aggression. The British Prime Minister was shocked by the request but, within a minute of speaking to Brezhnev, MoD were on the line advising the same course of action. The Prime Minister's decision was made easy for him. He gave his go ahead to an offensive strike with the objective of bringing down the renegade aeroplane.

Six senior service officers gathered around a large world map in the Combined Operations and Planning Room at MoD. An air vice-marshal looked across at Tony Widgeon. "What sort of plane are we dealing with group captain?"

"The Antonov 12 red 6 is basically a troop carrier, in this instance adapted to carry a nuclear payload and specialist troops. It's a bit of a plodder with a top speed of around 380 mph. Its NATO codename is 'Cock'."

"Assuming an average air speed of 350 knots and flight track 322 true where is the Antonov at the present moment?"

An air comodore navigator inspected his charts for about a minute.

"Flying on a 322 true track from the Seychelles they're just east of Bargaal and coming into the Gulf of Aden. I estimate they're three hours flying time away from their target. According to the coordinates they'll fly up the whole length of the Red Sea."

The navigator turned to his naval equivalent. "Are any of our Air Defence Vessels in the area?"

"We have two AD frigates patrolling the Red Sea and the Gulf of Aden. The nearest is HMS Probus just off Djibouti. I'll signal her immediately," and he left the operations room. The air-vice marshal made up his mind quickly. "We'll force her down into the Red Sea. A strike force of three FGR4 Phantoms from Akrotiri will fly to intercept the Antonov at a point about 800 miles south of Suez. They'll need K2 Victor inflight refuelling after the strike. We should be able to get our Phantoms to the target in an hour and a half. I'll signal Cape Gata to authorise the strike. We'll codename this mission Operation Cockspur."

The Defence Secretary made an obvious, but valid, observation. "We must avoid the plane landing or crashing in either Saudi Arabia or the Sudan. There's an obvious risk of an international incident and nuclear spillage."

"I've taken that aboard Mr Minister. My boys will aim to put her down in the water and, to play safe, they'll avoid using explosive and incendiary missiles and instead aim to blow off the Antonov's tail with cannon."

The air vice marshal was on his way to a sound-proof tele-communications room when he was waylaid by the naval commodore returning with information that HMS Probus had tracked a large air transporter proceeding north-westwards at 30,000 feet at an estimated air speed of 320 knots. The unidentified plane had passed out of radar scanner range at 0350 hours local time. Armed with this information he issued precise instructions to Cape Gata in Cyprus. At 0100 hours, London time, on March 17th 1976, Operation Cockspur was under way.

Tony Widgeon left the planning conference with a heavy heart. There was still an outside chance the Phantoms from Akrotiri might not find the Antonov and they might be too late to prevent the attack on Port Suez. It was a fifty/fifty situation. He had done all he possibly could to delay alerting the British strike force and he could do no more. Another pressing problem still remained. Why in hell's name was Mike Townsend flying to Diego Garcia? Was he about to blow the gaffe? If he did the finger would point directly at himself, Moscow's

163

agent at MoD. If Townsend was still alive he would have to be permanently silenced as soon as possible.

Antonov 12 red 6. The Red Sea
Captain Boris Voroshov had been seated at the controls of his cumbersome plane for four and a half hours without a break. Following the flight plan advised by the British commander at Gan he had snatched an hour's sleep when they were over the Indian Ocean and now they were a fifth of the way up the Red Sea and he was fully alert and in control of his aircraft. Owing to the lack of radio communication and his inability to pick up ground signals he had to rely on his antiquated nose-cone scanner which had a maximum range of 35 miles at 30,000 feet, distance enough to take avoiding action should anything fly dead ahead across his path. The sky was beginning to brighten on the starboard side and, in another 30 minutes, navigation by direct vision would be possible. He was flying at optimum speed to conserve fuel and his guages indicated he was erring well on the side of safety with more than sufficient fuel in his reserve tanks to take them on to Libya after the strike. So far, all was well, and they were within ninety minutes flying time of their target.

Apart from Gorky and Gagarin the crew were behaving impeccably. Gorky had secreted a bottle of vodka on to the plane at Gan and now, loud mouthed and truculent, he was getting impatient. Voroshov ordered him off the flight deck. Uri Gagarin was impatient for a different reason. He was anxious to prime his beloved weapon and needed constant reassurance there was plenty of time in hand. In about thirty minutes Voroshov intended commencing a gradual descent from 30,000 feet to 10,000 feet, the optimum height for releasing the nuclear weapon. His concentration was interrupted by his radar operator and navigator reporting three 'blips' travelling at speed from west to east at 33,000 feet and disappearing off his radar screen in 40 seconds. Captain Voroshov was only slightly perturbed, "Keep the scanner on constant search. Direct visibility will improve in about 20 minutes and we're well on schedule for the strike."

"I should bloody well hope so," Gorky belched, "Can't you push on a bit quicker?"

Despite his previous dismissal Gorky was again back on the flight deck. Captain Voroshov was livid. "If you think you can get there quicker you fly the damn plane!"

Twelve minutes later he was still smouldering over Gorky's behaviour. If Gorky had kept his mouth shut Voroshov might have devoted more attention to the radar 'blips' and he would have warned his rear gunners to keep their eyes skinned. As it was his normally vigilant gunners were dozing in their padded seats behind their 23mm NR cannons. A sudden loud crack at the rear of the plane and a shuddering of the airframe brought his thoughts sharply back to earth. His plane had been hit in the rear and started behaving abnormally and it took all of Voroshov's experience and skill to keep the Antonov on an even keel. Its nose-scanner did not cover the tail end of the aircraft and, when the attack came, the fighter planes streaked in from below and behind his blind underbelly.

Akrotiri, Cyprus. 17th March 1976

The order to scramble for Operation Cockspur came at 0420 hours Cyprus local time. Squadron Leader Richard 'Deadeye' Cadogan led three Phantom FGR4's into the night sky and made a direct beeline southwards, flying at 30, 000 feet over the Sinai desert, down the Gulf of Suez and to the Red Sea. As they sped along in formation at mach 9 his mind kept musing over his bizarre instructions. His Phantoms were ordered to intercept a target, an Antonov 12 Cock, and to force her down into the sea as far away from land as possible. And finally, if they had to shoot, the Antonov's tailplane and no other part of the aircraft was the target. He supposed the powers that be had good reasons for these precise instructions but they seemed daft to him. Still, 'His was not to reason why. His was but to do or die'. Known as 'Deadeye' for his prowess on the shooting range he was about to show the brass hats his reputation for accuracy would be bourne out in combat. He smiled under his oxygen mask and spoke to his wingmen, "Red Fox Leader. Keep your eyes skinned. I'm taking you up to 35,000 feet to get above the bandit. When we spot her hang back and let me go in first. Red Two will follow me in. We're here to knock off her tail and bring her down into the sea and nothing else. There's a gin and tonic behind the bar in the mess for the first man to spot her."

The Phantom FGR4 was equipped with a powerful nose-scanner capable of tracking aircraft at a range of 60 miles at an altitude of 30,000 feet. Squadron Leader Cadogan's navigator had identified the Antonov's unmistakable blip when they were 80 minutes into their flight. Deadeye led his wing in a wide sweep to starboard and, within three minutes, an excited Red Fox Two came on the air, "Bandit below at ten o'clock." Deadeye Dick adjusted his flying goggles and took the Phantoms in a wide, lazy turn, throttling back to 400 mph to come up about two miles behind the Russian aircraft. She was a sitting duck. The fighters stalked the Antonov for about 30 miles and, when he judged the time right, Deadeye took his planes into a shallow dive and accelerated upwards at an angled approach to the rear end of the Antonov. With a shout of 'here goes' he pressed the firing button and released a stream of non-explosive cannon shell. Within five seconds he was clear of the target and zooming upwards while, twenty seconds behind him, Red Fox Two pressed home his attack. The Antonov's left tail fin and a section of the tailplane came flying off and flashed away into the stratosphere. The striken plane began behaving peculiarly and, for the next thirty miles, it went steadily downwards in a gentle parabola. The Russian transporter developed a yaw and began a slow roll which Captain Voroshov expertly controlled by intermittent throttling and use of his ailerons. But there was a limit to the power of his engines beyond which the big plane's nose began dipping and she descended erratically in a series of low, flat, gentle spins, rather like a falling leaf. After 20 miles the spins became more frequent and protracted and, at 1000 feet, the Antonov went into a near vertical dive and plunged into the sea. On impact with the water one wing tore off and the plane's back broke. For about twenty seconds the smashed Antonov was visible amidst the mountainous spray and, within the winking of an eye, she disappeared under the surface to sink gracefully, with her human and nuclear cargo, into the depths of the Red Sea. Squadron Leader Cadogan took his fighters at low level over the crash site where a patch of turbulent, oily water and bits and pieces of flotsam floated on the surface of the water. As expected there were no signs of survivors.

"Red Fox Leader. Return to base. We'll RV with our Victor tanker in twenty minutes."

Deadeye Dick's navigator glanced at a chart strapped to his left knee. He worked out the coordinates and jotted down the exact site where the Russian plane had disappeared into its watery grave. The spot was roughly 220 miles south east of Port Sudan and a similar distance from the inhospitable Saudi Arabian coastline and the depth of the Red Sea at this point was 2000 feet.

Squadron Leader Cadogan and his Phantom crews were safely on the ground in Akrotiri by breakfast time on 17th March. A message was dispatched to MoD. *'Operation Cockspur. Mission accomplished. Bandit dispatched to Davy Jones' locker'* The Defence Secretary convened a meeting at the War Office at 4.00 pm at which Tony Widgeon was present and the Prime Minister himself presided.

"My Defence Minister informs me the Royal Air Force successfully concluded Operation Cockspur. The renegade aircraft is now safely entombed at a depth of 2,000 feet in the Red Sea. You may have been anticipating a violent reaction from Moscow. I can inform you that Leonid Brezhnev and his Politburo were in full agreement with our intervention. Brezhnev informed me in person the flight in question was carrying a nuclear weapon. In fact he begged the RAF to neutralise the plane and I thank you all for your prompt and expert advice and action in this crisis."

Tony Widgeon was dumbfounded. It was not in the nature of his Russian masters to admit mistakes and, much less, to agree to one of their planes and crew being sacrificed. He was interrupted in his reverie by the Prime Minister, "Is there any news of Gan's commanding officer, group captain?"

"No, Mr Prime Minister. We are in constant touch with Diego Garcia and, indirectly, with Gan. Regretfully he may not have made it. Sea searches from Diego Garcia in the vast, treacherous waters around the Chagos and Salomon islands are continuing and will continue a few more days."

Lost in deep thought, Harold Wilson sucked the stem of his unlit pipe for a few moments. "Gentlemen. I want this incident played down and I don't wish the Press in on it. Politically I have no desire to see the Russians with egg on their face. I suggest a discrete departmental inquiry headed by Group Captain Widgeon. And if the missing commanding officer is found alive, I wish to hear his version of events. Regretfully there were two casualties, a British medical officer and a Maldivian national. The Maldivian government will be handsomely compensated and will not make an issue of this incident. The medical officer's elderly mother lives in Birmingham and she will also be well compensated. I suggest we refer to the medical officer's death as accidental in the course of duty. I strongly recommend the actions and bravery of these two men be duly, posthumously recognised in next June's Honours List. If the commanding officer fails to turn up, or if his body is found, his death will also be designated accidental in the line of duty and his widow will enjoy full pension rights. So let's sweep this unsavoury incident under the carpet."

Group Captain Tony Widgeon's appointment to head the Gan inquiry played into his hands. Concerned Mike Townsend might appear from nowhere and spill the beans, he delayed his departure to Gan for nearly a week. A military investigation team and a home office pathologist were flown out on March 19th. Tony himself held out for five days and eventually flew to Gan on a VC10 on the 24th arriving five days before the official handover ceremony. The investigating team found plenty of evidence that the visitors to Gan on 15th and 16th March had been Russian militia. A rifle bolt and a beret were identified as belonging to a specialist spetcnaz unit and a torn shirt, with insignia, was of the type worn by Russian marines. A superficial post-mortem, conducted by the home office pathologist, confirmed that Squadron Leader Garvey and Reki had been shot in the back of the head by a handgun and death had been instantaneous. Russian cigarette and cigar butts, a soldier's pocket book and a well-thumbed erotic novel were recovered from the landing strip near the spot where the Antonov 12 had been stationary. A Russian stun grenade, which failed to detonate, was found under a jeep in the motor pool. Signs of trampling in the sand near the causeway and many discarded cigarette ends pointed to the certainty that the marine squad had come ashore, and had been evacuated, at this point. Eye witness accounts from the men held in the NAAFI and from Warrant Officer William Williams put a seal on the investigation. The secret inquiry concluded that, on the 15th and 16th March, the British airfield at Gan had been occupied for 32 hours by specialist cadres of Russian spetcnaz and marine commandos. During the occupation the base's commanding officer and a warrant officer and two airmen had been held hostage on the plane and the station medical officer and a Maldivian employee were executed by the invaders for reasons unknown. Furthermore, Gan's officer commanding, Wing Commander Michael Townsend, was missing and believed to have lost his life in a valiant attempt to seek help from Diego Garcia and to warn London of the dangerous nature of the Russian mission.

On 21st March Squadron Leader Clement Garvey was buried with full military honours on the golf course near the 5th green and close to the spot where he was executed. On the same day Reki's body was removed to Feydhoo by his family where he was buried in a traditional coir-based coffin. His passing was celebrated with a village feast which lasted 24 hours and is repeated annually, every April 25th and forty days after the date of his execution.

Group Captain Tony Widgeon stepped off a VC10 transporter at 1100 hours on 24th March. Tim Cosbey met him off the plane and Silly Billy insisted on providing a guard of honour despite their recent harrowing experiences. The airmen were well turned-out and WO Williams apologised that only three of them carried rifles as the rest of the station's firearms had been confiscated and dumped out at sea by the departing Russians. Tim walked the group captain across to Dr Clem's grave, marked simply with a plain white cross. Tony Widgeon spent his day in the officers' mess where he received reports from the inquiry team who were flying back to the UK at the crack of dawn on the following day. After dinner Tim had his first opportunity to speak to his superior officer, man to man, and in private. Tony Widgeon opened the batting. "Any further news of Mike Townsend? He's one of my long-standing friends and I was best man at his wedding. You know his wife Vanessa? She's taking all this very badly, especially as her father is in such poor shape."

"No sir," Tim replied, "The searches continue but as each day passes the hopes of finding Wing Commander Townsend alive are fading fast. The American colonel at DG intends calling off the search tomorrow. That is with you permission, of course, sir."

Tony Widgeon was silent for a while, "Yes. That seems in order. I doubt if anyone could survive in the Indian Ocean for longer than three, or at the most, four days. Poor Mike! He probably went down with his crate. It was a brave act on his part and to take off in pitch darkness was suicidal but if anyone could get away with it Mike was that man. He was an extremely talented pilot and his war record proves it. Poor Mike! He deserves a gong for his bravery."

They both sat in silence and toyed with their Maxwell specials. After a minute or so the group captain sensed the younger officer had something weighing heavily on his mind. "What's the problem Timothy?"

"Well, sir. I don't wish to appear insubordinate, and I hate speaking ill of a senior officer, but I believe Wing Commander Townsend was in cahoots with the Russians."

"What a ridiculous suggestion! That's a load of piffle! What evidence have you? I warn you what you're suggesting is a court martial offence in my book."

Tim faltered and froze. He was on the point of opting out but his conscience would not allow him to do so. "I have not mentioned a word of this to anyone else sir but on the morning after the Antonov landed I saw, and heard, Wing Commander Townsend advising the Russian pilot and navigator on the best flight path from Gan to Port Suez. That's how I was able to pass on precise details to Colonel Sheldon at Diego Garcia and to MoD."

"He was under duress!" Tony Widgeon riposted.

"No sir! He was smoking and chatting amicably with the Russians in the map room and it was only when they got back into their jeep to return to the plane that a spetcnaz officer held a gun to the commanding officer's head."

Tony Widgeon got to his feet and took a deep breath. "This is a serious matter Squadron Leader Cosbey. Thank you for telling me. What we do here is to wait and see what happens. If Wing Commander Townsend turns up he'll be able to explain his actions. If he is lost at sea we will achieve very little by exposing him. Confidentially, I can tell you the PM is anxious to sweep the whole affair under the carpet. If we blow the gaffe on this business the only person to suffer will be

Vanessa and she'd lose her pension rights and the disgrace would kill her. Let's settle this matter like officers and gentlemen and not mention your suspicions outside these four walls."

Tony Widgeon extended his right hand and Tim shook it firmly. A contract for silence was sealed by the handshake and, suddenly, it seemed as if a great weight had been lifted off their shoulders. They sank a few large Maxwells and toasted 'absent friends'. On impulse, imbued with a sense of honesty and fortified by alcohol, Timothy suddenly wished to unburden his soul to the seemingly trustworthy group captain. "I have not spoken to anyone about this. When I served at NATO Headquarters with Wing Commander Townsend he behaved in an odd manner which made me suspicious that all was not well. At a late lunch in the mess one day I found a highly confidential document stuck underneath my dinner plate. I reported it to Michael and he took charge of an inquiry. Two days later he advised me to forget all about it and I gave in. But, to this day, I'm not certain I did the right thing. I had my suspicions that Michael was in cahoots with a Jean Dupré, the head chef at NATO."

Tony Widgeon had arranged Sir Claude Bernard's visit to NATO and knew the French Connection quite well. He feigned incredulity and made light of the subject. "Mike should have reported the matter but there was no breach of security at the time and no harm was done. Rest assured, Timothy, you did nothing wrong and you have nothing to worry about."

Timothy heaved a sigh of relief. "Thank you very much for your advice, sir. I feel relieved now that it's off my chest."

The session went on for another hour and, unaccustomed to alcoholic excess, Tim became inebriated and loquacious and talked about his trip to Baros with Mike Townsend. By this time the group captain insisted Tim should call him 'Tony'. "And do you know, Tony, if Mike is still alive I'd hazard a guess as to his whereabouts."

"Tell me more Tim my boy."

Tim pulled himself together with difficulty and slurred, "It's only an idea but, if he didn't fly down to DG, he might have gone up to Male. There's a beautiful woman in Male he was a bit interested in. She runs a tourist agency and takes people across to Baros island resort."

The group captain's face remained placid and smiling but the information filled him with excitement. With his involvement and knowledge of recent events on Gan Mike was a serious challenge to his position at MoD and even a greater danger to his masters in Moscow. He had to be seen off, one way or another, if he was still alive. And now this stupid, drunken signals squadron leader was hinting Mike might be holed out with a Maldivian woman at Male or Baros. It was certainly something worth checking on. He burst out laughing. "Mike with a woman! A local bint at that. I don't believe it for a minute. He would never let Vanessa down and I can swear to that. Still it's very interesting, very interesting indeed."

Next day Group Captain Tony Widgeon announced he would stay on in Gan to take the salute and command the handover parade.

Handover ceremony, 29th March 1976

For a week before the grand parade the entire staff on Gan were preoccupied with preparations for the handover ceremony and with removal of all traces of the 32 hour Russian occupation. The timely arrival of a section of fife and drums and a pipe major of the Royal Scots Fusiliers, in transit from Hong Kong to the UK, added a musical dimension to Silly Billy's preparations. He managed to scrounge thirty American carbines, flown up from Diego Garcia on the morning of the parade. Early on the morning of the 29th March the Maldivian entourage, led by President Ibrahim Nassir and his Minister of Transport, arrived by boat and two VC10s stood on the runway ready to whisk the British contingent away after the ceremony. President Nassir inspected the airmen and the Maldivian cadre and, together with Group Captain Widgeon, took the salute as the parade marched past led by the Fusilier's fife and drums. Tony Widgeon offered a prayer for Wing Commander Townsend, Squadron Leader Clement Garvey and Mohammed Rekitutha. President Nassir proudly announced that henceforth the 29th of March would be officially celebrated as Maldivian National Independence Day. To the strains of the last post, the Union Jack was ceremoniously lowered for the last time and a Maldivian pennant took it's place on the flagpole. To a plaintive bagpipe rendering of 'Auld Lang Syne' Group Captain Widgeon marched along the runway leading his airmen to the waiting VC10's. As they passed the fifth green he ordered the parade to 'eyes left' in a last tribute to their fallen medical officer. As the VC10s took off, leaving Gan for the last time, the Maldivian employees stood in an orderly bunch on the causeway waving tearful 'goodbyes' to their British masters. The British Air Force was leaving Gan forever. They left behind a few happy memories, many memories of boredom and discomfort and the body of their medical officer. They also flew home without their commanding officer whom they assumed had lost his life at sea in a valiant attempt to bring help when the base was invaded by the Russian commandos. Aboard one VC10 two officers were in considerable doubt about Mike Townsend's gallantry during the occupation. The squadron leader was sworn to secrecy in the matter but the group captain fully intended to act when he got back to London.

Within a few days of settling back at MoD Tony Widgeon got in touch with Moscow. He let it be know that Gan's former commanding officer might be in hiding in Male or Baros and pointed out to the KGB that the fugitive was a danger to themselves but, of greater significance, Mike Townsend's continued existence was a direct threat to his own strategic position as the current director of operations at MoD and a hot tip for promotion to a higher command in the Royal Air Force. If Townsend was allowed to remain alive he would be a constant threat to Moscow's high-ranking agent in London. Tony Widgeon did not have to spell out the answer. If still alive, Wing Commander Michael Townsend had to be eliminated.

Chapter Twelve

The spetcnaz came to Ihuru

MIKE TOWNSEND TOOK ANOTHER LOOK at his fuel gauge. He had been flying in daylight at 2,000 feet for forty minutes and reckoned his fuel was low despite a generous margin of forty gallons in his reserve tank. He was not worried about reaching Ihuru. His present concern was that, if he needed to move on from Ihuru, there was insufficient fuel to get him anywhere near to the Indian mainland or Sri Lanka. Before he took off he had told the guards at Hithadhoo he was heading for Diego Garcia but thanked his lucky stars he had not done so as, with the mileage involved, it would have been a tight squeeze. He deliberately chose a devious route from Hithadhoo to Kaaf Atoll. Flying south, in darkness, for fifty miles he made a broad sweep eastwards and then changed direction northwards and well away from the chain of atolls that extend for 650 miles from 1° south to 4° north of the equator. Daybreak came two and a half hours after take-off when he was forty miles east of Male. His original intention was to make for Male but, within an hour into the flight, he decided to head for Ihuru despite a risky landing in its narrow lagoon. He continued northwards for another fifteen minutes and, swinging westwards, came down to 1,000 feet approaching Ihuru from the north. The island was shrouded in a misty haze but as he descended lower he saw his landing site, a light-green lagoon inside a coral reef on the western side of the island. The stretch of water looked remarkably narrow but he had no choice. If he put the seaplane down on the open sea there was no means of getting into the lagoon over the coral reef. Dark-blue patches of submerged rock were visible in the green stretch of water inside the lagoon and these blocks of coral were a hazard which he could not avoid once the seaplane hit the water. Gritting his teeth he bellowed, "This is it!"

The seaplane cleared the jetty by twelve feet and a couple of seconds later Mike depressed the nose of his plane. The floats hit the water in the lagoon at 105mph and the plane surfed for 100 yards reducing speed rapidly. The seaplane was almost at a standstill when its left float hit a submerged rock and a supporting stanchion snapped. The left side of the plane lurched sideways and its nose and spinning propeller were plunged underwater throwing up spumes of sandy seawater. And then, quite elegantly, the seaplane settled on its side with its tail sticking out of the lagoon and about 20 yards from the gently shelving, sandy beach. The cockpit immediately filled with water which came up to Mike's chest. He undid the safety harness, stepped out through the roof of the cockpit into four feet of water, and waded ashore. Sitting on the sand he took a look at the damaged seaplane, now belching pockets of air from time to time and surrounded by a widening patch of dirty-brown, oil-streaked water. Mike placed his head in his hands and contemplated his predicament. Why the hell had he involved himself with the bloody Russians in the first place? If he hadn't he wouldn't now be in this mess. He thought he might have got away with it on Gan and his fellow officers would assume he lost his life at sea in a valiant attempt to get help at Diego Garcia. That is everyone except Dr Clem and Reki who had seen too much on the Russian aicraft. They had been man-handled off the plane by the Russian commissar and Mike wondered what happened to them? Whatever their fate they deserved punishment for their unwarranted actions on the Russian aeroplane.

Sticking out of the water like a sore thumb, the useless seaplane was a dead give away. He would have to get it out of sight into the thick foliage at the lagoon's edge. But how? The answer to his unspoken query were standing behind him. All of Ihuru's thirteen inhabitants, men, women and children, were gathered in an awestruck semicircle looking at the big, noisy bird that had disrupted their morning ablutions and crashed on to their isolated little island. On recognising Mike the whole group, smiling broadly in welcome, broke into a bout of handclapping. His workforce had arrived unannounced. With an expertise born of many years of seafaring they emptied the cockpit of seawater, snapped off the undamaged float, floated the plane to the seashore and, using *coir* ropes, dragged it up the beach and into a dense thicket. They then salvaged most of Mike's belongings, removed all dèbris and surface oil off the water and eradicated the tell-tale gouging troughs in the sand. Within three hours all traces of Mike's startling arrival had been obliterated from Ihuru's lagoon beach. During this time Mike sat on his haunches marvelling at the ingenuity and simplistic lifestyle of native Maldivians. For survival they were wholly dependent on fishing and the products of the sea and palm trees. From palm leaves they made *cadjan*, a woven matting used for roofing and basket making and bound together by *coir* ropes plaited from the beard of the coconut fruit. Coconut juice provided a refreshing cool drink and the flesh of the fruit was widely used in cooking and for garnishing rice and a wide variety of spicy fish and meat dishes. Finally, at the end of its useful life, the tree itself became a source of timber and palm oil and is, not surprisingly, boldly stylised on the Maldivian national flag. The villagers settled Mike into cabin No 4 and to celebrate his arrival they sacrificed and curried one of their precious chickens. Having retired early, Mike slept fitfully and had vivid dreams and nightmares in which Sonitha featured prominently. He was awake at first light and lay on his bed staring fixedly at the *cadjan* and rafia-entwined thatch roof. There was only one thought on his mind – as soon as Soni was with him, and in his arms again, all would be well.

Masdhonis, laden with tuna after a night's fishing in the waters around Kaaf Atoll, started arriving in Male's inner harbour at around 11 o'clock. Sonitha was at her desk in the tourist office when she heard a commotion and excited chatter amongst the fishermen congregating at the quayside. Inquisitive as ever, she stopped writing and crossed the road. A masdhoni captain surrounded by a noisy group of fishermen was relating how, while cruising off Ihuru about an hour after sunrise, he saw a float plane flying low towards the island. He did not see it lift off again and assumed it had crashed and his story was vociferously backed up by one of his crewmen. Sonitha's heart missed a beat. Putting a seaplane down on Ihuru would be extremely dangerous and almost suicidal at the best of times and she could think of only one man who might attempt it and land safely in the lagoon.

"Captain Ibrahim. Are you sure it was a float plane?"

"Yes, definitely Miss Soni," the Captain replied.

"I expect you were tired after fishing all night. Planes cannot land on Ihuru. What you saw was probably a large seagull or was it the spirit of *dhevi?*"

The congregated onlookers surrounding the nonplussed captain burst out laughing as he stomped in a huff across a gangplank to his masdhoni. Sonitha returned to her office and outwardly she was her normal smiling self, though inwardly her thoughts were in a turmoil. Her instinctive reaction was to rush across to Ihuru to be near her lover but prudence and caution prevailed. She decided to wait for one day and if Michael was on Ihuru she did not wish to give the game away.

Sonitha routinely visited Baros two or three times a week to confer with staff and arrange client transfers between the resort and Male. Normally she went by dhoni with a senior seaman, the captain, at the tiller and a boy lookout at the prow. On March 19th Sonitha took the tiller and dispensed with the captain's services. At a Baros staff meeting the manager was full of a story about a seaplane landing on Ihuru. Captain Ibrahim's masdhoni had dropped into Baros with a creel of tuna before crossing to Male. Sonitha dismissed the improbable tale with a shrug. "By the time Captain Ibrahim came ashore in Male he had changed his mind. He now thinks what he saw early yesterday was a large seagull magnified in the early morning light. I'm going across to Ihuru later. I'll look into the matter when I get there."

Lurking on the fringe of the meeting was Fat Abdul who had once managed Sonitha's tourist office but now, demoted, was employed as an assistant chef in Baros' kitchen. Abdul did not accept Sonitha's account about a big bird and, if the chance arose, he was determined to get across to Ihuru and check for himself.

Standing on the jetty at Ihuru Mike saw Sonitha's dhoni approaching when it was still a mile offshore. There was no mistaking the straight-backed woman in a pink sari sitting at the tiller. Even at this distance Mike imagined she had a broad smile on her face and so as not to create a disturbance on the jetty he swiftly walked away to his cabin. The whole village met the dhoni and gave Sonitha a traditional, effusive welcome. They unloaded the weekly provisions and Sonitha ordered her 'boy' to moor the dhoni out in the lagoon to await her return. Sitting crosslegged on the floor in the headman's hut and sipping fresh coconut juice, Sonitha outlined her plans for Ihuru's further development. "Next week workmen will come across to start building a grand dining hall and two kitchen areas. When that's completed we'll build more cabins but it'll take quite a long time to complete the resort, maybe a year or two. Money is short and Baros is not doing as well as expected. That position will improve next May when we start using Gan to bring in tourists by air."

The headman nodded and smiled. Sonitha did not wish to appear too anxious but she could not stop herself asking, "We heard a plane landed on Ihuru yesterday. Either the dhoni captain is blind or he saw a big bird!"

"No, Miss Soni," the headman replied, "Captain Ibrahim is not blind. The Englishman is in Cabin No 4."

Sonitha was on her feet in a flash and running down the pathway towards Mike's cabin. He saw her coming and ran up the sandtrack to meet her and they fell into each other's arms clutching each other in desperation. Sonitha's smiling face was wet with tears of joy and relief at seeing her lover alive and uninjured. Mike led Sonitha into his cabin and laid her on his bed. There was no foreplay. The urgency of their reunion dominated all else and they made love urgently and uncompromisingly. By virtue of their primaeval urges the act of union was sustainable for only a minute and with Mike's climax came moans and whispers – 'darling, darling' and ' I love you'. Afterwards they composed themselves, lounging on the verandah on *undhoolis*, swinging seats constructed of cadjan and bamboo cane. Mike came clean without admitting his connection with Moscow and stressing the RAF authorities might come looking for him, "I have run away from Gan to be with you, Soni. We were due to go home in ten days' time but I couldn't bear the thought of leaving you. So here I am."

"That's wonderful!" Sonitha exclaimed, "you will be safe here on Ihuru. I can stop development for a few weeks and the workmen need not come across every day. When I can I'll take you to another remote atoll. I'll come across to Ihuru twice a week and bring fresh water and a chicken or two. I know you love curried chicken."

Mike took her hand and looked deeply into her eyes. "Soni. I love you with all my heart."

The old-fashioned expression of endearment struck a tender chord and Sonitha burst into tears. Mike took her in his arms again and consoled her and afterwards he showed Sonitha the shattered frame of his seaplane. Before she left it was agreed that Mike should lay low on Ihuru and, as soon as practicable, Sonitha would either join him or take him to an uninhabited island on another atoll where they could live together as man and wife.

Mike Townsend survived on Ihuru fortified physically and mentally by Sonitha's bi-weekly visits when the ritual was always the same – a torrid love session in Cabin No 4 followed by a swim in the lagoon and a meal with the villagers. Whenever a strange dhoni called, Mike disappeared and hid in his cabin or in the disused Buddhist temple at the north end of the island. Four unsolicited dhonis dropped anchor in the lagoon during the first fortnight, mainly itinerant vendors who moved from island to island selling their wares – salt, spices, bales of silk, kerosene and baubles and beads. They rarely came ashore, conducting their business from a floating market but one day a dhoni came to the jetty and three men disembarked. Fat Abdul brought two workmen along with him to start building an outdoor barbecue and cookhouse. Mike disappeared to his temple hideout and the work party stayed ashore until an hour before sunset. During the midday break Abdul befriended a playful, happy-go-lucky four year old boy. He played ball with the youngster and gave him a pomegranate and a fresh orange. Abdul pretended to be an aeroplane and, arms outstretched, he zoomed around the beach. The young boy was amused and quite innocently took Abdul's hand and led him across the deserted beach to the hidden seaplane. Abdul's suspicions were confirmed. He gave the youngster another orange and sent him packing. Once the work-party's dhoni was out of sight Mike rejoined the villagers at their evening meal and the headman showed him the newly-constructed log-burning barbecue. Mike thought it a bit Heath Robinson but as long as the workmen did not return he couldn't care less. He looked at the spit and sagely nodded his head. "Very good! Yes, very good!"

A spetcnaz hit squad arrived off Male on an Athenian registered 8,000 tonnes cargo ship. The Cerbes carried a load of timber and the ship's log recorded she was in transit from Manila to Piraeus in Greece. On April 15th 1976 she lay at anchor in the main channel three miles off Male. Though she displayed a Greek flag of convenience her connections with Greece were non-existent. The captain and crew were Vladivostok Russians and the Cerebes transported agents, arms and contraband to communist sympathisers in countries in the Pacific and Indian Oceans. Acting on instruction from Moscow she had been sent to the Maldives to apprehend and eliminate a defector whose continued existence could prove an embarrassment to the Soviet Government. To achieve this end she carried a squad of twelve highly-trained spetcnaz commandos and three high-powered inflatable dinghies. Concealed in her hold, amidst the stacked timber, was an arsenal of modern weaponry and ammunition. For a vessel ostensibly bent on peaceful trade the Cerebes was fully equipped to undertake a seabourne assault of limited proportions.

The Cerebes' captain and first officer, both in uniform, and two spetcnaz's dressed in white T-shirts and faded blue jeans, went ashore in a dinghy on the afternoon of their arrival. The ship was duly registered with the Male port authorities and the captain purchased a long list of provisions from a dockside chandler. The Russians then strolled around the fish market and harbour area and were disappointed at the lack of bars in Male. Next to the fish market they came across Sonitha's office where the seamen made inquiries about suitable bathing facilities for their comrades. Sonitha suggested Baros, Bandos or Karumba. None of the resorts apparently struck a chord with the sailors and, in broken English, one of the crewmen asked which was nearest to their ship. To promote her own enterprise Sonitha suggested Baros. One of the fair-haired, blue-eyed spetcnaz flashed a charming smile. "Okay. He and me. We go Baros. We wish go now," and, producing a wad of dollars, he paid for one night's accommodation. Sonitha hailed a dhoni and saw them on their way. Afterwards she paused and thought how quickly arrangements had been made and she had not even asked to see their passports. The language they spoke to each other was not Greek and she had always been under the impression that Mediterranean men were short, dark

180

and swarthy and flirtatious towards the opposite sex. The two men in T-shirts who had just left her office were tall with close-cut, blonde hair, bright blue eyes and were a model of propriety. Still, no harm was done. It was only for one night's stay and, if they thought they might find a bar, or women, on Baros, they would be doubly disappointed!

The following morning was Sonitha's routine visiting day to Baros and, afterwards, onwards to Ihuru for a brief reunion with Michael. She left Male early but when she arrived at Baros the two Greek sailors had already departed and an inflatable dinghy from the Cerebes had picked them up shortly after daybreak. Mr Saeed, Baros' manager, was under the impression that the Greek ship was due to leave on the afternoon tide.

"And what did you make of the two Greek sailors?" Sonitha asked.

"They were a strange couple. They were definitely not interested in the reef and didn't go swimming or snorkelling. They wandered around, nosing here and there, and spent a long time in the kitchen discussing recipes with your old manager, Abdul. I think one of them must have been a ship's cook."

Sonitha was only slightly perturbed. In common with seafarers the world over the 'Greek' sailors were only interested in women, food and drink. In view of the complete absence of booze and cooperative women on Baros she surmised they had returned to the Cerebes. Mr Saeed could well be right and the ship might be preparing to leave Male sound to continue her voyage westwards but there were no signs of this happening as yet. When she left for Ihuru the rusty old tub was still anchored in Male's main deep channel and showing no evidence of preparations to leave on the evening tide.

As soon as Sonitha set foot on Ihuru Mike was on the jetty to greet her. They were still uncomfortable displaying affection in public and the greeting was confined to a perfunctory squeeze of the hand. Even that light touch sent Sonitha's pulse racing. She went off on her own to speak to the villagers and later joined Mike in Cabin No 4 where they made love for an hour followed by a leisurely swim in the lagoon. Later Mike walked her to the jetty to see her off. During their time together that day Sonitha rarely smiled and Mike sensed there was something on her mind.

"Tell me Soni. Is everything alright?"

She gazed deeply into his eyes and flashed a fleeting smile. "Yes, Michael, I'm fine."

Sonitha paused for a few seconds, debating whether to continue, and then quickly made up her mind. "There's a Greek ship out there," pointing towards Male, "and some of the crew came ashore yesterday. Two of them paid for a night on Baros. They were an odd couple. They didn't look Greek and I'm pretty certain the language they spoke wasn't Greek. They had left by the time I got to Baros this morning and the manager told me they didn't go swimming but spent their time in the kitchen with Abdul. You remember Abdul? He used to work in my father's office."

Mike nodded and Sonitha continued, "The manger also told me they were picked up at the crack of dawn by a dinghy from the ship and they said they had to go because they're sailing this afternoon. But Michael, the ship is still there. You can just about see her on the horizon."

"What's the ships' name Soni?"

"The Cerebes," Soni replied.

"Well, now, don't worry my darling. I'm sure there's nothing in it. If anyone's looking for me they will be British and I'm not worried at all about this. Now off you go Soni."

Mike helped her into the dhoni and cast off. He then stood at the very end of the jetty and watched the small figure, in her brightly-coloured sari, disappear into the distant heat haze. Though he had not shown it to Sonitha, Mike was a worried man. He hadn't thought for a moment they, whoever 'they' might be, would not come looking for him. He had bargained on the diversion to Diego Garcia putting them off the scent but he was not expecting unwelcome visitors from a Greek ship. Before he turned in he went to check on the hidden seaplane and walked to the north end of the island to look inside the Chinese temple. In the seclusion of his cabin he took generous swigs from his rapidly-diminishing stock of scotch whisky. That night, April 16th , he slept fitfully, waking a few times in a cold sweat with a premonition that something disastrous was about to happen.

By the time Sonitha realised the lone, diminutive figure on the jetty could no longer see her waving hand her dhoni was a good mile out to sea. Her boy-lookout announced they were in a deeper channel and, instead of steering directly towards Male, she deviated starboardwise and made for the Cerebes. As she drew alongside there were no signs of activity on board and certainly no indication the ship was preparing to weigh anchor. And then, quite suddenly, six heads appeared over the upper-deck rail. Some of the crew of the Cerebes were sunning themselves and one or two waved, a few whistled and made catcalls, one stuck out and waggled his tongue and a large man, with a bare, tattooed torso, clenched his fist and bent his elbow in an obscene gesture. Sonitha looked straight ahead in disgust and opened the throttle to its limit, driving the dhoni at speed towards Male's inner harbour. By the time she reached her office she was still fuming and tried to make excuses for the seamen but could not fathom why they derived pleasure from embarrassing females. She always thought men from Mediterranean countries had a reputation for chivalry but not so that bunch on the deck of the Cerebes. And then she thought about her dear Michael, alone and lonely on Ihuru, a perfect gentleman. She had only left him two hours ago and already she was missing him. Her love for Michael was all-consuming and, one day, she planned to cross to Ihuru in a well-stocked masdhoni to pick up her lover and sail away into the sunset never to set foot on Male again. She looked northwards into the gathering gloom and blew a kiss in the general direction of Ihuru.

The Cerebes. April 16th 1976
At midday, on the upper deck of the Cerebes, Spetcnaz Captain Ivan Korsov gathered his twelve-man hit squad around a blackboard with a rough map of Ihuru chalked on it.

"Oscar and Sergeyi came aboard from Baros this morning with information that our target is on Ihuru, the island you all see in the distance about four miles away. The Cerebes will move closer under cover of darkness to anchor a mile offshore. We shall attack in three inflatables at first light. Sergeyi will take four men and make for the jetty and I will take three men into the lagoon through a gap in the coral reef. The third inflatable will remain outside the reef to prevent any attempt at escape. The island only measures about 800 metres by 500 metres and is surrounded by a fine sandy lagoon beach and its interior is thickly forested. There are four cabins along a path about 80 metres to the left of the jetty and a native shanty village at the jetty. Our main advantage will be an element of surprise. Sergeyi will take three men to flush out the village, leaving one man to guard the dinghy. I will take my squad through a gap in the reef into the lagoon and hit the cabins. The target should be in one of the these two places. If not, he may be hidden in the dense foliage and trees in the interior of the island. In that case we'll have to flush him out. And don't forget, he's probably armed and may have a hiding place in the interior of the island. So extra vigilance is necessary if we have to go into the forest. Any questions?"

"Yes," Oscar piped up, "do we shoot to kill or do we just capture the target?"

"My orders are we shoot to kill and bring the body back to the Cerebes. There will be canvas body bags in the three dinghies."

Captain Korsov lit a cigarette and looked around his eager-faced squad. Fit and highly-trained volunteers, they were all expert killers and he was proud of his commandos. He returned to the blackboard and wrote in chalk, *'Revallie – 0400 hrs Departure – 0520 hrs Dress – combat wet suits Arms – K3 submachine guns, grenades, stiletto daggers, cheese wire'.*

The captain stubbed out his cigarette on the blackboard easel.

"Rest this afternoon and check your arms. We probably won't have much sleep tonight."

Ihuru. April 17th 1976

Every morning since his arrival on Ihuru Mike Townsend was in the habit of rising an hour before daybreak. He found the pre-dawn hour silent, cool and soothing and he felt at peace with the human race and the world at large. After a quick brew-up and a ritual cigarette he invariably made his way to the jetty to enjoy the beauty of the sunrise over the palm trees in the centre of the island and to listen to the dawn chorus. And each morning, within a few minutes of the first rays creeping over the lush vegetation, there was the reassuring ritual as the villagers, facing west towards Mecca, prostrated themselves outside their huts and prayed to *Allah*. But on the morning of April 17th things were not quite right. Out at sea, in the vast blackness in front of him, he saw a tiny pinpoint of light. Night-fishing dhoni's carried flares but this spot of light was stationary and too high over the water to be on a dhoni. He ran back to his cabin and returned to the jetty with his service binoculars.

Puzzled at first, he began to get worried as the sky became lighter to reveal a grey hulk about a mile offshore and then, within a minute, the grey mass took the shape of a cargo ship. The steady pinpoint of light was in its rigging. Straining his eyes to identify the vessel, Mike suddenly became aware of three low-lying, grey-coloured boats, twenty yards apart and about half a mile away, approaching the island at speed. Thoroughly alarmed, he retreated off the jetty and sprinted back to his cabin. Thankfully the villagers were not as yet outside their huts attending to their ritual devotions and ablutions. In his cabin he turned off the kerosene burner, grabbed his service revolver and, as an afterthought, picked up a half-full bottle of scotch whisky. He then crawled through the foliage to the edge of the lagoon. The light was improving with every passing second and, after about two minutes wait, one of the grey-coloured dinghies came surging through a gap in the coral reef and made straight towards the southern end of the lagoon. There were four men, all dressed in black, in the dinghy and Mike clearly saw the glint from their gun barrels in the sun's first rays. He waited no longer. Under cover of the lush undergrowth he sprinted down the pathway alongside the lagoon, around the south end of the island and in four minutes he reached the derelict Buddhist temple. He plunged inside and re-arranged the cadjan matting and foliage screen covering the entrance.

The interior of the temple was dark and, at that early hour, dank and cold. The cold-blooded residents in their nest in one corner of the temple were dormant and listless. Mike placed his loaded revolver on a pedestal supporting Buddha's crumbling effigy and sank to his haunches, cradling the whisky bottle in his lap. Out of breath, he willed himself to calm down and took stock of his situation. Everything looked hopeless. The armed figures in black wet suits were obviously out to capture him but were they British, Greek, or possibly Russian and had they come from the ship Sonitha had mentioned? What was she called? The Cerebes! And Sonitha thought they were definitely not Greek, or British. That only left the Russians. Whichever, his chances of escape were very remote. He picked up his revolver and slipped off the safety catch. Perhaps they had only come to pick him up? But why come armed and in numbers? The more he thought about it the more he became convinced his visitors were an execution squad. It seemed he had three choices. Either he could make a dash for it, but where to? Or he could stand and fight and the third alternative, suicide, did not bear thinking about. He held his breath and in the creepy silence inside the tomb heard something moving in the darkest corner. Could it be a snake or a rat? It had to be one or the other as the two creatures were hardly likely to cohabit. While pondering the answer he heard a shout from the direction of the cabins on the other side of the island. Mike understood immediately what it was all about. The intruders had found his seaplane and the shouts were in Russian. So his masters in Moscow had sent their debt collectors to settle the score.

The Russian dinghies landed at two points on Ihuru. One, commanded by Sergeyi, hit the jetty to find the villagers on their knees at prayer. After a cursory search of the empty huts a spetcnaz was left to cover the prostrate worshippers whilst Sergyei and two commandos ran down the pathway towards the cabins. Captain Korsov and two spetcnaz, working their way up form the south end of the lagoon, arrived at the Cabin No 4 at the same time as Sergeyi. The six men crashed inside but the bird had flown. The kerosene burner was still warm and Mike's clothing lay strewn on the bed. The captain led a search of the outhouses at the back of the four cabins and almost immediately a loud shout announced that one of his spetcnaz had found the hidden seaplane. There then began a thorough and systematic search of all four cabins and the shanty village, but to no avail. All thirteen villagers were herded in a frightened group into the dining hall with the children crying and clinging to their mothers for dear life. Captain Korsov was losing his temper and attempts to interrogate the villagers proved futile.

"He must be on this bloody island somewhere. I expect he's taken to the forest. Spread out and advance through the woods in line abreast keeping about thirty metres apart. We've lost the element of surprise and he knows we're here. Use the Balakov tactic if you have to."

The Balakov tactic was a search and flushing-out procedure employed by Russian soldiers during the siege of Stalingrad. As they advanced, attackers tossed grenades into any potential hiding holes. All in all, three grenades were used by the spetcnaz during their progress across the island. Captain Korsov and five exasperated commandos congregated at the north-eastern end of Ihuru. Oscar was the first to notice footprints in the sand leading to an overgrown pathway. He gently pushed his way through the undergrowth and, within fifteen yards, came to the stone exterior of the temple. Cautiously he retraced his steps and made a sign to Korsov he had found a suspicious-looking building at the end of the path. The captain pointed to Oscar's grenade and made a lobbing motion with his hand. Oscar understood perfectly. Submachine gun in one hand and a live grenade in the other, he advanced stealthily towards Mike's hideout.

Thirty five long, anxious minutes had elapsed since Mike heard the searchers' shout on discovering the hidden seaplane. In a bath of sweat and swigging whisky from his bottle, he sat perfectly still on the earthern floor, his eyes glued on chinks of sunlight which, in three places, penetrated through the tendril screen over the entrance to the temple. When the searchers' grenades went off, one after another, Mike knew they were getting nearer and when one of the rays percolating through the entrance screen was obscured, he sensed there was a human body outside his hideout. He pointed his Colt revolver at the entrance, only fourteen feet away, and was about to fire when the ray of sunlight returned to illuminate a patch of earth two feet away from his outstretched legs. Mike took a last, generous swig of whisky and lay the empty bottle on the ground. In the fifty second interval before the assassin returned a hundred thoughts went racing through his mind. Just like a drowning man he had befuddled flashbacks from his previous life. He clearly saw the headmaster at Wellington school and Smithy, his rear-gunner in a smoke-filled Lancaster over Dresden. A blonde hippie girlfriend from the London School of Economics and Teddy, the smooth, well-dressed Russian agent who seduced him into joining the Communist Party, came to the forefront followed rapidly be Vanessa in her pink gown at the hunt ball and Tony Widgeon, his best man, on his feet making a scurrilous speech at his wedding breakfast in Cranwell College. Next came the communist thug, Arnaud

Baillier, and Monsieur Henri the timid buck-toothed agent at the Etoile Vert restaurant in Paris. Milli-seconds later he was in NATO Headquarters with General 'Monty' Baxter and the scowling double agent Claude Bernard. One second he was in the lagoon at Baros facing the ugly Russian agent and the next second he was making love to Sonitha in Cabin No 4 on Ihuru followed immediately be a vision of Gorky, the massive unshaven Russian political agent at the airbase, wielding a submachine pistol in the face of Dr Clem and Rekitutha. Within a flash he was back to conscious reality again and he re-focused his eyes on the raffia screen covering the entrance to the temple. His thoughts turned again to Vanessa and the perfidious Tony Widgeon and poor Dr Clem Garvey and Reki who had needlessly risked their lives on the Russian plane. And then Sonitha's beautiful face and winning smile overshadowed all else and he began to moan. He sat upright with a start. Why, oh why, were the Russians after him? He had kept his part of the bargain. That traitor Tony Widgeon was sitting pretty in London enjoying the status that was rightfully Mike's. What a 'best' man! More like a 'worst' man, the enemy within. If he survived he vowed to get even with Tony. And then a wave of panic set in. What were these attackers outside going to do? He knew the answer almost before the question crossed his mind. True to their tactics so far they were intent on blasting him out with a grenade. He was cornered and had no chance of escape and, when the sun's pencil-thin rays from outside were again blotted out, he fired two bullets through the raffia screen. There was a sharp yelp and a rustle of bushes as Oscar fell backwards into the undergrowth where he lay writhing, moaning and groaning. Seven seconds later the moans and groans came to an abrupt halt with a loud crump as a grenade, clutched to Oscar's belly, exploded and blew a gaping hole in his abdomen and the entrance screen into the temple. Now he had done it! He could expect no mercy. Mike shouted, "Come on you bastards" and sat staring dazedly into the bright sunlight outside waiting for the inevitable black, pineapple-shaped grenade to land in his lap. The thought horrified him and he could wait no longer. He pushed the revolver barrel up to the roof of his mouth and closed his eyes. Sonitha's smiling face flashed before him and, just before he pulled the trigger, another image surged to the forefront of his addled consciousness – Dr

188

Clem's puckish face was impertinently asking a question, "Why aren't there crows on Gan?"

His last thought before he passed into oblivion was "Now I'll never know."

Aftermath

THE CEREBES was well clear of Addu Atoll by mid-afternoon on 17th April. In its hold were two bodies wrapped in canvas bags and, two days into the voyage, a brief ceremony was held on deck and Oscar's remains was reverently committed to the deep. An hour later Wing Commander Michael Townsend's body was dumped unceremoniously over the side at a point some 300 miles to the east of the Chagos and Salomon Archipelago. The Cerebes then continued its journey homewards through the Malacca Strait into the South China Sea and northwards to its home-base in Vladivostok.

Gan has not been repopulated by Maldivians from nearby Feydhoo. The reason is obscure but the ghost of the British raj still lingers over the island and the Maldivian belief in *dhevi* and *fanditha* exercises a strong influence on the psyche of the superstitious islanders. During Maumoon Gayoom's presidency in the mid-eighties an attempt to promote a Gan Holiday Village met with failure. In 1994 the sergeants' mess was converted into an Ocean Reef Club which has blossomed into a thriving Equator Village Resort with the added advantage of direct flights from overseas airports. In a memorial garden near the site of the old NAAFI, and flanked by two second world war cannons, there is a monument inscribed 'Royal Air Force Gan 1956 – 1976' with a record of the RAF, Indian, Sri Lankan and Ghurka regiments who served on the island during these years. In 1985, at the instigation of Air Vice Marshal Sir Tony Widgeon and at a brief ceremony attended by Vanessa Townsend, a smaller plaque was unveiled at the same site to commemorate the ultimate sacrifice of three men whilst serving on Gan.

Wng. Com. M L Townsend CBE pos. DSO DFC and Bar   CO
Sqd. Ldr. A C E Garvey MBE pos. BSc MB BCh   MO
Hon. Sgt. M Rekitutha OBE pos.   Civ. Att.

The three victims of the action on Gan in March 1976 were posthumously acknowledged in the Military List of 1978. Wing Commander Townsend's citation recorded 'his gallantry during the occupation of Gan by a foreign power between 15th and 17th March 1976 and his courageous, but futile, attempt to seek help from the British/American airbase at Diego Garcia leading to loss of his life somewhere in the Indian Ocean'.

Air Vice Marshal Sir Tony Widgeon KBE DFC received a knighthood for his management of the Gan crisis and ended his service days in 1988 as Director of Tactical Operations at NATO headquarters, strategically placed to pass on highly secret and classified information to his masters in Moscow. In the same year Timothy Cosbey was promoted group captain signals based at MoD (Air) in Whitehall. Vanessa inherited Belvoir Hall becoming a wealthy, widowed lady of the manor on the death of her father in 1982. The same year she was unanimously elected 'Master of Foxhounds' of the Lincolnshire Border Hunt, warding off all attempts at takeover, or closure, by the more prestigious and powerful Quorn and Belvoir Hunts. By a quirk of fate, Vanessa and Tony Widgeon were thrown together in 1985 at the unveiling ceremony of the memorial plaque on Gan. In her anxiety to establish a lord of the manor at Belvoir Hall Vanessa swallowed her pride and overcame her abhorrence of Tony Widgeon and, the following year, they were married at a low-key ceremony at Grantham Registry Office. The union was a marriage of convenience in every respect. It gave cudos for Vanessa in having an air vice-marshal resident at Belvoir Hall and provided Tony Widgeon with respectability and a safe haven from which to conduct his nefarious activities and clandestine affairs with a succession of male partners of which Vanessa was blissfully ignorant. On retirement from the air force, Warrant Officer William Williams OBE ended his days as secretary general to a RAFA organization in South Wales which automatically gave him a seat on the RAFA General Council in London.

Over the years Baros has gone from strength to strength and is, arguably, the jewel in the crown of the eighty-six Maldivian resort islands. Its popularity is reflected in the large number of tourists that holiday in the resort and in particular the clients who return from year to year. A combination of first class luxury accommodation, excellent and varied cuisine and superb water sport facilities, make it a fascinating holiday destination. Added to this, and in common with all the islands in the archipelago, its idyllic setting, its crystal clear lagoon brimful with exotic fish and the attraction of an unspoilt coral reef, make Baros an irresistible magnet for underwater explorers. Work in converting Ihuru into a tourist resort was completed in September 1979. A miniature replica of Baros, Ihuru lacked the sophistication of its rival and the amenities for visitors were basic but more than adequate. Nevertheless Ihuru has its devotees, mainly independent travellers and honeymooners, and the quality of its waterfront facilities cannot be surpassed in any of the other resorts. In the twenty three years of its existence Ihuru, like Baros, has become recognised as one of the leading holiday resorts in the Maldives.

When Mike Townsend crash landed his seaplane in Ihuru's lagoon on 17th March 1976 Sonitha knew she was two months pregnant. Realising that her lover was in deep trouble she put off announcing her pregnancy until it was too late and Michael died ignorant of the fact he had fathered a son. She gave birth to a pale-skinned, blue-eyed boy on 4th November 1976. Young Mikeli wanted for nothing. At ten years of age he was sent to a private boy's academy in Sri Lanka followed by four years at Harvard Business School in America. In October 1998 he returned to Male and took over his mother's vastly-expanded tourist organization. Sonitha went into semi-retirement but maintained a controlling interest in her business. Every Tuesday throughout the year, weather permitting, holidaymakers on Ihuru are witness to the spectacle of a dhoni, carrying a single passenger, arriving at the jetty at around 11.00 am. The passenger, a strikingly beautiful, straight-backed Maldivian woman immaculately dressed in a pink sari and matching *palu*, walks slowly from the jetty along a sheltered pathway across the island to the isolated Buddhist temple. Sonitha has come to pay homage to her one and only love and the father of her only son and she spends ten minutes alone in the temple. The crumpled Buddha has long since been removed to a museum in Male while the unseen reptilians still lie, docilely hissing, in the darkest corners of the temple. Sonitha replenishes a long-burning candle and reverently lays a bunch of hibiscus flowers on the crumbling stone plinth. She then kneels in prayer for a minute. Grim-faced when she arrives, Sonitha emerges from the temple with a seraphic smile on her face. A brief communion with her God, and Mike's departed spirit, rejuvenates the handsome woman. Back in the village she mingles with visitors and drinks a glass of fresh coconut milk. Revitalized spiritually, she is then ready to face another week of loneliness living with the memory of the dashing British Air Force officer who came into her life and became her one and only lover all those years ago.